The Murder of Figaro

A Musical Mystery

by

Susan Larson

Savvy Press

SAVVY PRESS

All but a few characters in this novel were living people in Vienna, some well-known to us today, some not. Occasionally, they even get to say things they actually said or wrote. Although the main characters strongly resemble themselves as they appear in Da Ponte's and Michael Kelly's memoirs, as well as in Mozart's letters to his father and sister and his love-notes to his wife, I pretty much made up everything else.

Published by:

Savvy Press
Salem, NY 12865
http://www.savvypress.com

Cover art by:

Francois Thisdale

ISBN: 978-1-939113-33-7
LCCN: 2019902941

Printed in the United States of America

For Craig

ᖳᖰᖰ Participants ᖰᖰᖳ

Cast

Count Almaviva: bass: Signor Mandini (married to Signora Mandini, enamored of Signora Laschi)

Marcellina: soprano: Signora Mandini (tormented by her husband's philanderings)

La Contessa Almaviva: soprano: Signora Laschi (an Italian diva)

Susanna: soprano: Signora Storace (celebrated Anglo-Italian soprano favored by Joseph II)

Figaro: bass: Signor Benucci (the world's best basso buffo)

Cherubino: soprano: Signora Bussani (child bride of Signor Bussani)

Antonio: bass: Signor Bussani (free-lance spy, jealous of young wife)

Don Basilio and Don Curzio: tenor: Signor Ochelli (Michael O'Kelly, Irish *comprimario* tenor)

Barbarina: soprano: Signorina Anna Maria Gottlieb (infant phenomenon, 12 years old; also known as Anna, Nannerl, Nanette, and 'the ingénue')

Covering the part of Barbarina: Constanze Mozart (sister of Aloysia Weber Lange, Josepha Weber Hofer and Sophie Weber, all professional sopranos. Married to Amadé Mozart. Also known as 'Stanzerl' and by many other pet names)

Production Team

The composer: Johannes Chrysostomus Wolfgangus Theophilus Mozart (former infant phenomenon, currently a rising young free-lance genius, angling for a salaried post at court. Prefers to be addressed as 'Amadé' or 'Amadeo')

Archduke of Austria, King of Germany, Jerusalem, Hungary, Bohemia, Dalmatia, Croatia, Slavonia, Galicia and Lodomeria; Grand Duke of Tuscany, Prince of Transylvania, and sovereign of all the other Habsburg lands: His Imperial Majesty, The Holy Roman Emperor: Joseph II (also known as 'King and Kaiser,' 'Caesar,' 'The Emperor,' 'His Highness.' Principal patron of *Le Nozze di Figaro*)

Grand Chancellor of Spectacles Count Franz Xaver Wolfgang von Orsini-Rosenberg (Executive Producer of all the theatrical performances at the Court Theater. Instrumental in getting Mozart's smash-hit musical "*The Abduction from the Seraglio*" produced at court. Also known as 'Rosenberg,' 'Wolf-Bear,' 'Rosy Butt' and several other disrespectful names)

Count Rosenberg's deputy and chief financial officer: Johann von Thorwart (also Constanze Mozart's godfather and legal guardian. Known as 'Dear Godfather' or 'Thor-fart')

The Head Usher at the Burgtheater: Fritz von Drossel (collector and purveyor of information, in the employ of the Emperor in that capacity)

Chancellor of Education and Censorship: Baron Gottfried van Swieten (music lover, Freemason, son of the Imperial physician in the reign of Maria Theresa. Friend and patron of Mozart, patron of *Figaro)*

Arts patron, real estate magnate and financial backer of Figaro, Baron Wetzlar von Plankenstern

Assistant Musical Director: Stephen Storace (Mozart's composition student. Nancy's brother)

Imperial and Royal theatrical censor Wilhelm von Haegelin (rigid bureaucrat who enjoys cutting the naughty or near-naughty bits from plays. Loathed by everybody in show business. Deceased)

Featuring

Satiric Italian poet, fixer and factotum in the household of Chancellor Rosenberg: Giambattista Casti (wants Da Ponte's position at court)

Court Composer: Antonio Salieri (talented intriguer and slightly north-of-mediocre composer; jealous of, but not professionally threatened by, Mozart)

Court composers: Signor Bonno and Herr Starzer

Ultra-conservative anti-Enlightenment provincial Hungarian nobleman: Count Janos Szekely Gulas

Wardrobe worker and costumiere, widow and mother of Nanette the infant phenomenon: Frau Adelheid Gottlieb

Free-thinker and Mozart patroness: Baroness Martha Elizabeth Waldstätten (has a serious fancrush on the composer)

Grand Master of Freemasonry in Vienna: Ignatz von Born

Inventor of hypnotism and the theory of animal magnetism: Anton Mesmer

Venetian pornographer and thug for hire: Zani Diguri

Secret society promoting the Enlightenment: the Freemasons (encouraging scientific knowledge, charitable institutions, the arts, civil society, universal brotherhood and a few other things)

Secret society of political activists: the Illuminati (infiltrating the Masonic lodges, and purportedly fomenting revolution across Europe)

Various 'created' nobles and haut-bourgeois salonistes

Also Featuring

Pit musicians, actors, stage crew, stage moms, chaperones
The Vienna police and secret police, prison guards
A horse: Rosinante
Gravediggers

ᔐᕽᕽ Overture 1 ᕽᔐᕽ

A room in Judenplatz # 3, Vienna, Austria, June 16, 1783

Mozart makes an overture to his wife Constanze

"Oh! Ah! Ooo-hoo, yes! Oh, Loviekins, what a rush! I think it's going to make the baby come!"

"Three for the price of one, what a bargain! Now kiss me goodbye. I've got to run; I'm playing at Wetzlar's. I'll be home late; they make me play until the little bones stick out from the ends of my fingers. Where's that hair ribbon? It completes my outfit, and I have to look gorgeous tonight; important people may be there. Are you going out?"

"Under the bed, I think. Yes, I'm dining with Mama and my sisters; then we're going to a party unless I'm having the baby. Let me fix your hair, it's all mussed."

"Tell your mother that I'm working hard to become rich and famous and respectable. Kiss her for me. Kiss them all for me. Kiss me for me... Hopla, here's the little soldier, coming to attention again! *Gran Dio*, how I love you; I love you altogether and I love your component parts individually. I squeeze and kiss them all a million squillion times and yet I need to kiss them all over again. No! No, I say! I won't go out tonight, I'm staying home in bed with you!"

"You're going and I'm going, and you need to hustle; so tell your little soldier to stand down."

"If you must. If I must. If he must. I'll be a good boy and attend to business. I'll be home by one or two, with a dragoon and a hussar!"

⤳ Overture 2 ⤳

The salon in the house of real estate magnate and patron of the arts Baron Raimund Wetzlar von Plankenstern, later the same evening.

Lorenzo Da Ponte makes an overture to Mozart

The hot young musical sensation Mozart, resplendent in his brown silk suit with matching hair-tie, is helping himself to another dram of punch during a break in the music-making, when the baron himself approaches, carrying a be-ribboned guitar, and arm in arm with a tall, elegantly dressed man with glittering black eyes.

"*Mon cher* Mozart," says Baron Wetzlar, "How is your dear wife progressing? Splendid, I'll be round next week to view the new arrival."

"With your gracious permission, Baron, we're naming him after you."

"I am flattered."

"Baron, you look rather raffish, like a Spanish Gypsy, holding that guitar. Why don't you abandon it and let me give you some clavier lessons?"

"The guitar is the perfect instrument for both a Gypsy and a Jew, dear Mozart; both tribes prefer to travel light. And now before the music begins again, I would like to present you to *Herr von Abbé* Da Ponte. He has, as you may know, been appointed to the Imperial post of Poet to the Italian Theater and is already adapting a libretto for Salieri. I am certain you and he will have much to discuss."

Wetzlar beams, bows and moves on to greet other guests. The tall man fixes his dark eyes on Mozart's blue ones, and sweeps him an extravagant bow.

"Honored, I am sure. The name of Amadeo Mozart, composer of the sublime '*Seraglio*,' is on every tongue. Well no, actually, I haven't seen it, but it's only a matter of time, isn't it? It plays every five minutes, does it not? I am certain to adore it. Would you like me to write you an original Italian libretto for the court theater? I have the Emperor's ear, you know; he adores me. Such a splendid man, but a dowdy dresser as emperors go."

"Indeed. His Majesty spoke to me once, but I hope to meet him again soon. How is your libretto for Salieri getting on?"

"Ah, well, between you and me and the gate post, this old text that I have to doctor is abject crap. I'm panting to show Vienna what I can do, so I want you to think seriously about this: your brilliant music – set not to some dried-up old turd by Metastasio or whoever, but to something completely original, zippy and modern; to wit, my matchless poetry! It would be more than Sensational! The Emperor adores me, did I mention that? Only say the word and tomorrow I'll go knock on his door and persuade him to back us; are you in? I'm your man, I'm witty and naughty and irreverent. I got kicked out of Venice for being irreverent, and that takes some doing!"

"How many opera libretti have you written to date, Signor?"

"Oh, none, but really, how hard could it be? I'm a famous virtuoso in prose, poetry and polemic; the Italian language is my Elysian Fields; I frisk, I gambol, I cavort in it. When do we start?"

"Oh," *Mozart looks a bit vague,* "perhaps tomorrow? Come to my house, I'm in the Judenplatz. Number three. Baby arriving any minute, but we can work around that."

"Tomorrow then! It's a date! When's lunch? Two? Excellent! You have made a superb choice of librettists, my dear Amadeo."

"Choice?" *mutters the composer as Da Ponte sails away, tacking sharply toward a group of young ladies.* "On the other hand, he's quick-witted and ambitious; and he wouldn't be bound by the old formulas, because he doesn't know the old formulas…

"Could Da Ponte be my ticket to a court post? These Italians, they're such charlatans; they embrace you like a long-lost brother, then you never see them again. But he's on the make and looking for his big break, just like me. Could we work together? Tomorrow will tell…"

∾ Overture 3 ∾

The Prater – a former Imperial Park, now opened to the public by the grace of His Imperial Majesty, Joseph II. May 1, 1785

Mozart makes an overture to Da Ponte

"Abbate Da Ponte?" *shrieks the plump little man walking his plump little dog along the gravel pathway.* "Dear God, I hardly recognized you!"

The pale skeleton of a man sitting on a bench looks up into the eyes of the illustrious composer Amadé Mozart.

"Mozart, my dear friend, so lovely to see you. And your dog. Sorry I stood you up for lunch. How are you getting on?"

"I-I- you…"

"Go on, say it, just say it and get it over with. *All my teeth are gone.* They just melted like wax and fell out of my head. And you?"

"The baby died, but we have another. Thanks. Otherwise, incredibly busy; making pots of money, though. Sorry I missed your debut in the Burgtheater. I was ill with the dropsy when the play was running, but I did make an attempt to stagger out to see it one night. Halfway there I was sweating like a carthorse, so I reeled back home. How did it go?"

"Catastrophe! I was trying to doctor that shitsucking libretto in time for the premiere, while Monsieur the Court Composer Salieri took himself off to Paris; and the whole production went to hell.

"Singers are like wolves, you know, Mozart; they smell your weakness. Without Salieri there I had no clout. Sopranos started demanding whole new texts to their arias, complaining that I did not understand The Voice or The Grateful Vowels… Singers caught colds, were recovering from colds or were afraid they might catch colds, hence they could not attend rehearsal today or perhaps tomorrow, or possibly never..."

"Oh dear."

"There's more! After opening night's disaster, a torrent of broadsides appeared – the worst of them screaming for the Court Poet's execution, the more moderate demanding my resignation and retreat to the nearest Jewish ghetto, there to dine on Christian infants with others of my degenerate race. The screeds were all scribbled by Italian poets, led by that syphilitic sycophant, that pitiable poltroon, that Pygmy of Parnassus, Gianni Casti, who is hoping – indeed, doing all he humanly can – to winkle Da Ponte out of the post of Court Poet to the Italian Theater and insert himself into it."

Mozart sits down and takes Da Ponte's waxen hand.

"I'm so sorry I haven't asked after you at Wetzlar's. I was frantically busy, and – I suppose I assumed that you had forgotten about me, too. People do, at court."

"Ah, you are damned lucky if they *do* forget you at court! Because – O Mozart, they poisoned me!"

"God save us! Who at court would poison anybody?"

"Casti! May his tiny testicles wither like tomatoes in the sun and blue-black suppurating sores munch away his member, if they haven't already. If it wasn't him, then it was Salieri!"

"Salieri would never stoop to poisoning anybody, Lorenzo; he's too civilized."

"No, he'd hire it done. I know the man who handed me the poison. A Venetian thug-of-all-work named Diguri. He gave me a bottle of nitric acid, saying it would cure my tooth-ache. It did, God knows it did, but it nearly killed me."

"Are you getting better at least?"

"I heal; but slowly. But I will always have trouble digesting my food. The Emperor sent me to his doctors, real ones, not barbers or pig-castraters, but educated men from the Imperial hospital. They gave me calcined magnesium and milk enemas, and saved my life, if not my teeth. I owe my life to His Majesty."

"Listen, Da Ponte, I have an idea! Schikaneder gave me a play yesterday.

I think it could make a wonderful opera, but it's been banned from the stage."

"What's it called?"

"But it came out in book form, everybody has read it, and it's the talk of the town. We'll have trouble with the Imperial censor, he's such a prude; but we could go over his head to Baron van Swieten – or perhaps we could go straight to the Emperor!"

"What sort of a crazy idea is that, to set a banned play to music?"

"It's a *good* crazy idea. It's *Les Noces de Figaro*!

"You're kidding! Beaumarchais? George Washington's gun-runner? It's practically a revolution in five acts! Come to think of it, that clever Figaro is a lot like me; he says the most fabulously disrespectful things!"

"Oh, so you've read it, then! Come on, Da Ponte! Say yes! We'll take the town by storm!"

"You think *I've* had trouble at court, Amadeo? You, a free-lance composer, coming into the court theater with '*Figaro*, The Musical,' '*Figaro*, the Career-killer,' '*Figaro*, the Scourge of the Nobility'…"

"Listen a minute, Abbate; the Emperor is struggling to forward his agenda for modernizing the Empire; and who obstructs him?

"The nobil – ooh, Mozart, you wily little bunny you! Yes! Caesar might want our help lampooning them in public!"

" Oh, Renzo, let's go pitch the idea to him!"

"Better idea, Amadeo, let's write some of it first and then play it to him as a *fait accompli*! Wetzlar will back us!"

"If he does, we'll put some guitars into it, he'd love that!"

"*Carissimo*, permit me to ask – where did a composer get all these racy political ideas?"

Mozart strokes his dog's ears and grins.

"Well, you see. I joined the Masons."

༄ Program Notes ༄

Vienna under Joseph II was a cosmopolitan city, the capital of the far-flung Habsburg lands. In the streets, taverns, coffee-houses and concert halls of Vienna, all classes mingled closely together; one could hear Austrian dialect, Czech, Polish, Italian and Hungarian. Opera people spoke (and speak) a wild mix, switching between Italian, German, French and English, as the situation or level of emotion demanded.

Vienna was a chattering town. Commanding the art of lively conversation was almost as important as dressing to the latest fashion. There is no written record of any discussions between Mozart and Da Ponte during their fruitful collaboration, but whatever they said must have been interesting, erudite, smutty and hilarious.

There is some correspondence between Mozart and his wife Constanze, but they too tended to stay close together for the near-decade of their happy marriage. Music historians belittle Constanze Mozart, portraying her as stupid, crude, unaware of her husband's genius, and worst of all, money-grubbing. None of this is true.

Act I

❦ Scene I ❦

The audience house of the Court Theater,
Vienna, April 21, 1786, 2:00 P.M.

Amadé Mozart is directing a bunch of sweating students where and how — "Gently, GENTLY you donkeys" — to place his pianoforte, which they have carried to the theater from his flat. Mozart sits and begins to tune the instrument. The composer is short, pale and plump, his limbs tapering to small, almost girlish, hands and feet. He is dressed to the nines in a blue coat and breeches, buff vest, gold and mother-of-pearl buttons, gilt shoe buckles and an oversized lace "artist's" cravat. He wears his own abundant sandy hair professionally dressed in a dramatic pouffe and tied with a matching blue ribbon.

On the schedule for today is the first staging rehearsal of Le Nozze di Figaro, *to be premiered on May 1 by the Italian opera company. Opera rehearsals begin at 2:00 p.m., because the straight theater troupe rehearses onstage in the morning, and also because no Italian singer would ever consent to rehearsing before lunch, or to singing in full voice before dinner.*

Cast, crew, production staff and administrators stand around in the red-white-and-gold audience house. Special invited guests include the Court composers Antonio Salieri, Giuseppe Bonno and Joseph Starzer the ballet composer, and their friends and students, who cluster together according to their kind, speaking quietly at the back of the house. Chancellor of Spectacles Count Rosenberg, attended by his toady Casti, talks to the production manager and stage manager.

Rosenberg's chief assistant Johannes von Thorwart stands at some remove from his boss and regards the performers of the Imperial Italian Opera troupe (all of whom have arrived fifteen minutes late) with a less-than-friendly gaze. The troupe's members stand or sit on the backless benches in the Second Parquet of the house, flirting, gesticulating, chattering loudly and running through their vocal warm-ups.

Thorwart snorts in disgust and turns to Head Usher Fritz Drossel, who has sidled up close to him.

"You know, Drossel, I despise Italian people. They are frivolous, libertine, and totally untrustworthy. They are always late for their calls, always complaining and making excuses for themselves. And our so-called Court Poet Da Ponte – he is the worst! I can barely stand to look at him, toothless and practically dead, but still romancing other people's wives. It's disgusting."

"Yes, Excellency. A degenerate race. What have they ever accomplished?"

"And why do we have an Italian troupe here at all? What was wrong with the German musical, may I ask? Everybody says the musical is dead, but I say it was a thousand times better than these idiotic Italian farces with these loud hand-flapping foreign singers, preening and posturing all over the stage! And what was so wrong with Stephanie and the other German poets, that we were obliged to replace them with the likes of Da Ponte and ... well, Da Ponte?"

"Oh, he's their ringleader, Excellency. The worst Italian of them all..."

Giambattista Casti, the celebrated and acidly satiric poet and the librettist of Giovanni Paisiello's opera Theodorus, is chatting up the Court composer and singing master, Giuseppe Bonno, *who nods pleasantly, half-listening and half-misunderstanding what the poet is saying to him, although Italian is the mother tongue of both. However, Casti's palate has been eaten away by the French disease, causing his voice to emerge via his mouth and his nose at the same time: an incomprehensible mixture of sneeze and quack.*

"Mo-zhnart?" *says Casti.* "A one-hit wonder. *S-hneraglio* was fairly well-received, considering; I found it quite tedious, personally."

"Indeed,*" says Bonno, waving across the house at one of his singing pupils.*

"The shameless arrogance of the fellow! Last year he followed me everywhere, bragging to me that he was the best composer in Europe, imploring me to write something for him, all the while speaking the most *hhn-orrific* Italian! And where does he get those vulgar clothes? He glitters like the S-hnultan of Turkey. He thinks he is going to just strut into court like a peacock and own the place. Let me sp-hneak frankly. I knew Paisiello. I worked with Paisiello. He's no Paisiello!"

"Indeed?" *murmurs Bonno, winding his watch and smiling vaguely.*

"And his librettist, what's-his-name! Frankly, 'Seppe, the man can barely read and write!"

"You don't say," *says Bonno.*

"Just between us, Signor, you have nothing to fear from this provincial popinjay of a Mozart. He burned out before he was twenty, everybody knows that..."

Mozart calms himself by tuning his clavier. His nerves are on edge, but not because his creative juices are drying up, as his enemies believe or hope. He has a supreme and a totally justified confidence in his powers, which he does not bother to hide. His twitching nerves are caused by other things, including a healthy fear of sabotage by his or Da Ponte's rivals, and the mulishness of his cast. Some of the singers have been especially witless about performing his new lightning-fast style of theater music. He has thrown a few tantrums to get their attention: threatening several times to throw the Figaro score into the fire if his express musical demands are not met. There will be no compromising – well, as little as possible – with this particular opera.

Nancy Storace, the celebrated English soprano of Italian extraction, has been sitting in the parterre with her mother and her brother Stephen. Now she stands, leaves the parterre and strolls languidly down the aisle to stand next to the fortepiano.

"*Caro Maestro*! First time onstage, are you a little nervous?" *coos Storace in English.*

"To me it goes good, but nevertheless I have gross anxiety," *says Mozart in the same language, more or less; looking up into his prima donna's celebrated melting brown eyes, in which the amorous invitation is all too clearly writ. To himself he says,*

"*Drat, she's lusting after me, with both Benucci and, God help me, the Emperor infatuated with her. Do not, oh do not, encourage her in any way. Keep it cordial but cool and professional at all costs.*"

"*Dimmi, angela mia,* Tell me, my angel," *Mozart begins again, switching to Italian.* "Why is it that you and you alone never complain, in the charming fashion of prima donnas everywhere, that the airs I write for you do not suit? Why do you never demand that it be higher or lower or in a different meter or that I must re-write it so as to better exhibit your considerable gifts, or to hide your weaknesses?"

"*Perchè, cherubino mio,* Because, my little cherub, the Storace voice needs no gratuitous displays of virtuosity to make its power felt. And, although my heart, ah, God knows, may have its weaknesses, my voice has none. But most of all, because the airs you write are already perfect for me, and the ensembles are too delicious, I love every one I sing in, which is, dear me, all of them, isn't it?"

"I cannot bear to view the Burgtheater stage without you upon it, Madame."

"Amadeo, truly, you are a dramatic genius of the ilk of Shakespeare, and no one knows it better than Madame Storace. You understand the human heart better than anyone. You really *must* come back to England with us. So you must practice speaking English with me! I can teach you how to speak like a Lord, and – if you put yourself *entirely* in my hands – so many other things as well…"

"You have so right, *Susanna mia*. No doubts. Now go flirt with Benucci, who would love to go to England too, or go sing some scales, now must I tune this Goddamn clavier."

"*Oh, bravo, caro Maestro,* you know the most important English word already!"

"It is the equal in German. This very famous word was even in this opera for a while before the god-damned censor schnitted – snipped – it out. Go 'way now."

Enter Lorenzo Da Ponte into the parquet; a pallid, reed-thin figure in black silk, trimmed everywhere it is possible to trim a suit, with gold thread.

"Carissimi!" *he bellows to all assembled, his glittering eyes welling up with sentimental tears. He flashes the company a rosy pink smile.*

"How marvelous to see you all once more in good health and spirits! How acutely I have missed you! And you – *most* acutely of all, madame."

"Since yesterday, Signor?" *giggles Signora Mandini, taking his hand in her own and pressing it just north of her bosom. Da Ponte has been leaning backward in a fashionable pose supported by his cane, but now he sways forward like a willow in a windstorm and bends low over the hand of the pretty young soprano who will create the role of Marcellina.*

"I am in an absolute paroxysm of despairingly incurable love for you, Signora," *groans Da Ponte. The singer giggles and whispers in the poet's ear, and slides his hand directly onto the bosom. On the other side of the parquet her husband, the bass who will sing the role of Count Almaviva, glares at her. She sees the glare quite plainly and ostentatiously ignores it.*

"Herr Da Ponte, up to your usual shenanigans, I see!" *says Count Rosenberg.*

"Oh, Excellency, in the tender arts we all must bow to you," *smirks Da Ponte, bending low over the hand of* Signora Luisa Laschi, *who will sing the role of Contessa Almaviva, and professing his despairing and incurable love. A seat in the First Parquet is unlocked by Fritz Drossel for the Poet to the Italian Theater to rest in. He sits heavily and with a little sigh.*

"Ah, that's better. And how are you, my dear Court composers? Dearest Salieri, and my dear Bonno, and dear Starzer! Turned out to see our first stage rehearsal, have you?"

Salieri is even suaver and silkier and more gold-trimmed than Da Ponte. Salieri maintains a distant cordiality with his countryman, perhaps because Da Ponte wrote the libretto for his only unmitigated flop, Rich for a Day. *Salieri had, at some personal risk, sponsored Da Ponte for the Court Poet's position years ago, but now he is pleased to blame his opera's failure entirely on his erstwhile protégé. He is also not entirely at ease with the facile brilliance and cocky egotism of his young colleague Mozart. Salieri eases his pain by confiding sotto voce to Starzer, who is quite deaf.*

"Do you know, my friend, I live in the hope of this show's failure? Dear Maestro, believe me when I say that Da Ponte is the worst librettist in Vienna, perhaps in all Europe. I vowed I would rather die than collaborate with that gummy poltroon again. Then, curse him, he pulls off a half-baked success with Soler in *The Good-Hearted Geezer*, even with everyone toiling night and day to ruin the show. 'So exceptional,' the Emperor said, 'what a poet! He must write another one for Salieri!' What torment!"

"Ja, natürlich," *says Starzer.*

"Why the Emperor is so attached to Da Ponte is completely beyond me. I did not think Caesar would so warmly embrace such a charlatan, such a ribald, a gambler, and a Jew to boot."

Starzer nods and smiles approvingly and takes a little nap.

"I can hardly contain my delight," *Salieri confides to his dozing companion,* "that he and Mozart are collaborating. How charitable of me to allow him to stop scribbling on my libretto and encourage him to write for this preening bumpkin instead. Being saddled with Da Ponte will keep Mozart from enjoying any more success in Vienna, that is a certainty. Let me just make a note to send Da Ponte a case of wine. Or nitric acid, ha ha."

Salieri, having cleansed his spleen, rises and approaches the Poet to the Italian Theater, arms outstretched.

"Lorenzo, *poeta magnifico*, it is my fervent hope that you are feeling stronger after your dreadful illness." *The two Italians embrace like long-lost brothers and speak in their native tongue, waving their hands, showing off their pretty lace cuffs.*

Count Rosenberg slides an alert and professional eye over his Italian troupe, counting heads. When he has ascertained all the cast and crew are present and ready, Rosenberg gives the sign to commence the rehearsal to his production manager, who passes it on to Mozart.

"Also, incomminciamo, tutti i personaggi sulla scena per favore! All ze company on-staitch, pleece!" *Mozart claps his hands and shouts. He does not shout his request in German, because there is only one German speaker in the cast, and she is standing beside him.*

"Schnell-schnellste, mädl, auf die Bühne." "Quick-quick onstage, little miss."

He stands on tiptoe to kiss her forehead and pat her cheek; Anna, Nanina, or Nanette Gottlieb is all of twelve years old, but already taller than the composer. She is an actress and child prodigy soprano from the German theater company, who will sing the role of Barbarina. Her mother, Frau Adelheid Gottlieb, *a massive woman with ice-blue eyes and a braided coronet of mousy-blond hair, is sitting by herself in the parquet seats. She wears half-mitts, is ferociously knitting something, and frowns darkly.*

Mozart cues the stage manager to raise the show curtain. The man gives two sharp whistles, and then the riggers backstage haul on the hempen ropes to raise the velour, which is weighted with a heavy chain in its hem. The cast, having gone onstage through the side doors, begins to cross to downstage center. Suddenly Signora Laschi *emits several piercing screams and faints gracefully into the arms of* Signor Mandini.

"What the devil is going on up there?" *shouts Mozart.*

The cast surrounds the stricken soprano, babbling loudly among themselves.

The composer's voice rises to a shriek; "Signora Laschi, will you stop these out-dated histrionics! This is the Opera Buffa, so please to not dramatize yourself! Come down center please and prepare to receive some notes!"

Signora Mandini wrenches La Laschi from the arms of Signor Mandini, and dumps her none too gently on the boards. Signora Mandini vigorously slaps her fallen colleague's wrists, and, it must be said, her face. Signora Laschi revives, shoves la Mandini away, sits up and screams again. She points offstage down left, with a trembling, but statuesquely poised, arm.

"*O Dio, vedete la,* look, look there, don't-a you see? *O Dio mio, che scena orrib-ile!*"

"What are you doing? Stop screeching and embracing and falling down, all of you!" *Mozart screams.* "Such a display of ham acting! Attention please, I have notes for all of you and then we will begin!"

The whole cast is now staring transfixed and open-mouthed offstage left at the object entangled in the rigging, slowly descending until it stops about two feet from the floor. It is not the sandbag counterweight for the show curtain, but a human body, hanging by its neck. It is a man, his mouth and eyes open and his face pale blue-gray in hue. He is most certainly dead.

Mozart, who cannot see the body from where he stands, halloos and waves his arms to attract the performers' attention. More sopranos collapse. More basses and tenors offer their splendid chests for the women to nestle against as they hide their eyes from the grisly spectacle.

"Begging pardon. We cannot rehearse today, Herr von Mozart," *says the stage manager, appearing onstage left and taking a knife from its sheath.*

"I will not put up with another delay!" *howls Mozart, dancing with rage. But his cast is already staggering offstage, supporting one another, weeping, and holding handkerchiefs to their noses.*

"This rehearsal is cancelled," *says Count Orsini-Rosenberg, appearing suddenly from upstage right.* "Someone has died in our theater, and we must call the coroner, the police and the priest."

"What? What? Who's dead? What kind of nasty prank is this? What about my rehearsal? I need to rehearse my show!"

"Not now, Mozart. Go home. Do you hear me?"

Mozart continues to stare at Count Orsini-Rosenberg, his pale blue eyes bulging and mouth agape. Rosenberg turns his back and joins the members of the stage crew who are clustered in the wings. Spectators from the parquet are rushing to get onstage, jostling the singers who are rushing to get off. Elbows are thrown. Nasty words are exchanged.

The composer is left standing alone next to his clavier amid the empty orchestra chairs. Suddenly he squeals, turns and bolts for the exit. At the door he stops, turns on his heel and marches back down the aisle and up the stage left stairs.

The stage crew, having put another counter-weight on the curtain rope, and cut the corpse from its hempen noose, are arranging the body into a dignified position on the floor. Mozart arrives and stands on tiptoe trying to see over the shoulders of the crowd as they stoop over the corpse. He gasps, turns even paler and puts his hand over his mouth.

"Bless me, this is awful!" *says the composer under his breath.* "I've never seen a hanged man this close before. He's all blue-gray and his eyes are sunk into their sockets. There's where the rope has cut into his neck, and crushed his voice box. It left a thin little line of blood all around the front of his neck. Who can he be and why is he hanging around backstage at my *Figaro* rehearsal?"

"My dear Mozart, if I may hazard an opinion…" *it is Da Ponte, who has limped onstage.* "I believe the gentleman before us in that unfortunate condition is Herr von Haegelin, the Imperial theatrical censor."

"Know him well, do you?" *purrs Salieri.*

"Only professionally. Even in this condition I recognize him. We have crossed swords from time to time in the past. I was with him in his office just yesterday afternoon, poor man. We were having some words, and rather heated ones at that."

Da Ponte looks at Mozart. Mozart looks at Da Ponte. Mozart flushes violently and his brow contracts.

"You had words? About … this show?"

"Not about this show as a whole, dear fellow. It was about the third aria for Figaro, in Act I. You know, the one he wanted us to cut?"

"Third aria for Figaro in Act … *what?*"

"Threatened to kill him, that's what you did. Everybody in the building heard you. Now look at him. " *Signor Francesco Bussani states, in a more-than-usually resonant bass. Bussani is singing the dual role of Don Bartolo and Don Curzio, but he does other odd jobs around the theater, including reporting on his colleagues.*

"Stop sneaking up behind me, would you, Bussani? You made me jump!" *says Da Ponte.*

"Guilty conscience about something?" *Bussani booms.*

"All personnel off this stage at once, I will have order here, did you not hear me, Bussani? Get out!" *snaps Count Rosenberg. Nobody moves. He turns a pleading, pale and perspiring face to Mozart and Da Ponte. His mouth works but words do not emerge. Salieri gallantly picks up his cue.*

"Dearest colleagues, please, this is no time for show-doctoring. Would you be so good as to clear the stage for the police and the priests?" *Salieri gently shoos the younger composer and his poet towards the stage right exit.* "This poor gentleman does seem to be Herr Haegelin, who was charged with the oversight of your play, Mozart."

"But – must the police come here during *my* rehearsal time?" *whimpers Mo-*

zart, coming to a full halt.

"Certainly, the presence of police is customary in Vienna when there is a death – and especially a suspicious death, where a murder may have been done." *This from Assistant Chancellor Thorwart, glaring at the composer.*

"I say it's murder, murder most foul!" *roars Bussani, glaring at Da Ponte.*

"There will be no talk of murder here," *says Rosenberg.* "Suicide is not a crime, so we do not need the police, surely."

"Due respect, your Excellency," *purrs Thorwart.* "Suicide is both a crime and a sin, and as such the scene must be investigated to ascertain whether the deceased is to be denied a proper funeral and burial in holy ground. And of course if it is not a suicide…"

"You think it's murder then?" *gasps Mozart.*

"Oh, indubitably," *smiles Salieri.* "I don't see how Haegelin could have climbed up into the rigging unassisted and done himself in. He's not exactly young. And not exactly slim."

His Excellency Count Rosenberg is beginning to look very ill. His hands are shaking; his face alternates between livid red and pale gray. He struggles to regain his powers of speech, wiping his mouth with a handkerchief.

"Haegelin is-is- obviously a suicide," *says Rosenberg.* "Nobody commits murder in Vienna. Murder is almost unheard-of in this happy city!"

Da Ponte nods his assent. "If Herr Haegelin, a man famous for wielding his righteous pen to administer *coups de grâce* on countless *coups de théâtre*, wants to exit the world in a sudden fit of *felo-da-se*, I consider that he has, in one fell swoop, made both a fine *coup de théâtre* and a good career move."

Rosenberg bursts out giggling in falsetto, sits down abruptly on the lip of the stage, and puts his head between his knees. Thorwart purses his lips and raises his eyebrows as he inclines his head submissively in his boss's direction. Salieri tsk-tsks delicately.

"Your Excellency," *babbles Mozart,* "You are obviously right! I agree with you wholeheartedly. Suicide it is! If there's anything I can do … our first rehearsal onstage and now this terrible thing … a suicide, yes, how fortunate for us … no, that's not what I mean … *Excusez-moi*, I need air. Come with me to a Coffeehouse, Da Ponte, and let us gather our wits." *Mozart exits the stage, fumbles for his gorgeous gold-trimmed hat, which he had stashed under the clavier, and tucks it under his elbow. He turns and looks up at the Chancellor, who is still bent double between the footlights.*

"   Your Excellency, Count, begging your pardon, how long will all this priest and police business take? I simply must have a rehearsal today. Do you think we might get the house or a large room later this afternoon?"

"The stage house is a crime scene; and the rehearsal rooms are engaged all day and in the evening," says Thorwart, "so you will just have to wait your turn till tomorrow at the same time."

"If there is anything I can do, I am, of course, at your complete disposal at any time, night or day," *murmurs Da Ponte, bowing to the assembled gentlemen. He pivots on his cane, steering Mozart toward the door, with a hard hand under his elbow, saying* "Keep your mouth shut, Amadeo, till we get ourselves out of here."

❧ Scene 2 ❧

The streets of Vienna: a Coffeehouse, two minutes later

Mozart, DaPonte

The creators of Le Nozze di Figaro *have left the building. Having crossed the Michael Square they are now hustling through the dust of the little alleys, called 'Gassen' by the locals. They wordlessly agree to bypass the shiny new Court Pastry Shop. Da Ponte leads Mozart toward a café at a safer remove from the theater.*

"You know," *whispers Da Ponte to Mozart, as they careen around a corner and into another alley,* "I've never seen Rosenberg look so panicked. Perhaps he's worried that corpses hung up like salamis in his theater will reflect badly on his tight-ship management style. But he shouldn't worry; I have a premonition that the axe of Imperial justice is going to fall on me. I calculate that I have about an hour before I am detained."

"Really? Why you? Why not any number of people? Why not Salieri? Did you notice how quick he was to assume a murder was committed? I can see him killing Haegelin himself just to keep us from presenting *Figaro*! Did you see him smirking and insinuating? How he hates me! I just know he'll wheedle at Rosenberg to cancel the play and put up one of his godawful mediocrities in its place," *fumes Mozart.*

"Thanks, dear colleague, for your tender concern about my imminent arrest! By the way, we'd do well to speak in Italian: there are snitches everywhere, not that it makes any difference, as I'm a marked man." *Da Ponte hobbles even faster, wheezing audibly.*

"Why," *whines the composer,* "are you hustling me so fast down this dustbin of a *Gasse*? My shoes and clothes are getting soiled and I'm choking!"

"I desperately need a coffee and a really gooey sweet before they toss me into the dungeon, *if* you don't mind! I personally have formed no hypotheses about Salieri or other anti-*Figaro* factions, because everyone wanted to kill Haegelin, may God receive him in Paradise," *says Da Ponte*. "Because everybody hated him."

"Yes, the feeling was universal; but why are they…"

"Why will they detain me? Let's go in here. Coffee! Coffee with whipped cream, and the torte cart over here, *s'il vous plaît*, and make it snappy!" shouted Da Ponte.

"But Salieri…"

"If you ask me," continues Da Ponte, "Salieri would never kill a censor. Or even want to, more's the pity. Salieri never comes close to doing anything censorable, but in spite of that he's a very nice man. He and I have reconciled; all friends again. And he wouldn't lift a pinkie to ruin you; he is acutely aware that you're the genius and he's the hack; but he knows how to cater to his audience better than you. This frivolous Viennese society loves Salieri's music: those bland-but-catchy little jingles they can forget with no effort on their way home."

"He hates me, because even composing jingles strains his paltry gifts."

"That's not fair, he's quite capable of endless jingles. No, dear friend and darling of my heart, it is not you but I, the brilliant Lorenzo Da Ponte, who am hemmed in by enemies on every side; every dilettante poet in Vienna is snapping at my heels, or plotting to slip poison into my wine or slander me in pamphlets! By the pricking in my thumbs I'd say they're doing it again now. Anyhow, Signor Bussani and Deputy Thorwart did much more insinuating than Salieri."

"Bussani would denounce people for the sheer fun of it."

"I believe it was for more than sheer fun when he accused me of murder. He does snitch work for H.E.'s office, on commission; I shouldn't confide my secret hopes and dreams to him if I were you. Ah, here we are! So, Amadeo, let's just enjoy this excellent coffee *mit Schlag* and these commendable tortes before the minions of the law nose me out. Let's have a good talk about art or women or politics, or literature, or women; what do you say?"

"Why are you so certain you will be detained? Because of that thing Bussani said? That you had a spat with Haegelin?"

"The last of many, seemingly. There's a history. Starting with the epic shoutfest Soler and I had with Haegelin over cuts he made in *The Goodhearted Geezer*. Surely you heard about it, the town was abuzz for days."

"Soler is such a peach. It was so nice of him to give up his slot and let us put *Figaro* in for this season. Or was it your fight with Haegelin that caused him to postpone his show?"

"Well, Soler was trying valiantly to drag me out of the office, but I think he was glad for a chance to do some revisions on the score.

"But I was saying, Mozart: to Haegelin's way of thinking, if anything on-stage isn't an impropriety it's an innuendo. The man could find filth in punctuation. I asked him 'how many improprieties can one *old geezer* commit?' Then I cursed him and threatened him so violently that his whole family fell down. O bless you and farewell and Godspeed, thou wart-bestrewn obscurantist obstructionist obfuscatory bastard!"

"Did he open the cuts, having been persuaded by the force of your arguments?"

"Of course not. I have changed my tactics slightly. Entirely on your behalf, dear Mozart, I made another even more stupendous scene in Haegelin's office, just yesterday. Naturally I shook my feeble fist and shrieked at our censor, cursing him in Venetian style. No, of course I didn't strike him, I'm in no condition to strike anybody, and yes, people heard me, I took good care that they did."

"Oh dear God, Renzo. Why? Baron van Swieten oversees – oversaw – Haegelin's work on *Figaro*, and has restrained him at every turn, so why did you feel compelled to stick your oar in? Did that idiot – God rest him – threaten to cut the Second Act Finale again?"

"No. Not that. I heard through the grapevine that he was going to cut Figaro's arias in Act I, and I confronted him about that. But the sneaky bastard tried to throw me off guard first by raising a quibble about the top of Act III. You know that little recitative between Susanna and Figaro right after she offers herself as bait to the unsuspecting Count Almaviva?"

"*Eh, Susanna ove vai? … Hai gia vinta la causa?*" What's improper about that? All Susanna says is 'You've already won your case.'"

"Well, he didn't care so much about what she *says*. He noticed that she and Figaro *exit together*. This great ox – may angels fly him direct to Paradise – announced to me he would not permit Figaro and Susanna to exit the stage together, because that bit of business will lead the audience to infer that the two are going off for an assignation."

"Excuse me?"

"So I bellowed, at him *con tutta la forza*, "They ARE going off for an assignation, they're going to get married, you bone-headed granfaloon! Not only that, but had you been paying any attention you would have known Susanna had just MADE an assignation – right onstage – *with the count*, which we all hope she will not have to keep!"

"He saw reason, of course?"

"No. He became even more spiteful, and declared that the fandango in Act III would have to go. Not, as you would assume, because of the notorious ASSIGNATION NOTE that Susanna passes to Almaviva during the dance, but because there is no ballet permitted in the Italian opera, per the Emperor's orders!" *Da Ponte does a fair imitation of the late Herr Haegelin's stolid and malevolent drawl.*

"The fandango hardly qualifies as a ballet," *whimpers Mozart, who has begun visibly to tremble and tear up.*

"I told him that the singers themselves were undertaking the dancing, but that stinking son of a sow – may his soul be with God immediately – pretended reluctantly to back down, at least for the moment. Then he sprang his trap! Back he went to Act I, which according to my confidential sources, was his true prey! He said Figaro's First Act arias are too insubordinate and that he was excising them both immediately."

"'Fine,' said I, 'we happen have another Act I aria for Figaro, all ready to go, which is much more respectful.'"

"There is no such aria."

"But there *could* be. I had the idea for it three days ago, after I got the heads-up. It's really provocative; it verges on *lèse-majesté*. It would probably cause a riot in the theater."

"I hope you didn't use that argument with Haegelin."

"Of course not. I didn't need to. I just handed him the draft of the recit and aria. The poor donkey practically shit cobblestones when he read it. Would you like to see a copy?"

Da Ponte fumbles in his pockets and produces a crumpled bit of paper. Mozart reads under his breath:

"Manteniamo lampante queste veritadine;

che tutti uomini uguali creati son;

che son dotadi dal loro creator

di certi dritti inviolabili; che tra questi son

la vita, la libertá, e la ricerca della felicitá;

che per sicurare questi dritti Oh God …

il consento delgi governati … Oh blessed saints … *destruttivo* …

"Renzo, are you crazy? That's Thomas Jefferson's … Independency Thing! And the aria is … oh, *no*, that Beaumarchais speech about nobles being mere accidents of birth, the very first thing we agreed to cut from the play! God knows Beaumarchais is provocative enough, but setting Jefferson's Declaration right in front of it is death! I never will set this text!"

"They love the guy in France."

"Radicals do, maybe, but France is France and the Habsburg-Lorraine Empire…"

"Anyway, poor Haegelin was so shocked it made him forget everything; "Se vuol ballare," "Non più andrai," assignations, recits, ballets, finales. He took up his Almighty Pen and cut it in one swoop. Then of course I was obliged to threaten to kill him by several time-honored trans-alpine methods and other things much worse. I fought like a Turk for this particular non-existent air, aren't you even grateful?"

"Is my grate full? Full of ashes. Dust and ashes. My life, up in smoke. This is all too convoluted for me."

"Listen, Amadeo, let me whisper this in your shell-like ear. My secret source says Figaro's arias were on the chopping block after written orders – direct from the Spectacles Office – *on their letterhead* – were issued to Haegelin at the censorship office. They seem to have been signed by no less than Chancellor Rosenberg himself. Rumor has it that His Excellency suspects that you and I are ridiculing specific nobles at court. Are we?"

"Catastrophe! No airs at all for the title character in Act I! Why don't we just call it *Le Nozze di Bartolo and Cherubino* and be done with it? Why are you cooking up these Byzantine intrigues?"

"Amadeo, how about some love here? I needed to stop Haegelin from ripping the guts out of our play! I needed to keep Benucci from finding out that his arias might be cut. If word got out to Benucci he would have quit the production, trashed Haegelin's office, then killed him and eaten him with red sauce!"

"Benucci has never in his life had such brilliant arias to sing, and everybody who has heard him thinks that they and his singing of them are a goddamn miracle! Everybody loves them! Including Count Rosenberg, or at least so I thought."

"Except for Haegelin. And the Spectacles Office, evidently. And Bussani of course, who always claims Benucci's high notes are flat. Ah, Bussani, the company spy! I am always so delighted to think they aren't paying his salary on the merits of his singing. But I personally think he's much too openly accusatory for a snitch!"

"That's just a diversionary tactic, to throw you off your guard. You are familiar with diversionary tactics? As in, you threatened to kill the censor if he cut the arias for the title character in Act I?"

"No, aren't you listening, and what do you take me for? I threatened to kill him if he cut the Declaration of Independence. My feeling is if you're obliged to sacrifice something to the Thought Police, it's best to give up something that doesn't exist. One feels its loss so much less acutely."

"We *will* continue to claim, if anybody asks, that Figaro's first aria expresses his loyal wish to play guitar for his lord's dancing pleasure? That when Figaro calls his Conte Almaviva a 'contino' it's a term of endearment, and not an assessment of his boss's man-tackle?"

"The last thing I would have thought."

"Good. The second aria, "Non più andrai," "You won't be going around bothering women any more," is not about me warning Dear Godfather Count Thorwart to keep his hammy hands off my sweet wife, but Figaro's warning Count Almaviva to keep his hammy hands off Susanna, all the while pretending to send the little Cherubino off to the army, right? Any resemblance completely coincidental, our little secret, yes?"

"Naturally. Absolutely no topical references to the illicit lusts of the nobility, general or specific, in this play. Took 'em out. All gone."

"Oh, woe is me. I had a horrible feeling that somebody or everybody is laboring round the clock to prevent this show from going up. There's Haegelin dead and no staging rehearsal and Bussani crying murder while Rosenberg insists on suicide, both Thorwart and Salieri gloating at my discomfiture; and the cast going coo-coo. I'm sure they've forgotten their words, their notes, their ornaments ... the Devil curse all singers except Benucci, Storace, my wife and my sisters-in-law!"

"Never fret about singers, my dear, it is a waste of energy. No matter how bird-brained they are, they'll always rank ahead of the likes of you and me. They draw the fat salaries while we work for food and tips. All we can do with singers is wheedle, flatter and try to keep them confused but happy, with an emphasis on confused. Pray God we will be able to keep our enemies, whoever they may be, confused also."

"Oh, Renzo, there's such a swarm of them. It would be lovely to winnow them down to one or two. We're pushing the limits, politically speaking, with the content of this play, but I believe they can't harm us in the long run, as long as we keep the Emperor's favor. His Kingly Imperial Majesty will keep us safe, unless there is a real scandal. For instance – ah, if *a corpse suddenly joins the cast*."

"Or if they arrest the Court Poet. Honestly, you Viennese are so child-like in your belief that Caesar will make it all better. Even your "Enlightened" democratic-leaning Masons wriggle and widdle like lapdogs when His Imperial Majesty looks at you cross-eyed."

"I'm not Viennese. I'm a Salzburger. And so what if the Masons have put ourselves under the protection and jurisdiction of the Crown, what's wrong with that?"

"And you take your orders from the Enlightened Despot and his head spook cop Pergen now, don't you? So much for your progressive free-thinking civil society."

"Well, after all, we really have had some dangerous subversives infiltrating the lodges, so we have to be cautious..."

"Cautious! This isn't the moment for caution! Can't you smell revolution on the breeze? Isn't it fun to let some of it blow into *Figaro*? What a fire-breathing recit and aria Jefferson and Beaumarchais and I wrote! How terribly I miss it now it's been cut! It would have stopped the show!"

"I only pray God the show *starts*! But let's get something straight, I happen to agree with the Emperor about reining in the Freemasons, and I agree with the Emperor about no riots in the theater; and also about his rule about no ballet in the opera; once ballet dancers get onstage, you can't get them off again. I even like his new rule shutting down the endless encores. Since every number in this show is a drop-dead hit, we'd be there for months, encoring one after the other."

"You're just no fun at all."

"No encores! *Punkt*! It kills the pace! I want the action to rush and tumble forward on itself, zip-zip! No riots, for the same reason! I want all those counts' and nobles' asses in their seats, witnessing the dawn of the modern age! I need them right there!"

"High-bred backward ninnies, the lot of them."

"No, a lot of them are with us on this! Think of Count Thun, Prince Lichnowsky! And I like a lot of them, especially the new-created ones, like Baron Wetzlar. I count countless counts among my friends, Renzl. I frequent their gracious villas and urban palaces; I give lessons to their homely daughters; I eat their excellent food. And they treat me as an important personage, not as some mere lackey to tinkle on the clavier while they play at cards."

"Well, listen to you, Amadeo, sucking up to the nobles! And who would know you weren't a count yourself with those posh clothes and that gloriously architectural coiffure? And here I thought you were a republican."

"Shut up, don't say those words even as a joke. I'm a dedicated Monarchist modernist, please. Besides, you dress more fashionably than I do."

"And everybody at court dresses better than our King & Kaiser, and they all poke fun at him for being so frumpy! It's the fashion to disparage our Monarch."

"No it's not!"

"His parsimony. His moth-gnawed waistcoats, his darned-up socks. Does he mend them himself in the still watches of the night? No, he just lets the nobles spend their money to dress up, throw lavish balls, keep salons; it saves him no end of expense. No wonder they feel free to mock him. It makes them feel so democratic and cutting edge. Come on, let's put the aria back in. We'd be showing them a good time."

"There is no aria, nor will I supply one. Besides, suggesting any sort of popular uprising in the Empire gets a little too close for Caesar's comfort right now. Think of America, Renzl, of restless Bohemia, think of the horrible horrors of Horia; whole hunks of Hungary consumed in flames in that peasant uprising not two years ago. Think of the ominous tidings from France. We don't want to raise an outcry for a Yankee-Doodle Republic under our Emperor's nose, do we? Haven't we been over this already several times?"

"Don't worry, Amadeo, I'm only passing what is left of my freedom in honing my rhetorical skills. Just kidding, honestly. I adore the Emperor, and he me, did I mention that today? And I love the Austrian nobility too, who more than I? Like you, I grovel, I toady, I simper and smirk and make love to them all. I happily kiss fat perfumed princely ass, because I love them so. Like you, I ape their clothes; I copy their manners. I know from whence my living comes, and I'm grateful, so grateful…"

"That's more like it."

"But I can't help wanting to jab them with a sharp stick now and then. Particularly, I want to poke those backward provincial counts squatting on their vast medieval estates, stripping their groaning peasants down to the last turnip, raping their peasant wives and daughters, and beating their naked shivering arses with nail-studded clubs. These rustic tin-pot nobles, they're wedded to the land, they don't know shit about modern life. Ignoramuses! They don't read, they don't talk politics, nor do they even have the imagination to wallow in dissipation the way our fine corrupt Venetian nobles do. So hooray, I say, for the newly ennobled bourgeois business-barons the Emperor seems to love so much: these realtors and merchants and bankers."

"Hope is new-crowned!" *whispers Mozart.* "A modern civil society will arise to replace the medieval one we have now. It's in the stars! The new bourgeoisie lights the way forward, certainly. Even the moldering old nobles and the fat princes of the church will come to see it! The Common Good! Equality under the law! Trade! Science! Hospitals! Everyone will come to embrace modern reforms, but! They should be Imperial Reforms, not republican reforms."

"You think so, darling? Caesar can't reform his Empire without the old guard's consent, no matter how much he encourages the Viennese bourgeoisie. The landed nobility sustain the monarchy, and they're all happily stuck in the fourteenth century. Ah, the grand old ways! The Grand old Names! Esterhaza! Gulas! No man of power and consequence in the history of the world has relinquished his ancient privileges without a fight. Nor should he. There is such a thing as tradition, you know."

"Listen to yourself, Renzo. In two minutes you've reversed yourself and are now arguing the other side of the case, just to hone your rhetorical skills. Look at you, practically weeping for the passing of the Dark Ages. What a hypocrite you are. You also urged me to pander to those witless nobles and dumb down my music into mindless jingles too, didn't you? Right before you proposed I set the Declaration of Independence to music? Yes you did, yes you did, five minutes ago."

"Well, we've come full circle then, haven't we? Good. Let's have another coffee, and perhaps some marzipan. Alas, my cherished dreams evaporate like morning mist. The non-existent Act I *recitativo* "We hold these truths" is cut. The riot of titled twits in Michaelerplatz will not take place. The Russian tour is cancelled. Let us lowly minstrels be satisfied merely to titillate the sluggish humors of the Viennese bourgeois and upper classes and avert our eyes from the larger issues of the day. The world is stirring, but it's useless to expect these bird-witted people to understand. Give them meringues, and not harangues."

"Figaro is hardly a meringue; it's revolution and revelation *in musical drama! With real live all-too-human characters!* And people are going to love it. How can they not? It's fucking immortal."

"You have such faith in the Viennese bourgeoisie. They may be comparatively tolerant, even of us Jews; they may all pound on the clavier and toot into the flute and read music off at sight like Bohemians, but their minds have been lulled to laziness by their sweet fat life. But they are so mortally afraid of passion. Bitchiness, *Schmäh*, as they say, is as far as they will venture onto the treacherous seas of the emotions, and bitchiness is their chosen medium. They like their theater to be a little piquant, with here a little laugh and there a little tear, but not anything too American and radical in it, God forbid. They would stay away from *Figaro* in droves if they had any principles at all," *hisses Da Ponte.*

"You want this show to be a success, don't you? I certainly do," *says Mozart.*

"Nothing gladdens my heart more than to turn out a brilliant work and get a big fat fucking sackful of money for it! That's my philosophy of nut, in an artshell. It's good business to be entertaining and it's easy as pie for me. Deep currents of human truth and justice might run beneath the sparkling surface of *Figaro*, but there let them run, unremarked by the masses of asses.

"The *cognoscenti* will hear and be utterly transported. They will see the shades of Shakespeare, Aristophanes and Voltaire, stretching out their arms, welcoming my play to the heights of Parnassus!"

"*Pace*, Signor genius, show some modesty."

"You, Renzl, have gone out of your way to extract the most obviously sharp front fangs out of the French play, for which I am so grateful. But now you must not go around exposing its subtle back teeth. I'm begging you here."

"Don't joke about teeth, *carino*. It's too personally painful. But never fear; I will soon be incarcerated, and that scandal will probably divert all gossip about Thomas Jefferson."

"Stop saying that; it's too melodramatic. I notice that nobody has come to arrest you, and we're on our third coffee and our fourth torte. Promise me that during production week you will not do anything crazy? *Figaro* is the greatest goddamn opera ever written. Everyone with clean ears will know it in a week's time, and we'll be rich and famous. If, that is, if His Excellency ever permits us to rehearse. What did you do with the fair copy of our non-existent aria, by the way?"

"Balled it up and threw it at Haegelin. Sorry, Amadeo, I needed to do it, the scene cried out for it. I dangled a red herring in front of his nose."

"And soon the poor wretch dangled like a herring himself."

"God grant that he soon dangle among the Cherubim! I'd almost forgotten he died. The man has done a great service to the theater. But now mine enemies are drawing nigh. But listen! Forget Salieri. Watch Casti. Watch for more memos from the Spectacles Office! Don't turn your back on Bussani. Avoid the old nobility. Someone already made an attempt on my life, may I remind you; and I am almost certain that by now they will have denounced me as a subversive Jew and the executioner of our unlamented Herr von Haegelin."

✌ Scene 3 ✌

The same plus police officers

Recitativo

Enter two Police Officers, with their numbers printed on their kit bags.

"Herr von Da Ponte?" *says the uniformed Imperial Police sergeant.*

"*Si, certo, numero quarantasette, son io,* it's me, the illustrious poet Da Ponte, at your service."

"You are detained, sir. Please come with me."

"Wait a bit, Monsieur forty-seven!" *cries Mozart.* "He's the Court Poet to the Italian Theater! He has a rehearsal in a few moments! With me! The famous composer Mozart! His presence at the Court Theater is imperative! What has he done, anyway?"

"I'm afraid you're going to have to rehearse without this gentleman, Monsoor. Come along with me now, Herr Da Ponte, and don't make an argument."

"Oh God, Lorenzo, *che sciocca,* what a shock," says Mozart.

"Not really, Amadeo. Didn't I just mention that this was going to happen? I distinctly remember telling you before. Thanks for the coffee and the fine conversation. It's just what I needed before facing this latest reversal of my fortunes. Pay the bill, will you, there's a dear. My treat next time."

"Was there something we forgot to discuss, Renzl? Some small piece of unfinished business?"

"Possibly. Just beware. Trust no one. Perhaps some discreet snooping around the theater on your part, my dear, might enlighten us as to the origins of this macabre Haegelin prank, and who it was who instigated my removal to the *Polizeihaus.* They are surely one and the same! I am innocent of whatever you think I am guilty of, gentlemen, innocent as a lamb. *Addio, caro*, I know I can count on you."

"Snooping around the theater … Oh heavens, I have to get to the theater! If we can't do *mise-en-scène*, at least I can do some musical brush-ups in a studio … I'll set up some individual coachings … got to post a schedule … if no rooms available, then at my house…" *and Mozart turns his face toward the Michaelerplatz and the theater.*

ᴄᴠᴐ Scene 4 ᴄᴠᴐ

Michaelerplatz, outside the theater, ten minutes later
Mozart and Count Gulas: Aria di rabbia e vendetta

The city now swims in a golden haze of rush-hour dust from the many wagons and carriages clogging the streets, so the composer flags down a Fiaker cab, and has himself driven the short distance back to the theater. As he descends, a florid gentleman approaches him waving a cane.

Mozart thinks, "God save us, it's Count Gulas, with blood in his eye as usual, the very exemplar of the old nobility I wish to avoid most; where can one hide?"

"Mozart, goddamn, what in hell do you think you are up to? Where are your values? Don't you see where your goddamned anarchist play has led? Murder, that's where! Insurrection, Illuminati Jew agitation, revolt and bloody murder, that's where. This is what happens when them damn Freemasons bring their filthy free-thinking propaganda in. They actually propose giving the peasants special rights and privileges, like letting them marry when they please and wander around the country without permission – it's a slippery slope, I tell you! I know these people, lived among 'em, and I can tell you they're less than one step up from brute beasts. Show them leniency and they think you're weak, and they start imagining that their wretched lives and ours have the same worth except for a 'mere accident of birth!' Yes, I've heard all about your goddamned subversive aria! It's all over town!"

"I…"

Gulas pokes the butt end of his cane into Mozart's chest, leaving a manurey smudge on his beautiful buff-colored vest.

"How will I go on ruling my estates, as the Lord God so obviously wants me to do? What will become of order, eh? Of people knowing their place? 'Inalienable rights' indeed! In my county I decide who does what, and who goes where and when, and who is convicted of what crime and how they'll be punished. And now you and that Wop Jew are suggesting to them that they live their lives as they please? It's anarchy!"

Mozart skips sideways to avoid the deposit of another blot of shit on his clothes.

"I tell you right now that I am personally organizing a boycott of your subversive little play if rehearsals continue. Every loge rented by the nobility will be empty! You will lose your gate proceeds, and I hope you will lose your commission as well! I insist that you call a halt to the whole fiasco this very minute!"

"Fine, thank you, Count, and how is the lovely Countess?"

"Don't get snippy with me, you squeaking little poppet! All decked out like a prince, and spewing republican filth! I know what you're up to, with your Voltaire and your Beaumarchais and your ... your George Washington!"

"Really, Count, I just write the music..."

"Let me tell you something, you arrogant young puppy." *Gulas shakes the carved onyx head of his cane in Mozart's face.* "I hold estates in Hungary, vast estates, which could go up in flames tomorrow if the peasantry isn't kept down. Joseph made me free my serfs, and butted in about my tax laws, and I have barely managed to get by since, but I keep control as best I can. The iron fist, they call me. But now this! Masonic *lèse-majesté!* It's the death-blow! The End of Civilization!

"Oh come now, Count, you speak of the Emperor as if..."

"You keep His Majesty out of this! Do you think he's a damn republican? Do you? My household serfs – servants – can hardly wait until this *Figaro* thing goes up in the Burgtheater. They're all Bohemians, mind you; and a lazy, sullen lot they are, too. But each one plays an instrument or sings in addition to doing their household duties. So I get an orchestra and singers at no extra expense, any time I want to have a *fête,* or a little music at dinner, y'see?"

"How economical."

"But those goddamned swine don't know when they're well off. They fraternize with musicians in town when we're here, and they know all about your damn *Figaro* already! I know all about it, I read their letters, I pay my household spies, I know exactly what they're up to. I wouldn't be surprised if my whole family is hacked up and burned in their beds and hanged from the lampposts the night after the premiere! I warned that damn coward Haegelin in his office and again in the theater yesterday evening! Told him off good and proper! We're all in danger, I said. Do something or else, I said. Did he listen? Now look what's come of it! He's been murdered. It's this so-called "Enlightenment," and your damned Masons and Jews and your damned modern hogwash that's killed Haegelin, an Imperial public servant, and I am telling everybody that I blame that smirking Italian Jew priest, that libertine, everybody knows he did it. He's been in Berlin you know, and takes his orders from the anarchists there. I warned Caesar about his dirty doings, too. Shut your mouth and stop gawking at me!"

Mozart shuts his mouth but continues to dance on his toes, ready to dodge a blow. During the count's harangue Mozart is thinking:

"In a black rage … a murderous rage, maybe? Why did he tell me he had hot words with Haegelin? Why did he tell me he denounced Da Ponte to the Emperor? Is he confessing, threatening, or mouthing the latest slander from … from whom?

"He is angry enough to kill anybody with that knout of a cane … but I'm forgetting Haegelin was hanged … or wait, could he have been walloped and then hanged? I never thought of that. Hit in a blind rage and then hung up like a sandbag to throw the stink of scandal onto my play. Da Ponte has a cane too, but he's feeble and besides, why would he want to wreck his own show? And … AND … can Gulas insist on murder when Rosenberg insists it's suicide? Did Gulas do it? Is he that stupid? Say something to him or there may be a real murder done!"

The composer backs off and addresses his assailant: "Count, calm yourself, I beg you. *Figaro* is a French farce. Boudoirs, doors, assignations, et cetera. A harmless *bon-bon* set to music. But you say you went to see Haegelin yesterday, Count? In his office during the day, and in the evening in the theater as well? Did you see Da Ponte speaking with Haegelin?"

"Yes, damn his Jewish satanic soul to hell, he was ranting and screeching and threatening to beat Haegelin to a pulp, and worse, in full hearing of everybody! I passed him as he came out, and he was grinning and drooling from his naked chops as if butter wouldn't melt in his mouth. Smug, conniving, dirty…"

"Da Ponte is a man of the church, Count. And a personal friend of the Emperor, whose patronage my show enjoys. You say he was smiling after his fit of temper? That's peculiar. Did you have words with him?"

"I don't speak to Jews, priest or not."

"And then you told Haegelin about your – misgivings – about *Figaro* in his office?"

"Yes, as I said; and again last night at the theater. I marched right up to Haegelin at the interval and told him we had to do something to smother this dangerous unrest among the rabble, not throw fagots on it and start a damn bonfire."

"Did you, uh, threaten him at all?"

"I told him exactly – what? Wa-a-a-it a minute, Mozart, are you trying to implicate me? Do you think I murdered him in my loge during the second act? That's a good one! I had better things to do in there, and there's a chit from the Corps de Ballet who will attest to it." *Gulas puts his finger aside his ruddy nose.*

"I beg your pardon, Count, but Count Rosenberg has plainly stated that Haegelin committed sui…"

Mozart's protest is cut short as Gulas's cane sweeps an inch above his coiffure in a whistling parabola.

"I've killed men in my day, real men, you puny cockerel, killed them aplenty, and I still could if need be! But I never did in any civil servants, no matter how insubordinate they might be. Listen here. Haegelin looked hale and hearty at ten when I collared him at the entryway. I just made my point again, and plenty of people heard me. He ran away and headed for the palace and I followed him down the corridor. If I hadn't slipped on the stair I would have pounded it into his thick head! But he must have ducked into one of the offices or *garderobes*, the damn coward. Then I went out to dinner. Somebody killed him, but it wasn't me. I have nothing to hide from the likes of you, and I don't owe you an explanation of my movements either, you simpering dandified dwarf! Get out of my way!"

✑ Scene 5 ✑

The administrative wing of the Burgtheater, two minutes later
Mozart and Fritz von Drossel, then Count Rosenberg

Mozart, having dodged out of the count's way, betakes himself to the administrative offices, entering at the stage door and going through the connecting corridor to the palace itself.

"Why did that lummox count keep insisting on murder," *the composer says to himself,* "when it's obviously a suicide? Was he drunk? Silly question. Ugh, look at the state of this building, all these grubby little office cubicles. This used to be the ballroom, I think, in the days of Her Majesty. No grand balls in this palace any more, such a pity. The Emperor, God save him; what a skinflint he is, always paring down court expenses and instituting new economies. More like a civil servant himself than an Emperor.

"I suppose he had his bellyful of his mother the Empress's pomp as a youth, and as a result he nurses a compulsion to downsize. He allows the Viennese nobility to foot the bill for all the grand occasions in the capital, and he visits their palaces and salons and drinks their wine. Fine with me; it makes for more concert venues. Even some little opera venues, here and there. But dammit, I need to move beyond playing at card parties and benefit concerts! I want a job in the Court theater! *Hofopernkomponist!* I won't be intimidated by intrigue or – by murder neither. I want to grab the world by the balls and swing it around my head till it cries uncle."

The main theater offices, costume morgues, instrument storage and rehearsal rooms are in the wing of the palace just beyond the theater hall itself. From his relatively luxurious executive suite, Count Rosenberg and his second-in-command Johann Thorwart, the financial officer, rule over the diminishing world of the Court spectacles: theater, ballet and opera.

"God grant that I don't see Dear Godfather Thorwart! No love lost in either direction," *muses Mozart.* "Does he know he was the model for Osmin the harem-guard? He fancied himself the protector of my dear wife's virtue; he accused me of all sorts of unspeakable things during our courtship; seduction, abduction, obstruction; her undergarments under the bed in my apartment, and so on. Well, we were in love, so why not?

"Thorwart was frothing with outrage when he made me sign his damned odious marriage contract, so insulting to both Stanzerl and me; he made me agree to a payment of 300 florins if – when, according to him – I went back on my promise to marry her. He treated me as if I were Don Juan himself, who seduced and jilted a thousand and three women. *'O pagarla o sposarla':* Either pay her or marry her, indeed.

"The man practically frog-marched me into St. Stephen's for the wedding; stood over me, glowering, hoping I'd bolt. As if I would. I'm pretty sure he fancies my tender little wife as a side dish for himself, now that he is securely married-up into the first-tier nobility and answers to the name Count Johann and not Haensl … I wouldn't put it past the old goat. Would he like to see me fall on my ass in his precious theater? Yes, he would.

"If I cringe and make nice to him, maybe I'll have a dim hope of getting first dibs on a rehearsal room today after all. And re-confirm the Act I and II staging rehearsal in the theater tomorrow, run the rehearsals, then perhaps visit the dear baroness beforehand, to ask for her moral support. I must keep her on the boil, but at a safe distance. Flirting with her keeps the cash flowing, and is even amusing as long as she keeps her hands more or less to herself.

"Here we are; all right, *Signor Hofoperkomponist,* time to arrange the face into a lamb-like blandness, put a little more bend in the spine. Count Rosenberg himself, or his toady and moral guide Casti, may be lurking in there, as well as Dear Godfather Thor-fart."

"Excellency?" *Mozart knocks diffidently.* "Excellency, I need to report…" *He peers around the door into the room, and finds himself gazing into the reptilian eyes of Herr Fritz von Drossel, the Head Usher of the theater. Herr Drossel smiles wanly and inclines his head as slightly as possible in the composer's general direction.*

"*Servus,* Maestro."

"*Gruss Gott*, Herr von Drossel. I have to tell Monsieur Deputy Thorwart that we will be needing a room and a music rehearsal schedule for *tutti i personaggi* in *Figaro* this evening. For the entire cast?"

"With all respect, maestro, that will be impossible. I believe your ingénue has withdrawn."

"The little Gottlieb? Is she ill, or distressed by today's … well, of course she is. But she'll be fine tomorrow or the next day. I'll request an understudy. I'll need to inform His Ex…'"

"Oh, I rather think His Excellency is aware of the situation. Count Rosenberg was just discussing it with Herr Haegelin, God rest him, in the inner office there, late last night after the play. Herr Haegelin seemed to have a strong objection against such a young child's participating in your play. Corruption of her morals or something like that. They had a loud and extended conversation; more of an argument, really."

"You don't say?" *Thinks:* "Does the man stay here all night, resting his weary ears against office doors in the hope of hearing something saleable? And did the dear departed Haegelin wander the halls at midnight objecting to everything about Figaro? O Lord, now am I supposed to tip him for this information? What will he do if I don't? "

"Are you sure you mean *last* night? Signorina Gottlieb was in the theater not two hours ago, all ready to sing. Nothing was mentioned to me about her leaving the production. The child was taken home, by her mother I assume, after the – incident. I suppose the shock might have sickened her. Last night, you say?"

"Oh, it was last night, very sure. I usually come in here to the outer office after the show, to count up the tips. The tips, monsieur, you know."

"Ah, yes, one moment, here, you're welcome. Did you happen, in the course of your duties of last evening, to see Count Gulas at the play?"

"I came back to this office at night, to turn in a portion of my tips to the general fund and make an accounting. Yes, Count Gulas was in the hall. Barging around backstage making a scandal, threatening to do this and that. Drunk, you know. One hates to see the grand old nobles of the blood acting in this unseemly fashion, doesn't one? But now that there are so many newly ennobled bourgeois folk parading about, even sitting in the old nobles' loges, one doesn't know whether one is bowing to a person of ancient lineage or scraping to a Jew real estate developer now, does one?"

"Do you mean my dear friend Baron Wetzlar von Plankenstern? I thought not. Do not Jews eat, piss, and shit like the rest of us mortals; didn't Shakespeare say something like that?"

"I wouldn't know."

"One must take care; I myself find it's better to grovel to everybody, just to be on the safe side," *says Mozart, backing toward the door.*

"One doesn't wish to offend."

"And yet one so often does."

Stepping back into the hall, the composer feels something writhe serpent-like beneath the sole of his shoe. Something familiar, but from another place, not the floor. He looks down. He is standing on a cello string.

Mozart stoops and picks up the string. He thinks:

"Wire wound, thick. The C string. Flakes of lint or something stuck to it ... How long has it been lying here collecting dust? No one has swept the hall this week; there's dust in all the corners, thick as the leaves in Vallombrosa: one of Caesar's austerity measures, perhaps?"

"Herr von Drossel," *calls Mozart, edging back into the office,* "do you play cello?"

"No instrument," *says the clerk with an infinitesimal bow and a hostile stare.*

"The only person in Vienna," *giggles the composer. He thrusts the string into his coat pocket, backs up another step, and collides with His Excellency Count Rosenberg himself. Rosenberg's face is dead-white, and his hand flutters suddenly towards Mozart's coat pocket, then to his own lips. In a flash the count recovers himself and puts the hand into his watch pocket.*

"Gruss Gott, Mozart," *the words are barely audible.*

Mozart bows and scrapes.

"'*SS Gott*, Excellency. I came to reserve a studio, and post a remedial rehearsal schedule for the cast. I am told that there is a problem with the little Gottlieb ... I'm sure she will recover soon. But we might think now about the need to put an understudy into the cast for the interim. A chorister perhaps, Your Excellency?"

Count Rosenberg's eyes look past Mozart and into the middle distance. His tongue writhes in his mouth, but forms no word.

"Good day, Count," *says Mozart, bowing, and retreating to the bulletin board to post his notice. He keeps his eyes on the floor, looking, looking for — he knows not what.*

⤜ Scene 6 ⤛

Mozart's house, Grosse Schulerstrasse #4, near St. Stephen's Cathedral,
April 21, 4:00 P.M.

Mozart and Constanze

"Oh, Sweetie, you look all pale and sad! Why aren't you rehearsing? What has happened?"

"Jesus Christ with a Toothache, what *didn't* happen? My first staging rehearsal was cancelled and the cast sent home! Now they're all coming over here to do individual musical brush-up before supper."

"Heavens! Is there still more intriguing going on? Has Salieri gotten up another plot? What non-existent reason for cancelling did the man trump up this time?"

"Oh the reason existed, surely enough. When they rolled up the curtain they rolled down a dead body! A dead body hanging in the flies, not flies hanging round the dead body, which is the usual case!"

"Aaah! Bad luck!"

"Worse yet. The body flying in the rigging was the Imperial Censor for the Theater, Herr Haegelin, who had hanged himself, or been hanged – opinions seem to differ – to death – opinions unanimous."

"How horrible. But then again, how nice for all the playwrights, I suppose. They can open up all those Haegelin-imposed cuts: the *dénouements*, the curtain lines, the unkindest cuts of all … How did he get up there?"

"That's the question. His Excellency Count Rosenberg favors a suicide, the better for his reputation. Dear Godfather Thorwart and that Hungarian

Count Gulas and Signor Salieri like to think it's a murder, the worse for mine, and the worse for *Figaro's*. Even more horrible, Da Ponte has been detained at the *Polizeihaus*, and Gulas is complaining to one and all that it's an anarchist plot and threatening to organize all the country booby squires to boycott my play. And, the ingénue is taken ill, and I will have to run the first staging rehearsal tomorrow all by myself and probably sing her aria too. The cast will be as addle-brained as a herd of panicked sheep, I just know it."

"Da Ponte was arrested? In connection with the-the pendant pedant?"

"The Dangling Modifier? *He* seems to think so, but I don't know, the police never will tell you why they're arresting you. It's possible that one of Da Ponte's legions of enemies has taken the opportunity to denounce him in secret, which means no public charge, no trial, and no sentence, probably. It could be years before we see him again, and with his bad health … It's common knowledge that he and old Haegelin had hard words yesterday, and he made multiple threats of murder within the hearing of dozens of clerks and stagehands. Of course that wouldn't shock them; threats of murder are the usual mode of address used by every poet who has had his darlings eviscerated by old Cerberus von Haegelin. But I don't believe he's ever been actually murdered before."

"Do you think Da Ponte really killed him?"

"More likely drove him to *felo-da-se*, with his mad schemes to interpolate non-existent airs with radical American republican texts into the play. Look at this draft for a third-act rant for Figaro; it's the famous declaration by Thomas Jefferson, as a *recitativo accompagnato*, wed to an aria taken from the most scandalous speech from Beaumarchais. No, darling, it's not a real aria; it's some kind of a red herring Da Ponte wrote to distract Haegelin from making some other cuts in the show."

"You can't mean "Non più andrai" or "Se vuol ballare"!"

"Among others. If Haegelin *had* cut those airs, Benucci would have killed him, and failing that I would have killed him myself!

"No, you wouldn't."

"Neither would Da Ponte. He's not a violent person, and he hasn't the strength of body to hang a man who was not renowned for his spirit of cooperation. Poison wouldn't be a method Renzo would favor. Besides, he has no reason at all to do murder as long as his pen and tongue are sharp – and he had little means to do it that I can see. Yet they arrested him. I need him desperately to do the *mise-en-scène* and general diva pacification and crowd control! Some devilish plot is being worked to spoil my play! What am I to do?"

"Well, my poor sweet love, I tell you what. Give me a kiss now. Take a deep breath. I feel the urge to intrigue rising in my heart. Right here. So let me be your little *mouche* and go out and do some spying for you. How can your wifey-kins do this, you wonder? Listen and learn. You may be coaching singers to-night but don't think that I will stay home cuddling with Karl and warming the bed against your return. I happen to have an invitation to Countess Pergen's salon, for tonight, to sing some little cantata or other."

"Pergen's! The Police Minister? I never go there."

"I wasn't going to go there either, because – well, the musicians who do go there give the word 'amateur' a whole new meaning. Musical policemen, *ver-schone mich*! Out of tune, out of time, but so-o-o enthusiastic! And tireless! I may not be a real professional like my dear famous sisters, but I take some pride in my musical skills … I've even gotten over being jealous of 'Oysia, at least most of the time. She may have the thrilling high notes, but I have the composer and the composer's sweet man-thing, near to hand…in hand, as a matter of fact … and a bird in the hand is, oho, *alla breve*, we don't dally in dalliance do we?"

"You take away all sorrow, my love, and your voice is sweeter than all of theirs, and truer besides."

"Kuesst mich noch einmal. Hier, und auch hier, und daunten, wenn du willst."
General Pause.

"Anyway, as I was saying before, I'm sure Aloysia would trade a few high notes for the little man, but she's not getting her hands on him, not even on loan. And I was saying before that I'll immolate myself and go to Countess Pergen's and sing while you pound notes. And I'll keep my ears open, kiss both of them for luck, thank you … for any gossip ripped from the police blotters. The place always draws its share of clavier-pounding spies, flat-yowling tipster tenors, and ferret-eyed fiddlers who make their noise as respite from sniffing out enemies of the State. However! Nobody, not even His Excellency Interior Minister and Commissioner of Police Pergen, can keep a secret in Vienna. I'll encourage the countess to share a few confidences about the hottest gossip, which should of course be today's scandal. Mere mention of it should fling open her flimsy floodgates: It's not every day that the Court Censor is hanged in the theater or the Court Poet is a guest at the *Polizeihaus*."

❧ Scene 7 ❧

Mozart's music room, April 21, 6:00 P.M.

Mozart, Michael O'Kelly: Recitativo and Aria Buffa

"Ochelli, my dear friend. Thank you for taking the time. A brush-up before the first staging rehearsal is never amiss even for such fine musicians as those in my cast. Before we begin your aria I want to talk to you again about…"

"Have you heard the one about the two tenors?"

"I think I may have…"

"It seems an opera company had these two tenors. Tee-hee."

"That's it? Pretty funny I'll admit…"

"The *primo tenore* comes home one day and finds the *secondo* on his couch, fucking his wife, harf harf harf…"

"Hilarious."

"And the *primo* says…"

"There's more?"

"The *primo* says, 'what in God's name are you *doing?*' And the secondo, without missing a beat…"

"How un-tenor-like!"

"Without missing a beat, he says, 'Belmonte in Prague, Idomeneo in Paris…' harf, harf harf harf!"

"I *love* that joke! Loved it as a child! Love it still. Ha, ha. Now, Ochelli, we need to talk about – well, the Don Curzio matter."

"Maestro, haven't we been through this? I have been an *artiste*, a man of the theater, all my adult life; and I feel – strongly – that I cannot – *not even for you,* an acknowledged if untried genius in the field of music – compromise the integrity of my interpretation, not even in the Sextet.

"But my dear Kelly, I love your hilarious stutter in the *recits*, you know I do. I laugh till tears of mirth flow down my cheeks and moisten the keyboard. No one now living could possibly do it better than you. My objection to the stuttering schtick in the Sextet is that, well, it puts you a little behind the beat, dear fellow."

"But I have explained and explained, maestro. That stutter is my *character note*. You surely cannot ask me to come out of character, *not even* in the ensembles. Not I. Not ever. Once *in*, I don't come *out*. What of verisimilitude? What of holding a mirror up to nature, as the Bible dictates?"

"Shakespeare," *murmurs Mozart. To himself he thinks,* "Tenors. They're all the same. Next time I write a role for tenor, the phrases will be so goddamn long that no tenor will have breath left to speak this kind of pigshit to me."

"No, Kelly, you are right; I see that now. You must stay in character. The others must adjust as they can."

"Oh, Mozart, I am so glad you finally see my whole point."

"Ha-ha. Yes. I yield to your cogent argument. Speaking of the others adjusting … this terrible tragedy, the body in the theater, how is everybody coping? Some are saying Haegelin is a suicide, some say it's murder! Da Ponte is detained by the Imperial Police, you know, on charges unknown. I fear for him, being in such delicate health. I need his counsel badly this week, because we are still up in the air about, well, many things. Your aria, for instance … Is it in, or will they cut it? Da Ponte *really* wants to keep it in; he's such a fan of yours. But the Emperor says people will be getting hungry if we let the fourth act go on too long. Who will advocate for you with His Majesty if not Da Ponte? Do you know if the singers discuss the scandal among themselves? Those that are speaking to one another, that is?"

"Well, I don't know if I should … repeat … it's only …" *Kelly rolls his eyes and puts a finger aside his ruddy snub nose.*

"Please, Ochelli. Tell me, I'll do anything you ask."

"Well, actually, there *is* something I'd like to ask. I do a little composing myself, you know."

"Don't they all," *thinks Mozart struggling to keep his groan on the inside.*

"Just some modest ditties, pop tunes in the Celtic tradition; no large works of genius, like you or Salieri …"

Mozart winces. "Scribblers, he thinks. Each one worse than the next. Salieri included."

"Do you indeed? You must show me your work some time."

"Well, I happen to have a little song right here with me …"

Mozart feels his heart sink another fathom. He takes up the paper and glances at it. He thinks, "Worse than I imagined. Weak. Clumsy. Obvious." *For the next two minutes, Mozart pretends to study the canzonet while he thinks about what in hell, if anything, he can extract from Kelly in the way of helpful information.*

"I was rather hoping," *says Kelly,* "that you might give me a course of counterpoint lessons. If I have a weak point, counterpoint is it, ha-ha, get it? I need instruction if I am to succeed. But I do have the Irish gift for melody, though, don't you think?"

"What? Oh, yes, yes, you certainly do. Just what I was going to say. Melody, yes. So much so, that I believe instruction in counterpoint would actually hamper your natural expression. Melody, you know, is like … like a fine racehorse, and counterpoint like … a draft animal of no breeding, who works … pulling canal boats. All drudgery and haulage, you know. You must let the melody run on and on, noble and unfettered by the hobbles of academic counterpoint."

Kelly's nose glows even redder, and a smile breaks out on either side of it.

"Just so, just so, Mozart. How well you understand me, how sympathetic you are. I'll take your advice and just 'run on,' then, following my natural bent."

"I can't begin to tell you how pleased I am. Now, dear Ochelli. About the situation at the theater. What are people saying?"

"Everyone is eyeing everyone else with suspicion, you know, and almost all chat has stopped. But right before this thing happened, the hot gossip was all about Casti."

"About *Casti*?"

"They were saying that Johnny Casti, our real-life Don Basilio, has begun to make sheep's eyes at that *garderobe* lady with the ingénue daughter, you know, old Frau Gottlieb. He's been seen passing the woman little notes."

"Dedicating some light satiric verse to her, is he? A waste of time. No reasonable woman would take him on unless she were blind – and deaf."

"They say that she did not look all that indignant about it. I only repeat what I hear, maestro. Mandini jokes that Count Rosenberg is smitten with her and Casti plays the go-between. He says that the count is afraid he'll end up eaten away by syphilis like Casti, so he turns his affections toward a respectable widow, somebody good and old and ugly and nasty, guaranteed not to tempt anybody else…"

"Oooh, that's uncharitable, Ochelli!"

"I'm just repeating the joke, Mozart. But that woman is a Basilisk. She'd gnaw Casti's balls off – assuming of course that they have not rotted off on their own. And she's definitely not the count's type; he likes them slim and pretty."

"Fresh young prossies right off the farm?"

"Oh, *'a quel che tutti dicono, io non ci aggiungo un pelo,'* I don't embellish what people say; I just pass it on. Go ask Mandini, why don't you? But wait, there's more. I don't know if I should tell you this, because Thorwart *specifically* told us not to. Casti's new Juno didn't show up at the theater this afternoon, to do her work in the *garderobe* for the matinee of the play. And neither was the daughter present, and she's the understudy for three roles.

"Mandini said that little Mamselle Gottlieb probably had the female vapors, but the gal don't even have tits yet. Rumor has it that she has *gone mute*! Harf harf harf! Her brother scrapes the viola or something in the pit in some flea-bitten suburban vaudeville theater. And *he* told his stand partner – in strictest confidence, of course – that the gal is struck dumb and can neither sing nor speak! So by now every hurdy-gurdy man in Vienna tells the tale. Her Ma has evidently put her to bed, and doses her with black powders. Say, Mozart, what's the matter? You look rather ill."

"Mute? She's gone *mute*? I imagined she was shaken up, but mute? Why didn't you say so immediately? Why didn't Thorwart want me to know? The premiere is in nine days! She can't have gone mute!"

"It's only a rumor, a little suspicion; I really don't know, myself. I don't lower myself to speak to pit musicians or street beggars, ha-ha. And I never, *never* involve myself with stage mothers or juveniles, if I can help it.

"Sa-ay, Mozie, would you like me to do one of my famous impersonations in the Basilio role? I did a take-off on Da Ponte once onstage, in *Musica/Parole;*

do you remember? He was so furious he threatened to kill me. My, he has a temper, doesn't he, and now look where it's got him! In the clink for murder! I can do a great Casti too. Sing through the nose, and so on. It would be such fun."

"Oh no, Ochelli, not Casti, no! Let's not bite the hand of the man who licks the hand that feeds us, eh? Why do you say that Da Ponte is accused of … oh, why do I even ask? I must go see him if I can, and also I've got to see if the little Gottlieb is recovering, before tomorrow's staging rehearsal."

"Why worry about her? Get somebody else to sing the part if the gal don't show up. As for the Jew…"

"Thank you, Kelly, for your expressions of sympathy regarding your artistic colleagues. I'll certainly pass them on."

"Oh, no trouble. We theater folk must stick together."

"And now can we sing the 'Ass' aria, please?"

∽ Scene 8 ∾

The same, 7:00 P.M.

Mozart and Signora Laschi: Argument and Aria

Laschi is rolling her eyes and fanning her bosom, which she is displaying for the compos-
er's benefit as she stoops down and points at the short score on the music rack.

"Theez aria, Maestro, these-a "Dove Sono", it eeza justa so soffffffocating, so opprrrrressive. Of course I sing it divinely but eet eez-a not worthy of my gifts. Rrrreally maestro you have given me no opportunity to insert-a my best ornaments into it. Cannot I, I beg you again, be allowed interpolate-a dear Salieri's air instead, that one he wrote-a specially for my voice, into Act-a III? I can't add annnnnything-a to theez one, for all it eez-a so dull, and-a besides, the phrases are sooooo looooong that I have-a no breath left for a brilliant-a cadenza. It's all I can-a do to sing it as-a written!"

"And, dear lady, it is more than sufficient to sing it as wπritten, exactly as written. This aria is the dramatic crux of the opera. All eyes, all ears, all ador- ing hearts, turn to you at this supreme moment. This air demonstrates, by its form, by its musical color and structure alone, the maturing will and passion of the Countess—by far the most important character of the entire opera. All you have to do with this air is lend it your celestial tones and endlessly flowing legato, and the effect will be – overwhelming!

"Do you rrreally think-a so? May I come downstage center to sing it?"

"Of course. Just what I was going to suggest. Shall I tip my cheering sec- tion to encore you?

"Oh God, *no*! I can't sing-a the damn thing twice!"

"All right then, at your specific request. No encore. Tell me, are you calm in your mind after the terrible events of this morning? I know how much the discovery of Haegelin's body in the theater has ruffled the sensibilities of my cast."

"I am sufficiently recovered-a from-a the shock. It was I who saw him-a first, you know. Perhaps it's-a not-a right, but I feel I must-a mention it ... Signora Mandini behaved extremely oddly. She leaped upon me like a beast-a, and slapped-a my face several times. I happen to know that if you look closely you will find that she was involved-a with Haegelin ... they have been seen-a together several times, you know. Drossel mentioned it-a to me. Perhaps-a she had a hand in killing him. I wouldn't put anything past-a that-a bitch. You might want to hint-a to dear Count Rosenberg that-a she is constantly intriguing to take over my roles, and she does-a my schticks onstage; what's more, she steals-a my cadenzas."

"That's hardly murder, though, my dear."

"*Worse-a* than murder, if you ask-a *me*! I believe-a she was involved in an amorous intrigue-a with the poor dear deceased censor, a man I very much-a respected. Her husband, Signor Mandini, suspected-a something too. What a life that woman has led-a poor Signor Mandini. I gather from his discreet hints – he confides in-a me, you know, the poor darling – that she was not terribly cheerful about fulfilling-a her marital obligations-a, if you know what I mean. That sort of woman will never sing with deep emotion. Cold, is what I call her."

"Ah, yes. Marriage brings bitterness with the joy, does it not? And now that we are in the proper frame of mind, shall we sing "Dove Sono"?

❧ Scene 9 ❧

The same, 9:00 P.M.

Mozart and Benucci

Benucci sings through his whole role with joy and brio and pinpoint accuracy, and cannot throw any light at all on the latest Burgtheater scandal. Mozart, whose ears are ringing from having received far too much information, is grateful.

∽ Scene 10 ∾

The same, 10:00 P.M.

Mozart and Madame Nancy Storace

The illustrious soprano sings through her airs with great beauty, passion and style. Her brother Stephen sits at the fortepiano and accompanies her. Mozart listens to her in a state of rapture, curled up on the windowsill on the far side of the room, as far away from the diva as he can get.

❧ Scene 11 ❧

Pergen's salon, 9:00 P.M.

Constanze, Countess Pergen: Duetto

A ballroom. A break in the musical activities at the Pergen salon; refreshments are being served. Constanze, dressed in her second-best gown, a crimson one which sets off jet-black eyes sparkling in a rosy heart-shaped face, stands in a corner sipping punch and trying to ignore the ringing in her ears caused by the excruciating cacophonies of the amateur musicians. She is preparing those much-kissed (by Mozart) and much-tortured (never by Mozart) auricular organs for their next task: information-gathering. As luck would have it, the over-brimming Countess Pergen is panting to know how the Mozart household is bearing up under the dual pressures of production week, and the discovery of a dead body in the flies. She takes Constanze by the elbow, and they walk up and down in a large parlor.

"My dear Madame Mozart, you do sing exquisitely. Your voice is so true! Surely you could have had a big career, almost the equal of your sister's. But motherhood is so much more fulfilling, and certainly more respectable, don't you agree? How are your children?"

"Little Karl is flourishing, thank you, Countess." *Thinks:* "Bitch! Sow! She knows well enough that poor little Raimund died!"

"Call me Gabrielle."

"You flatter me … Gabrielle, you really do. I really am terribly rusty. Being a matron now I certainly don't get to practice as much as I used to, so I like to use these low-pressure dilettante evenings to get myself back in some sort of trim. (*Thinks:* "Take that, you bleating old sheep.") But taking care of my dear chubby little cherub occupies most of my thoughts."

"Speaking of your husband, how is the play going? Is he terribly upset about the scandalous goings-on in the Burgtheater? I would have been prostrate with shock, I assure you, had I seen such a sight. Imagine, an Imperial civil servant killed – hanged in the Court theater! And to think that horrid Italian poet would do such a thing. These Transalpine people are all emotion, aren't they?"

"So unfortunate, to be sure. However. Count Rosenberg himself has assured the company that Herr von Haegelin is a suicide. As for our dear Da Ponte, Amadé and I got the idea that he was detained owing to a small inconsistency in his immigration papers. Can it be that he is also implicated in the Haegelin matter?"

"Well, my dear, certain sources ... close to The Source ... are inclined to say 'murder' and not 'suicide' at all."

"No! How shocking!"

"Of course I'm not at liberty to speak of police business ... but even on the street every housemaid tells the tale. Come sit on this divan, darling; why should you, who have so very much to lose, remain uninformed? Come close by me. We don't want the guests to hear ...

"Well. It seems Da Ponte actually threatened Haegelin to his face, and threatened to kill him in front of two reliable witnesses. Then they found a very subversive political writing, in Da Ponte's own hand, covered in blood and clutched in Herr Haegelin's cold, dead fingers. There's proof! Some say he, Da Ponte I mean, is mixed up with the Berlin Illuminati and *plotting to overthrow the Monarchy*! There's more yet! Listen to this! This very afternoon, officers were sent to search Da Ponte's rooms and they found – oh, you'll *never* guess what they found there ..."

❧ Scene 12 ❧

Mozart's bedroom, midnight
Mozart and Constanze

"What, *what*? Stop impersonating Countess Pergen and just tell me, will you?"

"So then that fat, simpering, sweating bitch purses up and says, '*Pornography!*' Yes! Copper plates, engraved with pornography, and several runs of absolute-ly *scandalous* prints! You know what the Emperor thinks of pornographers! And for good measure they found a half-empty bottle of *aqua fortis*, a well-known poison, which is usually used for cleaning copper plates, but never mind! An anarchist and a pornographer and a poisoner, a murderer, *and* with a post at court! His Majesty won't put up with *that* sort of betrayal! This is the worst outrage: these dissolute Jews and Italians and blah blah blah, oink oink oink! So says Madame sow, judge and jury."

"*Aqua fortis*? That's the same stuff some man tried to poison *him* with, two years ago! Da Ponte must have kept the bottle, probably with an eye to finding his enemy and spiking his coffee with it. But pornography? That's ridiculous! Da Ponte is a literary man, not a graphic artist; everybody knows that. This is a put-up job certainly. There's much too much evidence, and all of it is fishy."

"But why are they doing this to him?"

"And me? What about me? Oh, my poor poor play! One scandal in this multitude of scandals will stick to *Figaro*, I know."

"And to Lorenzo too, *Schatzi*. Stop tearing out your hair and tell me – do you think there is any chance at all that he is a murderer or an anarchist or a pornographer?"

"He's a reprobate, a gambler, a libertine by all accounts, especially his. Hot-tempered, certainly. But murder and smut? Why would he do either? He doesn't have the time."

"Never mind why, for a minute. Could he have done it?"

"Let's snuggle up and imagine out a scene. So. He threatens Haegelin. Then he offers him poison. Haegelin, hoisting the bottle and crying '*Prost!*' knocks it back at one go … no, not logical."

"Let me try now. Renzl meets Haegelin backstage. They climb up into the … no, he hauls up the curtain, thus revealing his intended crime to anyone loitering in the house. He removes a sandbag or two from the counterpoise loop and persuades Haegelin to stick his head into it. He lets go of the curtain rope, and if Haegelin weighed less than the remaining sand, he would be yanked up and hanged."

"Same problem as before, Stanzerl. Da Ponte is quite feeble and would not win in any kind of struggle, so getting his victim to cooperate has some merit. It just remains to imagine what possible blandishments he used to get Haegelin to stick his head into a noose. I can think of millions."

"I know! He knocks Haegelin on the head with his cane, then rolls up the curtain. And proceeds as before. He would have to do it late at night, after the crew had struck and set the stage for next day and gone home. Say, midnight?"

"My dear little blackbird, what would either of them possibly be doing in the Palace Theater stagehouse at midnight?"

"Love tryst? Duel? If duel, where are the seconds? Spying on each other? I don't know."

"Could anybody not on the stage crew perform such an operation as hanging one's rival – in the pitch-dark?"

"Lit a candle? No. At dawn, then?"

"There *are* some small windows backstage. Painted black."

"He's an unlikely candidate, sweetie."

"Most important, could he keep quiet about it after? He can't keep a secret to save his life. The evidence is totally ridiculous and phony; the rumors of secret plots; then the dirty pictures and *aqua fortis*. The Haegelin death may be irrelevant, but someone is denouncing Renzl as an enemy of the State."

"You need to go talk to him. Do you think Warden Beer would let you see him in the prison? He is an old shit-for-brains but he's such a fan, and he loved *Seraglio*. The man can't resist plays about captives and escapes."

"I'll go over there tomorrow morning. I'll tell Herr von Beer I'm there on theater business, an exigent production staff meeting, the show must go on, and so forth. God have mercy, I devoutly hope it will!"

ॐ Scene 13 ॐ

The Polizeihaus, *Vienna, April 22, 9:00 A.M. A stone cell, one barred window, admitting a pallid light. A rough table, a low pallet in the corner. Two guards stand dozing on either side of the door.*

Mozart and Da Ponte

"Renzl, thank God they let me visit you. I had to practically give Beer a blowjob to get in here. I couldn't go on without your input, so crucial to the show's *mise-en-scène*. Production problems. Text re-writes. Cast morale, and so on. He likes music, you know; he came to every performance of *Seraglio*. Dear God, what a terrible time this is for me, you can't imagine!"

"Can I not?"

"Yesterday Count Gulas told me he was going to organize the nobility to boycott *Figaro*. Then he practically confessed to Haegelin's murder while trying to lop my head off with his cane. Then that lizardous usher man, Drossel, confided in me that the ingénue has withdrawn, she's out of the cast, and then I couldn't get a room to do any staging work, so I had to do brush-up coachings at my house, and La Laschi practically refused to sing "Dove sono", and I am at my wits' end with her."

"Fine, I'm fine, thank you for asking. The bed is a bit skimpy and the food lacks a certain savor, and I lack pen and paper, books and newspapers; but otherwise I'm happy!"

"Oh, sorry. When it comes to my work, you know…"

"By the way, SSSHHH, don't blather about your sufferings quite so loudly. This is a prison, if you had not remarked on it before. Best to speak Italian; we can't be too careful. Even these ugly, scrofulous guards whose panting, squealing, slut pigs of wives I screwed up the bunghole only last week, might speak Italian, although somehow I don't think so."

"Do they at least tell you what the charges are?"

"I've had several unfruitful conversations with the police. They don't ask me anything of consequence, because they don't know shit, and don't want me to know what shit it is they don't know. So I respond as little as good manners permit. When one is denounced in secret and packed off for an indefinite sojourn in jail, it's best not to say anything at all.

"Have they – tortured you? Oh My God, Renzo, *they've pulled out all your teeth!*"

"Mozart, that is in such execrable taste. You really can be a little pill, you know that?"

"Sorry, but my nerves are gone and my good manners are following suit. You know it could be death unless you cooperate, Renzl."

"Oh, no, not death, surely. There's no death penalty here, and besides I'm a foreigner. They'll probably just escort me to the border; '*non più andrai, farfallone amoroso…*"

"There's usually no death penalty here, unless the Emperor feels the sudden urge to make an example of somebody. For instance, somebody who had won His Majesty's trust and favor and has since been denounced, possibly for committing a brutal murder upon one of His Majesty's civil servants in His Majesty's personal theater. Do we know anybody who might be thought to fit that description?"

"There was no murder! And if there had been, His Majesty wouldn't just assume that I did such an absurd thing!"

"And, Renzl, do you not recall the Baron von Zahlheim case, the scandal that had the town buzzing, only last month? The young man who murdered his old landlady and stole her money?"

"Vaguely…"

"He was convicted, *schnip schnap schnur.* He was due to be gang-pressed into the provincial army, but then Caesar interceded. He claimed that killing an elderly lady was so horrible that he was sorry he had abolished the death penalty. So guess what? He restored it again, just as Almaviva restored the *droit du seigneur* when he wanted to fuck Susanna!

"Can he just abolish his own law like that?"

"Noodle, he's the Emperor. We live and die at his pleasure, and his plea-sure in this case was that Zahlheim die in the utmost torment. 'I don't need anybody's permission to do good,' he said, right before he decreed that chunks of Zahlheim be ripped from his bones with red-hot pincers. After which the murderer would be broken on the wheel and displayed to the public on a gib-bet. Didn't you go? Everybody went."

"I was busy, Amadé. Writing a brilliant libretto?"

"But Zahlheim's torments were quickly over, relatively speaking. If you ask me, he was dealt a punishment easier than the usual one for murder, which is *worse even than death*! You pull boats!"

"*Scusi?*"

"On the Danube! In Hungary! Against the current! They put you in leg chains, fetter you to some other criminals, throw you into the muck and make you haul barges back upstream. They feed you thin gruel, just enough to keep you from dying, but you die anyway, sooner than you'd expect but later than you hope!"

"*Gran Dio*! I'd live two hours, at the most. But how Draconian! In Venice, they just poke your eyes out and throw you into the lagoon in a weighted sack; if you're a citizen in good standing, that is. But then we're not as Enlightened as you are here. You know Venice?"

"I was there as a youngster, for Carnival. I dressed up as Harlequin."

"I'm sure you stood out amongst the hundreds of other Harlequins."

"Stop joking around, Da Ponte! Don't you even care about yourself? Don't you care about *me*? Don't you want to write another play with me?"

"I would hate to inconvenience you in any way, dear Mozart: I know how it would distress you if I should miss rehearsals, if I did not appear on opening night, if I were torn apart with hot pincers or died in the riverbank mud. So yes, I care deeply."

"Good."

"And, if I may speak of my own paltry inconveniences, I'm languishing for female company. You know, the warders told me that this building used to be a convent. Ah ... just think of all those sweet little nuns, right in this room, praying, doing penance, washing their chaste undergarments, doing whatever nuns do – *Gran Dio*, I can almost smell them. So, after you get me out, and I slake my lust for female charms, what shall we do for our next opera?"

"Stop being evasive. Why? Do you have any ideas?"

"*Don Juan*, of course. I could have sworn I told you."

"*Don Juan*? We can't do that in the Court theater! It's a low-class pornographic puppet play for bordellos and peep show booths ... but then again, why not? It's a terrific story."

"Why not write it and produce it somewhere else, Amadeo? London, for instance. Prague. They'd eat it right up. Picture it. Rape and murder in the dark! A grand ball, drinking, dancing, *with* another rape offstage ... not unheard-of at grand balls, now that I think of it ... oaths of vengeance ... apparitions! A singing statue, seeking revenge for its own murder ... hellfire breaking through the floor!" (*Mozart hears three trombones, D minor, playing under the stage!*) "All humanity, plus the denizens of heaven and hell, all united against the Dissolute Don of Seville!"

"Stop, stop, I'm all excited! I like it ... *I love it*! We'll do it! But this is not the time for workshopping, Renzl. I have to think of a way to get you out of here. Perhaps if we understood why you're in here ... Question: do you have any idea at all why you came to be denounced?"

"The only Jew, probably. The convenient scapegoat for somebody else. I have no civil rights at all, just the Emperor's benevolence. So I am denounced, although I am a humble, a simple, a harmless and a peace-loving man, a gentle voice amidst the howling mob of poets and playwrights who had every reason to brutally murder a man who committed suicide."

"The police found the draft of your Jefferson/Beaumarchais pastiche on Haegelin's person."

"*Scandale*! So they surmise that in addition to committing a fictitious murder I am single-handedly fomenting revolution in Vienna? You'd think these oafs would recognize the texts, even rendered into coruscatingly brilliant Italian verse by me. Stealing other people's stuff for use in libretti isn't a crime. It's common practice."

"But, Renzo, there is – *shhh* – some other incriminating evidence, that Constanze heard about. Manufactured evidence, I'm pretty sure. The police searched your rooms and found some dirty engravings, plus their copper plates, with a bottle of *aqua fortis* standing nearby."

"The same corrosive they poisoned me with? *O numi pieta, sono in trappola!* I knew it! It's Casti and his crowd; the identical fiends in human shape who tried to kill me before, now brazenly claiming that *their* murder weapon is *my* murder weapon! And – *o dio*, possession of pornography: that's a really serious offense in Vienna … that settles it, I say nothing, nothing! Amadeo, you have to help me! They're going to kill me!"

"Renzo, *calmati*, eh? Let's think this through. Your threats to, ah, murder the deceased – can we start there? How did you come to cross swords, or pens, with Haegelin? Did you not tell me yesterday that somebody had given you a heads-up about some directives from H.E.'s office to gut Act I? Who is that somebody? Perhaps if I talked to him I could find out who is behind this plot to ruin the show and, um, even what happened to Haegelin."

"Whoever killed him performed an important service to the Theater."

"May I ask again who fed you the story about Spectacles and Haegelin and the Act I arias?"

"I have my little sources, Mozart. I am no stranger to intrigue myself."

"Quick question: *you're* not the one intriguing against the play, are you?"

"Certainly not!"

"And you're not in league with the Berlin Illuminati?"

"Is *that* what they're saying?"

"Gulas."

"I'm not really a joiner, darling, I'm more of a free-lance gadfly. International politics is not my thing. So no. Let's confine ourselves to the enchanting and magical world of the theater, shall we?"

"All right. Your little source. What exactly did he say?"

"Well, just what I said before. That … that His Exxie, Count Rosenberg, sent a memo to Haegelin, instructing him to cut Figaro's Act I arias because he had come to believe that you were maliciously lampooning the Austrian nobility."

"That is so hard to comprehend. We've had a cordial relationship in the past … but I suppose if one holds, as 'twere, a mirror up to the nobility, one or two of them might actually recognize themselves … So! Count Rosenberg – behind it all! He's betraying me! He wants to murder *Figaro*! He must have murdered Haegelin!"

"Sweetheart, that is totally asinine; they were on the same side."

"Oh, right, on the same side. Against you and me, it seems. I get so crazy when my work is threatened. So. When your source whispered these unlikely rumors to you, did you casually mention that you were going to write an even worse aria than the existing ones, then go directly to the censor's office and offer to kill him if he refused it?"

"Well. I might have ... preened. Thumped the chest. I was feeling very vulnerable, and needed to make an impression on her."

"Ahhh."

"I can't help it, Amadeo. They throw themselves at me."

"An enamored lady, passing you secret information about a plot originating in the Spectacles Office, and the matter ending with Haegelin's death and your being arrested! Why are you so indiscreetly amorous?"

"Couldn't help it. Love danger. Pitied her. She is so unhappy with her husband."

"They're all so unhappy with their husband."

"Amadeo *caro*, you know how I adore all womankind, I really don't care what their motivation is. "'*Voi, che sapete, che cosa e amor!*'"

"Is that some sort of dark hint? Oh *no*, not our little Cherubino!"

"Mozart, I always wanted to fuck a woman dressed up in men's clothes."

"Oh God, Renzl, are you completely crazy?"

"She loves me, she loves me, I'll swear to it."

"And yet here you are, denounced; here you are, incarcerated. You told me yourself, she's married to a spy! What if both of those cursed Bussanis cooked up this whole cutting-the- Act I arias story just to make you lose control of your world-famous Italian temper in a matter of honor, and then ... then ... well, and then *what*? You're sure you didn't kill him? In some sort of fit?"

"Reasonably sure, yes, you little ass."

"Well, if one pursues this train of thought much further ... one has to assume that *they* killed him! Oh God, murderers in my cast! Oh woe is me, SHHHHH! Renzo! We've got to keep this a secret!"

"Yes! The show must go on! At any cost, evidently. Perhaps you would prefer that I confess to an imaginary murder so that you can have your breakthrough Burgtheater triumph? Or is it sufficient that I continue to languish here with a padlock on my lips? Hm? Hm?"

"I-I- well, would you mind? There's really nothing left for you to do now."

"The poet, having poetized, is expendable. As good as dead. His name will not even appear on the poster. Of *course* I mind, you self-involved imbecile; I'm eating thin soup and sleeping on flea-infested straw!"

"Sorry."

"I pardon you. Let's think a minute ... It's quite easy for me to spin you a tale that does not include a murder, nor impugn the lady. How about this? That wretched Bussani may have finally worked it out that his is not the only sausage warming in his wife's oven, and decides to make his rival go away ... he allies himself with Casti and his goon Diguri; and they manage to break into my rooms and plant some porn and Casti's old calling card, the famous bottle of *aqua fortis* therein. Then he calls in his police pals."

"But what about Haegelin's remains? There they lay in full view onstage, while His Excellency and Bussani debated about whether he had killed himself or was killed by, well, probably, you."

"Bussani, in all his eagerness, thinking he could further besmirch my character by attributing Haegelin's demise, obviously by his own hand, to the last person who threatened to murder him."

"Count Rosenberg was holding firm for suicide, though, wasn't he, Renzo? And you'd think he would embrace your guilt whole-heartedly if he were truly interested in wrecking the show, tossing you from the Court Poet's post and putting his little fixer Casti into it."

"Not so easily done as you think, Amadeo. His Imperial Majesty is still the patron of this play. H.E. can't just sabotage Caesar's darling *Figaro* all on his own, without offering up some sort of cogent evidence of my guilt! No, the gradual disappearance of the opera still seems the more prudent course for Rosenberg to take; he gets to keep his ass covered and his hands clean while he soothes the wounded sensibilities of Gulas and the mob of rustic Austrian nobles who are yowling around his office door."

"But how did Signora Bussani find out about ... well, she could have heard it direct from her husband, I suppose. He spends time lounging about said office, waiting to tattle on people and collect his thirty pieces of silver. Maybe *he* did the murder to stop Haegelin cutting his tiny part."

"The man's a snoop, not an assassin. We have to assume he has at least a financial stake in this show's success, seeing as he is still working in it."

"But Renzl, what about Count Gulas, acting on his own? He boasted to me that he has killed men before."

"Gulas is too stupid to pull it off. Just blunders around drunk, swopping at things with his cane, and missing."

"But – I know he was chasing Haegelin backstage on the night before he died, insisting that he shut us down; because he boasted about that, too."

"Notice, dear Mozart, that I now continue to help you sort these things out, in spite of your callous disregard for my welfare. But let me ask you a favor: do not dwell on murder, or who did murder, since I am still the prime suspect. Suicide is my strong preference. In this, Count Rosenberg's heart and mine beat as one.

"As for your most urgent matter, namely the plot against *Figaro*, my money is still on somebody or everybody, from Spectacles. I trust my source; the nibbling will continue. The death by a thousand cuts! You can expect H.E. or his minions to strike again, in an attempt to bait you into withdrawing the play. I go further and prophesy that their target will be the Act IV finale. If they come after it then you know that H.E. is behind it all. How do I know this? Because she swore it was so.

"But why Act IV, for heaven's sake? Oh, wait; because of all those assignations happening onstage?

"Yes indeed. Your susceptible friend admits that he boasted to her that he had, in a courageous act of defiance, crammed the show's finale with the largest number of assignations ever before seen in the theater, starting with Cherubino's impudent groping of the countess (disguised as Susanna), up to and including the one where the count commits adultery with his own wife in the *côté court* pavilion. She was deeply impressed at my audacity."

"But why should anybody care about assignations? Haegelin was the only one who cared."

"But wait, there's more! Even more important than those assignations! My darling told me that the real hot issue for Spectacles is not the ridicule of the nobility in Act I, nor the ballet, nor the assignations; but the dread spectacle of a real purebred Count kneeling to a mere commoner and begging her for-giveness, right out there in public. Almaviva's surrender is more bruising to the tender sensibilities of the high-born than anything else in the show!"

"*What?* How dare they ..."

"Don't interrupt me! These backward-facing oafs see their personal supe-riority vanishing the very instant the silken Almaviva knee hits the floor! '*Perche siete un Gran Signore,* Just because you are a big fat Lord, you think yourself a big fat genius! Nobility, fortune, rank, position, all that makes a man proud! And what the hell did you do for all these advantages? You took the trouble to be born, and nothing else.'"

"Quoting that bit of Beaumarchais is not such a good..."

"How *dare* anyone depict a noble debasing himself like that! No matter how many stupid knuckle-headed things he has done, he's still better than the common herd! And he is deeply offended by the egalitarian notions of Thom-as Jefferson, Beamarchais or our King and Kaiser Joseph II!"

"Pipe down: even these ox-brained non-Italophone guards will wake up and figure out somehow that you are committing treason."

"Just practicing my curtain speech. Or my gallows speech. So, back to our conundrum; if The Spectacles Office cuts '*Contessa, perdona!*' You'll know for certain it's the bumsuckers over at Spectacles, colluding with the feudal lords, doing their best to drive the Enlightenment back into the shadows, and inci-dentally to ruin Mozart and Da Ponte in Vienna. May they all roast in hell and be served up on red-hot platters smothered in cayenne pepper..."

"If any of that is close to true ... the rest is silence. They can't cut that bit. What's the sense of doing the opera anyway if we take that bit out? That bit is the whole point. Everything devolves on those few measures. My life is over. Over, I tell you. What can I possibly do if this happens, but withdraw?"

"Well, Amadeo, should this Act IV thing happen, you must go to Caesar and accuse the Chancellor and his crew of conspiracy to murder *Figaro*, and incidentally, the entire Austrian Enlightenment right along with it. You have to start thinking like a snitch, or a cop."

"Oh yes, I'll just run to the King, and the King will make it all better. Didn't you recently mock me for thinking like that? I can't go tattling to the Emperor. I won't. I have no solid evidence of either the Murder of *Figaro* or the Murder of Haegelin. Haegelin, murder or suicide seems like an entirely unrelated problem…"

"Not to me, they don't, Mozart!"

"But! If *those people* cut *that piece* – if they do this horrible, *sinful* thing – I *will* withdraw. I'll leave Vienna forever and put the show up in Prague or London. Being in this Court theater is like attending a cheap dog-fight, with street-curs fighting over *Figaro* like a scrap of meat, and I'm not letting these bastards tear my work apart."

"Good to get that off your chest, wasn't it? You must find some sort of solid evidence, dear man. You must save your opera. And you must save me, your devoted collaborator. I implore you. Something is rotten in the Spectacles Office. Keep a weather eye on *la famiglia* Bussani-Casti-*e-forse*-Diguri. I still feel in my bones, such as they are, that the Haegelin death, while *not* a murder, is intimately connected to these people and to our troubles. I will remain here, your humble servant, awaiting our next briefing."

"Renzo, if only I…"

"I predict that my little Cherubino is honest; she is telling the truth about His Excellency and all the little Excellencies' plot to whittle our masterpiece to sawdust. They want to stop the play from going up."

"But wait, Renzo, I just remembered something. Maybe His Excellency himself knows something about Haegelin's death. That Drossel man over-heard him and Haegelin shouting at each other the night before the staging rehearsal. He could have had a hand in the murder; or perhaps he's shielding the real killer!"

"Suicide. Suicide. Unless you cast Casti, his puling putrefying pet poet, in the assassin's role. I would happily endorse that theory … but is protecting the Pygmy of Parnassus worth the trouble of such an eminent man as H.E.? Poets come cheap; they can be bought and sold, or thrown into dungeons at the flick of a hanky, evidently. The more I try to sort this out the more insane it gets. Sort it out for me, will you, darling, and get me out of here. Then we start work on *Don Juan, or the Dissolute Man Punished!* That's all I ask."

"Yes, I'll do it. We'll do it. Now I've got to carry on as if *Figaro* is actually going up in ten days. Perhaps it will after all, but! Not as a mangled torso, and not without the Act IV finale, *lo giuro*! So excuse me, Renzl, I have to go and examine the ingénue; she's lost her voice. And then I have to run the staging rehearsal from the keyboard. I'll keep quizzing the Italian singers when I see them, but I doubt that they are aware of anything that doesn't pertain to their all-consuming personal lives. Excepting, perhaps, our tender little *Cherubin d'amore.*

❧ Scene 14 ❧

The Gottlieb apartment, in a working-class quarter of Vienna,
April 22, 10:30 A.M.

Mozart, Frau Gottlieb and Nanette Gottlieb: Recitativo
and duet for Mozart alone

Mozart rings the bell to the Gottlieb apartment. After some time, Frau Adelheid Gottlieb appears. She is a tall, massive woman with large calloused hands. She starts when she sees the composer on her doorstep, but quickly recovers herself and arranges her face in a scowl of aggressive disapproval. Mozart sweeps off his hat and bows low.

"*Scusi, Madama Gottlieb, si può...*"

"Don't fling that Italian jabberjabber at me, Herr Mozart. We're not in the Italian Theater now, and I refuse to understand one word of that tongue. I speak German like you, and I'd feel much better if there was still a *Singspiel* in Vienna, a theater in German for Germans, and not one crawling with oily Dagos."

"I feel the same way *exactly*, Frau von Gottlieb, forgive me. I'm all for the National Theater and German musical comedy too, but it's closed, isn't it, and one works at the pleasure of him who closed it. Strange, this vogue for Italians, isn't it? But Northern Italy is Austria too, after all." *Thinks:* "What a fire-breathing basilisk she is. Bad luck for Casti, if he loves her, because she doesn't seem to favor the Southern Races. She's wearing those mitts, as players do in cold rehearsal rooms. Does she play? Or is it a new fad? "

"Dear Frau von Gottlieb, I would like to pay a sympathy call on my favorite little soprano. Is she recovered enough to receive me?"

"No, Herr Mozart, you may not see her. No one may see her. Her health is very fragile at the moment."

"Yes, Frau von Gottlieb, so I have heard; but not from you, whose duty it is to keep the music director informed about your daughter's readiness to perform. Miss Nannerl is contracted to sing in my opera in a few days, so my visit is official. I need to assess her vocal condition and determine if she is fit to remain in the cast. If she is not, I must find and prepare an understudy, and notify the front office and the printers. I will brook no delay in this. Do you want your daughter to sing in Vienna hereafter? I thought so. Then please admit me."

Beat. They stare at one another.

"If I must. However, I insist on being in the room with you when you speak to her. I have her modesty to protect. I know how you men of the theater are, and I never relax my vigilance for one eye-blink. My daughter is my jewel, Herr Mozart, and I guard her talent and her integrity with my life."

"It must be a great source of consolation to you, dear lady, to know that – if it is carefully guarded and nurtured – your daughter's prodigious musical and histrionic talent will pay your bills and comfort your declining years. And I assure you that if the child continues to sing as beautifully as she does now, many more roles will be written for her by the personal pen of the celebrated Amadé Mozart. Now, let us go and greet her."

The woman's Cerberus scowl gives way a little; as ambition, avarice and anxiety vie for full possession of her face.

"Wait here," *she snaps, and slams the door, leaving the composer on the landing. Mozart is tapping his fingers on the door post and humming the second theme from a little trio for clarinet viola and piano that he plans to write and then play with his best pal Anton Stadler and his favorite student Francesca Jacquin at an upcoming benefit concert. By the time Frau Gottlieb returns, the theme is nicely developed.*

The woman leads him up one flight of stairs, down a dim hall. The apartment is a first-floor suite, close to the noise and dust of the street, and to the smells of the shops and stables below. It is the customary floor of artisans, teachers, musicians. The pair enters the apartment and proceeds through the parlor. Mozart sees a small clavier; a battered violin case; a battered mandolin case; a Spanish guitar with faded ribbons around the neck, hanging on the wall; a music stand. Frau Gottlieb unlocks a door and swings it open. Nanette is cowering against the far wall of a bedroom, pale and rigid, her eyes downcast.

"Her left cheek is red," *muses Mozart.* "But not the right. Does she have half a fever? Or has she been slapped? The latter – and recently, and hard, I am guessing."

"It's Herr Mozart, Nannerl, come to see you, he won't be long," *says her mother. Folding her hands, the woman settles herself on the bed next to the door. Mozart approaches two steps, stops and holds out his hands to the child. She comes to him but keeps her hands behind her back. Together they move toward two wooden chairs by the window.*

"Now, Nannerl, my dear. Nannerl is my sister's nickname too, do you remember? You do? Good. I think of you as a second sister, my little, little sister. I am so fond of you, and you are such a lovely singer, such a good musician. Would you like some clavier lessons after the show opens? Every singer should have a good keyboard technique; it is so useful. You can accompany yourself, and others.

"They tell me you have been ill. We were all so shaken after the other day, weren't we? Are you very ill? Don't weep, my dear; it can happen to anyone. You have a few days yet to regain your voice. I will ask my dear wife to sing the part in rehearsal until you get better. She knows it very well, because she has sung the whole opera through with me.

Beat. During which, Mozart has an inspiration.

"Or, tiddly-piddly! I could sing it myself! I sing *falsett* extremely well. Do you know, I sang your air for the Emperor himself, when it was just His Majesty and me together, the very day he told me he would be the patron of our show. Yes, that is true. At pitch, yet. Listen!"

"L'ho perduto, me meschina, ah chi sa dove sara ... ah, see, you are almost smiling! Here's the rest!" *Mozart continues to sing in a clear, true falsetto.* "Che t'ha avvenuto, che hai veduto? Che hai veduto, che ha avvenuto, meschinella, ah! chi sa dove sara? Cosa e venuto, se e forse male, meschinella, io t'amo come sorrella, in verita! Sei mia cugina, sono il padron, cosa dirai, cosa dirai?"*

The child's eyes widen as Mozart begins sticking new words into her aria. Nanette flicks a quick glance at her mother, then stares at the composer.

"She has picked up enough Italian," *Mozart surmises,* "to know that I am asking her, 'was it something bad that happened to you, what did you see,' that he wanted to make her feel better, and couldn't she tell him, and best of all, he loved her like a sister, like a cousin, he was her patron, what can she tell?"

The child's eyelids squeeze shut. Her mouth opens and her throat convulses, making a sound like a hiccup. But no words form on her tongue and lips.

"Paralyzed with terror," *Mozart says to himself.* "It's clear her mother has commanded that she not speak. But! The old Gorgon does want her to be singing, and bringing home her salary. So…"

"Frau Gottlieb, this child has had a terrible shock. She needs a doctor. I will send a messenger to Baroness Waldstätten and ask if her personal physician may see her tomorrow."

"It is very generous of you to offer to pay for a doctor for my child. But I insist on witnessing any intercourse between her and this medical person."

"But naturally, Frau Gottlieb. We are in total agreement; we will bring her to the doctor ourselves."

"Now get out."

Frau Gottlieb shows the composer out the door and hustles him down the stairs with a hard mittened hand under his elbow.

"May I remind you, Madame, that your daughter is in a production that enjoys the Emperor's favor and imprimatur. I will expect your full cooperation in all matters pertaining to Nanette's performance in my opera, and in future ones, do you understand?"

"Of course I understand, you dolt. Do you think I don't want her to advance herself? But I will not have upstarts and Italians and bohemians like you and that crazy Waldstätten woman meddling with her without my say-so, all clear?"

༄ Scene 15 ༄

A square in Vienna, April 22, a minute later
Mozart and Casti

"Something odd going on there," *thinks Mozart, adjusting his mouse-colored overcoat and settling his gold-trimmed hat gently upon his coiffure as he stands in the street. A string quartet timbre drifts through his mind ... no, it's an aria, in 6/8, strings, flute, oboe ... G minor, a lament – sung by a wounded heroine? A heart-rending appeal to a beloved who cannot, must not speak ... Mozart writes a quick note to Baroness Waldstätten, finds an urchin to deliver it and sets out for the theater.*

He has not taken a dozen steps when a man who has been loitering in a shadowy door-way falls into step with him and greets him in a quacking rasp.

"G-hnrruss G-hnott, Herr h-Mot-hnart."

"Excuse me? Oh, *Gruss Gott*, Signor Casti, it's you. What are you doing in this part of town? Were you going to stand under some virtuous matron's window and serenade her? Where's your mandolin?"

"Walk with me a few paces, signor. I am here on an official errand. Isn't it a shame about *Abbé* DaP-hmonte?" *Casti smirks.* "He won't be attending the final rehearsals or even the premiere, evidently."

"Oh, I am pretty sure he will be released very soon; he hasn't been charged with anything and he is a favorite, a *great* favorite, may I say, of His Imperial Majesty."

"So they say. But you, H-maestro, you now must carry the burden of production all alone without Signor DaP-hmonte's valuable help. I am sure you are toiling like Sisyphus night and day to ensure the success of your show."

"I-I..."

"Consequently, I have a duty to inform you – as a well-wisher, you understand – that the Spectacles Office is monitoring your professional behavior and has found much that is wanting. His Excellency Chancellor Rosenberg wants to extend a friendly warning to you that you are on probation."

"His Ex-?"

"You may assume that he is telling you these exact words through me. This is what he charged me to say: The insolence and lack of deference in this show's subject matter has been brought to His Excellency's attention. Some have come to him saying that the libretto as well as the music harbors an anarchic political message. Others have commented on your professional comportment. You behave in a much too familiar manner with persons above your rank. You presume that you are already an *employé* of the Court. You flirt in an unseemly manner with Madama Storace. You laugh too loudly and at too high a pitch."

"Excuse m…"

"Speaking for myself now, I find your music rather tuneful, and the finales in this show have a nice pace to them, so they're over really fast, which is a great virtue. It's a nice little play you have there, and it would be a shame if anything happened to it."

"What are you…"

"A word to the wise, maestro. Eyes are on you always. Any misstep might cause you and your play to be withdrawn from the theater. The Office of Spectacles has standards to keep up at court. You understand me?"

"No, I-I…"

"Good. I'll just be going, then."

Signor Casti fades down a narrow Gasse and into the shadows. The composer stands like a stone statue in the square, the blood draining from his face.

❧ Finale ❧

Burgtheater stage, 2:00 P.M., April 22, 1786

Mozart, the cast of Figaro minus Fräulein Gottlieb

"So, my *enfants de joie*, here we are again," *giggles Mozart,* "squirming with anticipation to get this little skit onstage, and eager to draw the veil of oblivion over yesterday's, ah, unfortunate incidents. As you all probably know, the Court Poet is indisposed and cannot be here today, so you will have to sing the words as they currently appear in the libretto; there will be no chance of last-minute re-writes, sorry.

"Now. The ensembles and recits go extremely fast, unlike those in the old 'Seria' style. I know that you have all seen our excellent acting troupe performing Goldoni, and their style exemplifies the lightness and lack of bombast I wish for. Signori Benucci and Bussani and Madame Storace know just how to do it, having performed in *The Barber*. If you would all just model yourselves on them.

"Madame Storace, will you instruct your *costumière* to remove the padding from under your skirts? You are portraying a ladies' maid, are you not? Then they must dress you as a ladies' maid, who must be able to pass through doors with trays in her hands."

"So much for the notes; Figaro, Susanna onstage, Bartolo and Marcellina stand by, thank you!"

Nobody moves. The Imperial Italian Opera troupe stands huddled together staring at the composer with blank, sheeplike expressions.

Beat.

"Maestro," *says Madame Mandini,* "can you not tell us if Da Ponte is coming back soon? Is he implicated in Haegelin's death? I simply can't believe he would do such a thing."

"He's been jailed for doing something wicked; that's certain," *booms Mandini.* "My guess is that Da Ponte hanged the censor."

"He *has* said 'the censor be hanged' often enough in his career, hahaha," *Mozart's laugh is verging on the hysterial,* "but if saying this constituted a crime, our jails would be stuffed to the bursting point with playwrights. Besides, I was personally assured by His Excellency the Chancellor of Spectacles that Herr Haegelin's death was self-inflicted, God rest his soul. Please, Figaro and Susanna, onstage."

"How could that be?" *says Benucci.* "Who would hang himself in the Burgtheater rigging, and how could he get the curtain down again after he did it?"

"No, don't you see?" *roars Mandini, running into the stage left wings.* "The curtain was up, he put his head in the loop like this, un-clipped the sandbags, like this – and – HOPLA! Up he goes!" *An alarmed stagehand rushes over and puts the sandbag back on its clamp, thereby preventing Mandini from hanging himself and bringing an early end to a fine singing career.*

"Ah, I see now; the curtain would fall because he weighed less than the counterpoise," *says Benucci.*

"*Did* he weigh less than the counterpoise?"

"Must have."

"Why are you so sure? Did *you* do it?"

"No, I didn't. Did you?"

"Maybe he killed himself because he feared he was going to lose his job when Swieten found out what a scandal it was going to create."

"Swieten backs the play; he knows all about it, remember?"

"Perhaps," *tinkles Signora Laschi,* "perhaps it was an unrequited-a love-affair with a beautiful actress, and he hanged-a himself in one last-a, grand-a, despairing-a gesture."

The whole cast turns to stare at her.

Beat.

A slow blush dawns on her bosom and works its way upward to her face.

"You know, like in-a *Le pene del giovane Werther.* The book," *she adds.*

"*Werther* is a *banned* book, Signora," says Bussani.

"Which we have all read, Bussani," *sniggers Mandini.*

"People, *please*, can we start the show or I will personally test the Mandini theory by hanging myself on the curtain rope and *I mean it!* This is not a coffee-house; this is not a card-party; this is the *first mise-en-scène* rehearsal of the *greatest goddamn opera yet written*, so off the goddamn stage now, *now*, NOW!" *Mozart's voice rises into that soprano range of which the Office of Spectacles is said to disapprove.*

The opening duet begins, and at long last, Le Nozze di Figaro *begins to unfold its miracles onstage. In five minutes everyone has settled down to the task of staging the ensembles of Acts I and II, and by the second-act finale, poor dead Herr Haegelin is forgotten completely.*

Act II

❧ Scene 1 ❧

Mozart's house, 10:30 P.M., April 22
Amadé and Constanze: Duetto

"*Weibchen, sposina,* where are you?"

"*Hier bin ich, komm ins Bett und küss mich!*"

"But Wifey, Wifina, where's my nightcap?"

"Have you tried under the bed?"

"Aha. Now. Whew! What a very odd and frightening day I have had, but All's Well that Ends Well, we had a good rehearsal and the first two acts are put on the stage without incident."

"How is Renzl getting on in prison?"

"Oh, he complains about everything. He's working on a new libretto for us, though. But as to why he is detained, he thinks that his arrest may have been instigated by either Bussani or Casti, or both, who hate him for personal reasons."

"What personal reasons?"

"Well, he's sticking it to Bussani's wife, and Casti wants his post at court. On the other hand, we think the intrigue against our play may have its source in the Spectacles Office. His Excellency could be instructing Haegelin to whittle the show down to nothing but the overture and the final chorus, in order to get me to withdraw the production – and myself – from the Court theater."

"'What need you five and twenty, ten, or five?' 'What need one?' But why on earth does Rosenberg not want it to play? He backed *Seraglio,* and he laughed his ass off at *The Impresario.* He must see a sure success in this one."

"Something to do with the anti-establishment tone of the piece, which he seems suddenly and only recently to have noticed. Or maybe it's the too-apt caricatures of the upper classes. I didn't believe it of H.E., he's too high and mighty to care what we think of our betters, and he's a man of the theater after all. But then a very odd thing happened on the way to rehearsal. It got me thinking..."

"After you went to the prison?"

"Not immediately. After I interviewed Renzo I paid an official visit to my ingénue, Miss Gottlieb, who still seems truly incapable of speech or song. Her mother is a first-class dragon – every time I see her, my cock and balls shrivel up and hide inside my stomach, and my asshole snaps shut with a crack. The beldame is keeping her daughter locked up, and she is also smacking her face every so often. The child is distraught; she was as white as a sheet under her bruises. Maybe she is only worried about losing her part in *Figaro*, but I think her fear is more, well, deathly."

"Deathly!"

"Something must have happened to her yesterday morning. Perhaps the Haegelin corpse reveal? Did she know that Haegelin had been arguing with Rosenberg about taking her out of the show? If she *did* know it, she should have been delighted to see an obstacle, namely the censor, removed from her career path. I was totally mystified. But then I got my own dose of the horrors."

"There's more?"

"Listen to this. After having been rudely bundled out of Frau Gottlieb's lair, I found that the loathsome Signor Casti had –alakazaam! – magically appeared at my side. He said he had a personal warning for me from His Excellency the Grand Chancellor of Spectacles. What he said confirmed Renzo's theories about our having enemies in the Spectacles Office, and then some. Casti was delighted to relay a message from H.E. that the play, and not only the play, but *me*, Amadé Mozart, a professional musician and entertainer of royalty for twenty-five years of my life, are on probation – for having revolutionary ideas and crude manners, respectively. One false move and it's over for you, Casti croaked, like some rotting raven from hell. What did he mean? Is it even remotely true? Does he or Rosenberg just want to keep me off-balance? If yes, what for? Oh God. I need another kiss at this point. Maybe throw in a hug."

"There you are, sweetie. This is all very confusing."

"You had to be there. I confess that in my worst moments I think Da Ponte did it after all. Even worse, sometimes I wish he had. Damn him! None of this would have happened if he hadn't thrown his phony tantrum in Haegelin's office, and written the perilously scandalous decoy aria to keep the man's paws – may they change to angel wings in heaven – off the other two merely mildly scandalous arias in Act I. That caper may be what landed him in jail. Renzo thinks His Excellency Count Rosenbutt may have turned – or been turned – against the play and that my only defense against him is to denounce him to the Emperor if things get worse. He is probably right about that but I don't have the nerve to do it. Do you think he's giving me good advice?"

"Now, darling, Da Ponte is a nuisance, but you know in your heart that he is a good-hearted man, a clever man, and very, very loyal to his friends. You know he has no motivation for this so-called murder, don't you? All he wanted was to divert the censor's attention like a conjurer at the fair who tells you to watch the cards while he picks your pocket. He did exactly what Figaro does!"

"Hmmm?"

"Well, what does Figaro do when he discovers Almaviva's scheme to rape his wife?"

"Sings two of the greatest arias ever penned. Then – ah! He sends the count a false note saying that the countess is going to receive a lover. He creates a diversion to keep the count busy trying to nose out the non-existent lover instead of forcing himself on Susanna. A clever ruse, not that it works all that well for anybody…"

"But consider now, Punkatititi-pooh, who in the theater is creating the largest, loudest and most elaborate diversion? That person or set of persons might be the one with the most to hide."

"Hide what? The Murder of Figaro? The Ruin of Mozart and Da Ponte? It could be anyone; they're all hiding things. Singers divert me by talking about their sex lives; censors threaten me with cuts to crucial numbers; somebody diverted me by arresting the Court Poet on murky charges, including maybe murder! It should be a murder, and not a suicide, with all the hiding and diverting that's going on."

"*Pace, pace…*"

"And, wifelettina, who didn't have a reason to kill Haegelin? Only Haegelin! He was an obscurantist in the age of Enlightenment, an obstructionist in a time of greater freedom of the press! He drove everybody crazy. He was lenient with *Figaro*, because Swieten stood over him, telling him that all the *personaggi* were just the usual stock comedy characters: the dissolute counts, stuttering lawyers, cat-fighting women, betrayed wives, wise-cracking servants and saucy housemaids we'd seen on the stage a thousand times before. So, who is blocking this hum-drum same-old same-old farce from getting on stage? Da Ponte says it's Spectacles. But why?"

"Well, sugarbug, I can tell you one reason why anyway, it's because your music makes those same-old stock characters human and all too human. People recognize themselves in your characters. They take offense. The fact is that this Figaro is not just another smart-aleck servant, like he was in *Barbiere*. Your Figaro is visibly smarter than, and a better, more moral person than, his noble master. Maybe, by implication, people think that you are better and smarter than everybody, and they suspect you are thumbing your nose at them. They think you are a little upstart from a little town, and they can't stop seeing you as a little boy. They resent you."

"Oh, sweetheart, sweetheart, I just want to be famous and make a shitload of money, is that too much to ask? I hate being punished for doing my best! We need to go to London or Prague or somewhere else!"

"All right, love, the next opera will be in London."

"Or Prague."

"Kiss me. Harder."

"But this unquenchable hue-and-cry of murder! In the theater of all places. Theater people love drama but don't do murders; they'll skewer you without mercy with bitchery, but they leave you writhing and alive. Maybe Haegelin was robbed and killed by a passing footpad and … but then why was he flying in the wings? But even Haeglin's cameo appearance might be a diversion of some kind. But a diversion *from what*, and to what end, and by whom, I can't imagine. I tell you I am coming close to committing murder myself, I am so frustrated. If I only knew who it is that I want to kill most."

✍ Scene 2 ✍

The same, April 23, 1786, 7:00 A.M.

Mozart and Constanze

A messenger knocks at the Mozart flat with a note from Baroness Waldstätten. Mozart tips him and throws himself on the divan to read.

"My Adored Amadé, etc., etc.!

"Never mind my usual physician," *the baroness had written.* "Great luck for us: the great Doctor Mesmer is here in secret from his exile, and is staying as a guest at my house. He and Count von Thun have commandeered my drawing-room, and they are doing really extraordinary experiments in hypnotism, animal magnetism and healing by the laying-on of hands. I tell you, this man is the wave of the future! A genius! Mesmer will know just what to do in this child's case. I will send the carriage to your home this morning – better yet, I will also come myself to chaperone La Petite Nanette. I need not remind you to keep word of A.M.'s presence to yourself. My Barouche will be at your door at 8:00."

"Lovey, I'm going out with the baroness; where's my hair-ribbon?"

"*Liebes Mandel, wo ist's Bandel?* Have you looked under…"

"And yes! Here it is!"

"What a vampire the woman is! See that she keeps her hands off you."

"No worries, wifekin. She's good-hearted, an eternal fan. And donor to the Mozart career wardrobe fund. She just wants to rub elbows with the *artistes*."

"Elbows only, please."

❧ Scene 3 ❧

At the Gottlieb's door, 8:30 A.M.

Mozart, Frau Gottlieb, Baroness Waldstätten, Nanette

The carriage containing Mozart and his patroness arrives duly at the lodgings of Frau Gottlieb. The widow and her daughter are at the door, dressed for travel.

"Can we exclude her from the party?" *whispers the composer.*

"Nothing easier," *smiles the baroness. She leans out of the carriage and greets Nanette and her mother.*

Although La Waldstätten has a reputation as a kook and a free-thinker (she appears at this moment to be more than a little blowsy and dust-strewn, since she has left her home sans traveling cloak and cap, having grabbed up and carelessly wrapped herself in a gaudy oriental shawl), she can still crank up a fine show of patrician condescension. She aims it right at Frau Gottlieb in the form of a warm and yet patronizing smile.

"It gives me enormous pleasure to tell you, Frau von Gottlieb, that a noted Physician who is visiting our city from Paris, has consented, at my urging, to attend your daughter. He has had great success in France with exactly this sort of illness. However, the great man has told me he must forbid you to attend his séance. Your magnetic animalistic vibrations and Nanette's, being so similar in nature, will disrupt one another and he will not be able to use his marvelous methods and restore her to speech if you are anywhere in the area."

"Where she goes I go."

"Only stop, dear lady, and think of your daughter's career, of her chance to present herself to the public as a prodigy in a work of the divine Mozart! Surely you will allow me to take charge of her for these few hours. I am, as you surely know, a patroness of the arts, Frau von Gottlieb. The Emperor relies upon my taste. I am always interested in exciting new talent. I am certain you can trust me to treat your daughter as my own."

After a few more dances around the bush, followed by the gift of a folded Irish linen handkerchief which clinks like a tambourine when transferred from hand to hand, the baroness's and Frau Gottlieb's desires sing in harmonious accord. She receives little Nanette into her carriage and places her on the seat next to Mozart, to the extreme displeasure of Frau Gottlieb.

⨕⨕ Scene 4 ⨕⨕

A villa in a leafy suburb of Vienna, 9:30 A.M.
Mozart, Baroness Waldstätten, Nanette, Anton Mesmer

Arriving at the baroness's door, they descend, allow the maid to brush the road dust off their outer garments, and enter a parlor on the first floor. They wait silently for the famous vitalist Anton Mesmer to make his appearance. Ten minutes later a light footstep echoes in the hall.

"Er kommt, er kommt," *thinks Mozart, hearing syncopated arpeggio in his head.* "Not in a cloud of smoke and flashes of green fire as he would like, but in a pretty fair approximation of a mage's grand entrance. What fun he is. I hope he can get this infant phenomenon singing again. I have Act III finale staging rehearsal to run this afternoon, and Act IV tonight. Having her back in form would be a help. And maybe she knows something about the Haegelin thing too."

"*Ma chère* Baroness, and *cher* Mozart, lovely to see you. You've grown up, I see, Mozart!" *Mesmer, resplendent in a tasseled fez and garnet-colored velvet robe, embraces them both in the French manner.*

"And when are you going to put me and my magnificent magnets into one of your operas?"

"Very soon, I promise; just as soon as I rescue the present opera from imminent oblivion, Monsieur Mesmer," *says Mozart.*

Mesmer then turns to Nanette and takes her hand, looking deep, deep into her eyes.

"Dear child, have no fear; my methods involve no pain or suffering at all. Can you not speak? You may signal or nod, my dear. Don't worry about anything, and soon you will be able to chatter like a magpie and sing like a nightingale once again. Would you like to come and look at my magnets? Your friends will be right outside the door, in this room."

The tall pale child goes willingly with Mesmer, leaving Mozart and the baroness alone together.

Beat.

"Vous êtes mon cher ami, Amadé."

"Yes, Baroness, *je sais bien.*"

"You know I love you. I can say that to your face because I am so old and so silly and because you are so married. It is a little ridiculous of me to have such sentiments for you, but it is still true. I have learned my bitter lesson since the night when I encouraged your wife to follow my example and exhibit our calves and legs at my little party. It was not such a fine joke after all, was it? Herr von Thorwart was so angry. You can trust me now, not to make you, nor Constanze, nor myself the object of censure ever again. I so wish for this opera to be a success for you, and that you write many many more in Vienna. What can I do to help you?"

"Dear Lady, you know my heart as few do. Our long and outrageous flirtation has been but a tinsel ornament upon the pure gold of our mutual friendship. There are two things. I am very disturbed about this hanged man who has joined the cast of *Figaro*. I have an uneasy suspicion that he was hanged in the theater to cast a shadow on Da Ponte and myself. Da Ponte is detained; I am sure the charges are false, but someone has secretly denounced him as having done a crime against the State, perhaps the murder of the hanged man, perhaps something else. He could be in prison until the Emperor notices he is missing, and perhaps longer if powerful people work against him. Count von Rosenberg has declared Haegelin to be a suicide, but the rumors fly. Can you keep your ears open for a word dropped, an eyebrow raised, especially in the Emperor's presence, or The Chancellor of Spectacles's?"

"Yes, dear Amadé. I can do that. I have no small experience with court intrigue, as you know. And the second?"

"Could you, if it becomes necessary, keep Nanette by you for a while? I believe that her mother means her no good. She is beating her and frightening her, for reasons I cannot comprehend."

"This also I will try to do for you. And for the child. She has the gift, I have heard."

"Yes, she does. She is a terrifyingly good musician, and her dramatic skills … Oh God, is he hurting her after all?"

Screams and sobs and a babble of words pierce the heavy oak door.

"Amadé, he's done it! She's talking!"

"But how upset she is! What has happened to the girl?"

The door flies open, and Nanette runs into the room. She makes a bee-line for Mozart, then veers sharply, throwing herself, weeping loudly, into the baroness's arms. Mesmer follows, in great agitation.

"Can you not tell the rest to me, please, Nanny?" *he coaxes.*

"*No! I can't! I mustn't!*"

"Will you speak to Mozart?"

"No! Only to her. Only to her." *The poor girl continues to yell and sob without restraint. The baroness twitches her head, signaling the men to leave them alone together.*

Mozart and Mesmer step out into the garden, leaving Nanette to howl into the silken lap of her new patroness. The baroness offers her yet another linen hankie. Nanny mops her tears, blows her nose and calms herself.

"You will understand, my lady. I can't say it in front of them."

"Oh my dear, you may empty your heart to me. Think of me as an older sister."

"She gave me to him for money. He made me sit in his lap and he passed his hands all over me as if I were a horse at the fair. He put his hands up my petticoats and in my drawers and then he hurt me and I bled. I am surely ruined, and now I can never marry Mozart. And I wanted to so much."

"So did I," *murmurs the countess, as she strokes Nanette's hair. The child wails afresh for several minutes before her breathing becomes regular again.*

"We both love Mozart, my dear. But we can't marry him; his wife would be so annoyed. But, little songbird, you have been so hurt and betrayed. You may never forget, but you will heal in time. Then when your feathers are smooth again, you can do something even better than marrying Mozart. You can act in Mozart's plays and sing the sublime music he writes just for you. Few can count themselves so fortunate. You will be immortal, as he is, if you sing his music."

"And you? What will you do, since you can't marry him?"

"Well, my child. I-I'll take him shopping. He loves fine clothes, and he depends on my taste and largesse to keep him looking like a success. I am happy to do it. People who want to work at court have to dress the part."

"He is so sweet-looking in that blue coat and ribbon."

"Yes. He is an elegant-looking, a poetic-looking young man, and so kind and good. Now, can you tell me who the bad man was, and the woman?"

"I tell only you. It was Count Chancellor Rosenberg who bought me. I saw the money. He gave it to my mother. She told me I needed a protector at court and I should do her bidding and go into his office alone with him and let him do what he wants to me. She said it happens to every girl and I would get used to it, and I should be quiet about it forever or I would be very sorry."

"And you were very, very quiet, weren't you?"

"I couldn't even remember it until just now. My mother said she needed to pay the rent. My brother needed to repair his instruments and re-hair his bow. She said we had to have the money, so be quiet, don't make a fuss about it."

"That's all right."

"Am I truly ruined?"

"No, my dear. Mozart loves you like a brother, like an uncle. You will sing so beautifully, you are so pretty; and one day a man – just your age, and tall – not like Mozart – and dark – not like Mozart – and handsome – not like Mozart - a man who is not married to Frau von Mozart or to anyone else, will appear before you, and instantly fall in love with you, and win you, and marry you and treat you like a princess. And I promise I will do my utmost to protect you until then, but only if you wish it."

"Can I see Mozart?"

"We'll go and find him together."

❧ Scene 5 ❧

At the Gottlieb's door, 11:30 A.M.

Mozart, Baroness, Frau Gottlieb: Terzetto di rabbia

"I think you had better let her stay here, Mozart. She is fast asleep now, and Mesmer said he would like to treat her once more with his magnets. You should firmly inform Frau Gottlieb that I have her child for safekeeping; perhaps you should mention that she is not fit to be the child's guardian at all."

"O come with me, will you please, Baroness? The woman does not trust me, and I for one am terrified of her. Perhaps your presence might calm her. Besides, I want a true witness if she accuses me of anything."

"I will tell you more of what Nanette said as we go."

"There's more? Isn't it enough her mother sold her to Rosenberg and he violated her? How can anyone be expected to stay in good voice with this sort of trafficking going on? Did the mother just abandon her to him?"

"She says her mother told her what to do – and not do – before sending her into a room alone with him. She said at one point that another man entered the room and that he pointed at her, scolded her and called her nasty names, and threatened to put both her and her mother in prison for their sin. She thought that Frau Gottlieb also entered the room at that point, but it may be she only wished for her mother, as terrified as she must have been."

"How awful for her. I gather she was not at her home when this violation took place? She was in H.E.'s palace?"

"She said she was in the Spectacles Office."

"Ah … How did the child and her mother get home afterwards?"

"She says she went home in a carriage. Very fast."

"Sounds like Rosenberg, driving to endanger. What a monster he has turned out to be. Capable of anything. Oh heaven help us, here we are. Let me cower behind your skirts, Baroness, my knees turn to water before that woman."

The coachman rings the Gottlieb bell, and soon Frau Adelheid herself appears on the landing. She remains there, staring across at the composer and his patroness, who have elected to remain in the coach.

"I am glad to report to you, Frau Gottlieb," *says the baroness,* "that dear Nanette has recovered her power of speech. No, she was too fatigued to make the return trip, so I left her sleeping in her doctor's care. I think, Frau Gottlieb, after such a trial as she has endured, your daughter will need several days to recuperate at my villa. She is quite welcome there; the doctor was quite insistent that she remain."

"I cannot permit this! I insist on going there immediately! I won't be parted from her!"

"I understand your maternal feelings, Madame, but my appreciation for them is lessened since Nanny told me that you were willing to exchange her young virtue for a monetary consideration."

"How dare you accuse me of such a thing!"

"Do you deny it?" *shouts Mozart.* "You were both seen and heard by the head usher Fritz von Drossel, entering the count's office three nights ago, late! You have an arrangement with His Excellency, do you not? He is a man of the world and a powerful figure in the theater, to be sure. But you! How in heaven's name could you have offered that tender child up to him like that?"

Frau Gottlieb stands like a marble monument. She stands for a long time, as if waiting for more. Her face and posture soften when it becomes evident that there is no more. Then she speaks with an icy calm.

"Yes, I accepted His Excellency's kindly offer of protection for my daughter! And what of it? You are a man of the theater too, so why are you pretending to be so shocked? His Excellency showed an interest. Nanette needs a patron at court if she is going to advance herself. Both my children need money to keep themselves and pursue their careers. Nanette, being the most talented, must do her duty by her family."

"But woman, the girl is not yet out of childhood!" *shrieks Mozart.*

"You little hypocrite, how dare you question me? Tell us all, why don't you, where you spent *your* childhood, eh? Did you play at shuttlecock or hobby-horse on the town square in Salzburg? Oh no? I know where you were, all the world knows where you were. Your dear, loving parents dragged you all over Europe hawking you to every court that would receive you, and you spent your years of innocence slaving to support them!"

Mozart stares at her, his eyes bulging, mouth agape. Eight high C's, staccato, a twice-rising arpeggio to F in alt, stab like hot needles in his mind's ear … He says nothing. Frau Gottlieb goes on.

"I've heard your father kept you on short rations so your growth would be stunted and he could go right on exhibiting you as a *Wunderkind* until you were thirty! I've heard they rented you out to Padre Martini for his fuckboy! Legs not long enough to reach the organ pedals, indeed. I know what that means; I'm not stupid."

Mozart glares at her, pale and shaking with rage. The baroness sits mute and deathly pale. Frau Gottlieb takes her cue and continues.

"And what about your dear wife? Every soul in Vienna knows you bought *her* for 300 Gulden, so that her loving mother Caecilia could pay her tab at the wine-bar. And they also know that your dear good mother-in-law sold her oldest daughter to that decaying old Count Seeau for a good deal more than that! Her artistic patron, my ass! Anything to help Aloysia's singing career along! And after his lordship got tired of her, he married her off to an actor who paints portraits on the side and who wasn't too particular, isn't that so?

"And *you*, you bug-eyed little rat, all tricked out and pouffed up like a prince, and so full of yourself, you pretend to be so outraged at what I did because now it's your little play that is missing a singer, and it's your golden reputation that may tarnish, eh? Don't you dare lecture me about my daughter; all you care for is your damned opera!"

"My damned opera?" *shrieks Mozart.* "You flaming bitch from Erebus, may the devil suck the marrow out of your bones! I won't have you *or* your daughter in the opera, or anywhere near the theater as long as I am in it! She is dismissed! Any girl in the city can sing that part, and many would pay to do it! How dare you repeat the gossip of the gutter-rabble to my face! Get out of my sight, and be glad that I for one do not spread calumnies, or tomorrow you would have your head shaved and be forced to sweep the streets for procuring and traducing youth!"

"You just go ahead and try it! You won't be in the theater long enough to take a piss! His Excellency will cancel your pathetic little play today and replace it with any number of other, much better ones, and you will never set your dainty little foot inside the Burgtheater again! That stopped you cold, didn't it, my little provincial prodigy? I've been around the theater all my life; do you think a little cock-a-whoop from Salzburg is going to outflank me? Get your rig out from in front of my door!"

"Leave off with your disrespectful talk, good woman," *cries the baroness.* "Do you know what *great genius* you are addressing?"

But Frau Gottlieb has withdrawn and slammed the door.

᧖ Scene 6 ᧖

Mozart's bedroom, April 23, night

Mozart e Constanze: Duetto d'amore

After having conducted the Sitzprobe in the afternoon and staged the ensembles in the evening, dined with Constanze and friends at Count Thun's, and after having dandled little Karl on his knee while singing "Non piu andrai" to the child's immense delight, and having kissed him good night; the eminent composer Amadé Mozart now tears off his clothes, flings them against the wall, and hurls himself onto the bed, whimpering and moaning and clutching his temples. Constanze takes one look and goes to moisten a cloth, which she slaps on her husband's forehead.

"You look awful. Are you ill?"

"I drank a bit too much at dinner, and forced a bit too much jollity."

"What's wrong now?"

Mozart relates his adventures with Mesmerism and his bruising encounter with Frau Gottlieb, tactfully leaving out that lady's scabrous remarks concerning the morals of the Weber family.

"And if that were not enough for one crazy day … Oh, Stanzi, hold me tight. Stroke my brow. We got the rest of the ensembles blocked, and then we had the Sitzprobe from hell. The orchestra was as nervous as a flock of fowls; they rushed; they forgot all the *szorfandi*, the *pianissimi* and the *crescendi*. The wind band's playing would have curdled new milk. *And!* Even with their parts propped up in front of their faces, the singers made imbecilic mistakes, sang *sotto voce* and feigned indisposition."

"Poor, poor Pookybear!"

"Then I was forced to swallow a quadruple dose of the bitterest *Wiener*

Schmäh! No, not aimed at me this time, God be thanked. All the singers are using the happy opportunity of *L'Affaire* Haegelin to improve their positions in the company, or to take revenge on other singers for past slights, or perhaps just to keep their teeth and claws sharp. To wit, they are all *denouncing* one another! Madame Mandini took me aside and accused Madame Laschi of having done the murder, which is, officially, of course, a suicide. La Laschi accused La Mandini of stealing her *abellimenti, and* doing the murder. Then Bussani accused both Da Ponte and Benucci of vague villainous things ... but that, at least, I expected. I wanted to kneel down and confess to those assembled that I had strung poor Haegelin up there myself, just to shut them all up."

"Da Ponte would love a roommate..."

"Sweetie, things are so impossibly tense. I'm sure none of the singers had anything to do with murdering anybody. At least, somebody who is not another singer."

"Cats!"

"And rats."

"Here's a strange thing: when the *artistes* aren't denouncing each other to me, they are trying to be invisible, a hard task for opera singers, to the spies and mooches and police spooks who are floating around in the theater, also trying to look invisible. Everybody in the cast, crew and production staff is acting furtive and guilty of something. Why are the cops hanging around at all? Maybe Da Ponte did murder after all."

"But don't forget Rosenberg and the child, and what followed. Some other game may be going on."

"Yes ... Mesmer has unlocked the Gottlieb's secret, which puts a shadow of suspicion squarely on His Excellency. Our dear count bought Nanette; he took her without so much as a how-d'ye do. He was overheard by Fritz Drossel having a set-to with Haegelin the night before our first staging rehearsal ... and then Haeglin turns up dead."

"So your patron the count is the one with something to hide, with urgent reason to hustle the censor into his grave as a suicide, before people get around to thinking too hard."

"God knows I'm happy with his decision to obscure the events of that evening; that is, if it means *Figaro* will play. I'm surely not going to denounce him!

He must know that, and yet he sends his mouthpiece to threaten me anyway. We used to be so friendly. Why is he warning me off?"

"Well, he doesn't want you snooping around the Gottliebs', that's clear. The other accusations about your manners are just to distract you."

ᐖ Scene 7 ᐖ

Tiefer Graben, a fashionable street,
April 24, 9:00 A.M.

Van Swieten and Mozart: Recitativo

"Mozart, wait up, halloo! How are you, dear fellow? What are you going to play for us at the next meeting of the Cavaliers?"

"Baron van Swieten, *gruss Gott*, lovely to see you. More Bach, assuredly. I can never get enough of the Well-Tempered; I play a prelude and a fugue every day before breakfast. Allow me to express my condolences about Herr Haegelin."

"I am just now on the way to offer my sympathies to his aged parents and sister."

"Let me walk with you a while; our ways lie together. When is the funeral?"

"Oh dear, no obsequies I'm afraid. Only a burial in the prison field, attendance forbidden, even to the family."

"The coroner ruled him a suicide, then?"

"Swiftly and decisively. Poor Haegelin. He was such a dedicated employee. Rigid mind, but a decent, a hard-working person. He gave us very little trouble in the matter of *Figaro*, and what little objection he raised I was able to smooth over."

"Oh, well … he still wanted to snip a little here and there."

"I would not have thought he was the sort to kill himself. Suicide is a young man's pastime, especially if the young man has recently read *The Sorrows of Young Werther*. That was why I decided to ban the book. Too many self-inflicted pistol wounds, agonized farewell notes, buff-colored waistcoats, and so on. The novel was a danger to the youth of Vienna."

"Haegelin was not young, but he *did* have a note on his person," *says Mozart.* "Unfortunately, it was written by Da Ponte, who threw it at poor Haegelin to forward one of his crazy intrigues; and Haegelin put it in his pocket. I wish to God Da Ponte wouldn't do those things; now he is detained. I am deeply puzzled as to why the poet to the Italian Theater would be detained, presumably on suspicion of the murder, if Haegelin is officially ruled a suicide?"

"Da Ponte fell out with Haegelin, didn't he?"

"Threatened to kill him."

"These Italians. Let me ask you, did you happen to see Haegelin's body when they found it in the theater?"

"Oh, yes. I couldn't resist peeping. It was horrible. His eyes were open, frozen in horror, sunken in and all glazed over. His face was gray and had odd black specks in it, like pox, and there was a thin red mark, like a crease passing right over his voice box, which was crushed. The singers didn't like to look at it."

"Face pale, you say? Not at all livid? A V-shaped bruise, thick like rope, higher up on his neck? Around the ear, say?"

"No, not that I saw. Gray face. The mark was definitely thin and horizontal."

"Odder yet. If you have observed truly and carefully, then Haegelin was *not* killed by hanging."

"How do you mean? He was distinctly dangling, high as Haman; everybody saw."

"I mean – murder. From your description, I surmise that he was killed by garotting, fracturing the larynx from behind, obstructing the airway, leading to suffocation. Then someone hanged him up in the theater after he was dead."

"Murder? Garrotting? How can you be sure?"

"I am the son of my father, Mozart. He was the Imperial Physician under the Empress. I have seen many horrible things, including suicides and executions by hanging, and other things I do not like to think of – including the effects of the garrote. If you have observed well, then the face is the wrong color, and the bruise is too low on the throat and the wrong size and shape for death by hanging. And let us not forget the fractured larynx. Horizontal bruise, you say?"

"Oh, horizontal, I am almost sure."

"Was it not a rope mark, thick and mottled?"

"No, I tell you it was thin and string-like … about this thickness, actually."
Mozart draws a cello string out of his pocket and holds it up.

Van Swieten starts, looks long and hard at the string, then takes it gently by one of its ends. He traces his finger down the whole string, especially along the fuzz of residue at the middle. He rubs the substance under his fingers, holds it to his nose, and touches his fingers to his tongue.

"How did you come to carry this string in your pocket?"

"I picked it up off the floor in the corridor in front of Count Rosenberg's office the day they found the body. Then I bumped into H.E. himself, and I just put it in my pocket, so as not to look ridiculous holding it, I suppose."

"The substance clinging to the string is skin, Mozart."

"God save us, I thought it was dust-bunnies…"

"This cello string could easily have been the means of poor Haegelin's tragic murder."

"Murder? Murder? Why do you keep saying that? It was suicide a minute ago."

"Yes, I think we had better proceed cautiously here. The unseemly haste, the pressure from certain people in the coroner's office to render a verdict of suicide … I … we … may be in dark political waters with this."

"The theater is always a spawning ground for intrigue."

"No, not the Court theater … I mean national, perhaps international politics. There was an animus between – well the Freemasons and Haegelin dating from last year. It started with the Günther affair. It was Haegelin who denounced Günther to the Emperor. Poor Günther, His Majesty's own private secretary!"

"Everyone knows the tale. I believed it once myself. Haegelin made the wild claim that Günther was selling state secrets to the Freemasons and their allies in Prussia. The whole thing was a stupid hoax."

"Alas, Mozart, Haegelin never gave up believing it was true. And there were consequences. You remember the Freemasonry Act, written up last year?"

"What did Haegelin have to do with that? It was our freely offered promise of the Freemasons' complete submission to the Crown, all our secrets revealed. Secretary von Born and you yourself wrote up that document."

"Haegelin added a word to it, Mozart."

"Haegelin? Added? What word?"

"He struck out the words 'ancient rites' and inserted the word *'chicanerie'* into an otherwise benign document. When that word appeared, the brotherhood took it for the Emperor's own, and it struck fear in them. Good men, men of power and position and influence, began to resign from the lodges. They read the Emperor's animus – the handwriting on the wall – in that little French word."

"Are you saying that – the *Freemasons killed Haegelin?*"

"Quiet, quiet, Mozart. That is not a conversation for the public street. Whether a murder was done or no, whether it was one person or another, or many, it's a bad thing for our movement. I tell you now that there are … provocateurs … who have joined our lodges; I name no names, but they are not above dishonorable and secret doings to accomplish their political ends in this Empire. I speak of" *(he lowers his voice to a whisper)* "*revolution*. We must be circumspect."

"Baron, I am flabbergasted."

"Come into this doorway for a moment. Speak softly. So. Let me ask you some more questions about the body, while your mind is fresh. Were there signs that Haegelin had been violently handled? Clothes or hair in disarray? Shoes missing?"

"Not that I recall."

"When one is attacked from behind, there often are no signs, especially if the strangler is strong, or has the element of surprise in his favor. Of course his garments could have been re-arranged before the hanging."

"By whom? Our lodge-brothers? Freemasons are not murderers! Da Ponte isn't a murderer!"

"Shhh. Are you sure? These southern people are so hot-blooded."

"Da Ponte is an invalid, the victim of a horrible, near-fatal poisoning; he is frail; he can barely walk! Besides, he is an intellectual, a man of words! And my friend and colleague! Why in the name of God would a person producing a show in the Burgtheater do a murder in the Burgtheater and *hang his victim in the Burgtheater?* There is no logic in it!"

"Calm yourself. We don't really know the murder happened at the theater, do we?"

"No. We don't. But perhaps – on second thought – I am not so sure about the marks on the throat or anything else, after all…"

"Ah, Mozart, I understand. It's a shame I was not allowed to examine Haegelin's remains. He is already lying in his unconsecrated grave. His family are all terribly upset, but all their appeals to the Emperor were rebuffed. His Majesty shouted at these poor distraught people, and threatened them with a clenched fist."

"But surely the Emperor will relent when – well, on second thought, probably not. Once he has made up his mind, unmaking it is like un-brewing coffee. Murder! It can't be murder! Over the last few minutes I have become almost certain that I was completely wrong about the thin bruise, and this cello string probably belongs to somebody who practices too hard."

"Dear Mozart, courage. Truth! The string is new, long and unworn. Look at the ends; they are totally straight, and they have never been put on the cello, never wound around a peg."

"You are right of course, Swieten. Oh God, what am I saying! Let's not talk about this! Murder, not suicide! If this gets out it will ruin *Figaro's* chances! Da Ponte could be deported, or worse! The Freemasons! Secret plots! But wait! Poor old Haegelin buried in a criminal's grave! Was there to be no priest; were there no prayers?"

"No. Haegelin, right or wrong, is going to Judgment without benefit of rites or the clergy."

"Well, perhaps we might both offer a prayer for his soul."

"Perhaps we might. However he died, Herr Haegelin is not damned; remember, Mozart, God knows the truth, and God will take care of his children. God doesn't need the intercessions of priests nor the prayers of Masons to know what to do with Haegelin's soul when the day of Judgment comes."

"No. But I feel the need, for my own peace. After all, he was working on my production, or against it, actually."

"It appears, Mozart, that you are the only true witness to the marks of strangulation on Haegelin's body, and you may hold in your hand the instrument of his death. Yes, put it away. Hide it. Thank heaven for your keenness and curiosity. Your observational powers are so accurate; you are the only person who can dispute the coroner's verdict."

"But I really *don't* want to dispute it, though," *mutters Mozart.*

"Neither do I. But I fear greatly that we may be called upon to do so. And then, where will we find our resolve, our loyalty to the truth?"

"Let sleeping truths lie! Poor Da Ponte! Poor Haegelin! Poor *Figaro*! This is getting very confusing."

"Yes, it's very possible that these events may be connected somehow. Let us guard our knowledge and swear only to use it if Da Ponte or some other innocent person is falsely accused. The truth! The truth! The truth is our best tool for illuminating dark corners."

"Please, let's keep those corners dark for a while until we see what happens next. I for one don't want to risk … my God, it's production week! Curse my curiosity and my perspicacity! I have to get my opera on the stage!"

"And clear your friend's name. And protect the brotherhood. And serve the truth."

"Oh, well, yes, of course, certainly. I must go to the theater immediately. Adieu!"

⤳ Scene 8 ⤶

At the Freemasons' house,
April 24, 10:00 A.M.

Mozart and Von Born: Recitativo

Mozart wanders across the Bauermarkt *and into the narrow* Gassen, *weaving in and out of the crush of delivery wagons,* Fiakers, Pirustches *and municipal water carts spraying the streets to keep the dust down.*

"I wonder if what the Emperor believes about the Freemasons is true. It's hard to imagine; our ideals are so in tune with his – rationalism, just laws, practical humanity – my own lodge, "Beneficence," raised funds for the deaf and dumb hospital! We take up collections for flood victims; we hear lectures on the latest science and technology ... Caesar lets us go on doing good works and promoting higher learning, but I suspect that now he mistrusts us too."

The composer looks up and sees that he has wandered into Landskrongasse. *He stands directly in front of the Freemasons' house, which contains the meeting rooms shared by all the lodges in Vienna. Membership has declined to the point that this one house can now accommodate all the chapters.*

The door opens suddenly; the chiefest Freemason of them all – Ignatz von Born – stands on the threshold (Mozart hears brass, in the redgold key of E-flat major – a serene and majestic fanfare ... ta-taaaaaaaa...). The two distinguished men regard one another; the elder man speaks first.

"Mozart, lovely to see you. I so enjoyed your music for the funeral. What a pity that the Masonic movement in the city has come to such a sad state, when we have such loyal brothers as you giving of their talents."

"Master von Born, you are too kind. I am surprised to see you here in the house. I was informed you had withdrawn from our activities entirely. Is this true?"

"Brother, if I may still call you that, it is so. But I store my specimen collections and scientific notebooks here still. But so many catastrophic things have occurred. We are infiltrated by subversives – the Rosicrucians certainly, and – perhaps – others more unsavory. I am frankly quite frightened for the Freemason movement – and for all men of learning and good will. And for the future of our empire."

"Master von Born, I have just spoken with Brother van Swieten, about the – the recent mysterious death of Herr von Haegelin in the Burgtheater. I have just learned about his role in discrediting the Freemasons and turning the Emperor against us … I am very confused about how the affair will play out. I fear it will harm the chances of – well, my play."

Von Born's expression freezes and the warmth and welcome in his eyes fades. The two men stand silent for several minutes. Finally the master descends into the street and speaks, in a barely audible voice.

"The Emperor believes that the Austrian Freemasons are run out of Prussia, by those who are plotting his downfall. He fears the Illuminati, the Rosicrucians, and perhaps some international Jewish republican revolutionary plot. Masons have always … advocated for enlightened ideas and practices on the international stage. Some of us work through the power of learning, and by moral suasion. Some are impatient and want more immediate results, and they are perhaps not choosy about the means of achieving them. I … some of these men were involved in the Netherlands disaster, where their mission failed. Others had a hand in fomenting the Hungarian uprising, where so many nobles were slaughtered by the mobs. We have lost control of our movement, or so it seems."

"The emperor is right, then?"

"He receives very biased reports. Count Gulas has his ear about ongoing Masonic subversion in Hungary. Gulas is an arch obscurantist and would do anything to prevent the future – or the present – from encroaching on his feudal prerogatives. You can see his point, though; having a hundred of your fellow nobles cut down by a lawless mob is reason enough for him to inveigh against the Masons, or anybody at all with up-to-date ideas about the rights of humankind."

"He is trying to stop my opera from going forward."

"But Caesar does not heed him in that regard, does he?"

"Not at the moment. But I am nervous about Gulas anyway. He doesn't take well to ideas and facts of any sort. Should I quit the Masons, Brother – Monsieur Von Born?"

"If you want to enter government service, or work at the Imperial theater, you should strongly consider it. You cannot be a court composer and a Mason any more."

"Is-is revolution coming?"

"Not to Austria. I believe Joseph is something of an aberration, and I will always support him and pray that his benevolent reign continues. I know he is a willful tyrant and his trade policies are truly lamentable, but his zeal to modernize and to end the barbarities of feudalism make him very valuable in the long run."

"The long run to what?"

"To liberty, equality and fraternity. To a free and just and humane society."

"You are a noble and far-sighted man, brother; it's an honor to speak with you thus. I'm mostly concerned about the short run right now, or just the run … of my show, I mean. I want my opera to run, and I can't think about international politics this week."

"Keep a watchful eye on Gulas. He hates free-thinking, and he's not above a little larceny to get his way."

"Do you really think so?"

"I am afraid I do."

✦ Scene 9 ✦

The Spectacles Office
April 24, 11:00 P.M.

Thorwart and Mozart: Duet at cross purposes

Mozart enters the theater. He walks down the office row, his eyes once again sweeping the floor. He sees in the gathering dust – "Couldn't that gaggle of buxom housemaids hanging around the palace put in some time dusting, just to keep up appearances?" – *the tracks of the casters of costume trunks, the footprints of staff and musicians. The corners where the dust lies thickest contain bits of ribbon, stray sequins, brass buttons, hair, both horse and human … a whalebone corset-stay, a scrap of lace, an entire sausage roll* … "Can any of these lost bits be connected with the – the death? If so, how could I possibly tell? Was I lucky or unfortunate to pick up that cursed C string? Is it really an instrument of murder? Here's H.E.'s increasingly notorious office; best to knock – who knows what goes on in there any more…"

"Mozart, how tiresome, what do you want now?" *The chief financial officer, Dear Godfather Johannes Thorwart, stands at a desk in the outer office. He glances up at the composer, and down again at his ledger.*

"Fine, thanks, Dear God-father-in-law; and how is your lovely lady wife? I am the bearer of good news; I have secured the services of an understudy who knows the ingénue role. She will be in the theater, completely off book, this evening. I came to inform H.E."

"You can inform me; H.E. is indisposed and I am in charge of this office now." Thorwart continues examining the columns of figures in his great book.

"Well, it's Constanze."

"She won't do."

"Why not? She sings as well as anybody, she's still slim enough, she knows the whole opera cold, and she's good to stand in right now."

"I don't approve of my god-daughter appearing in the theater and mingling with theater people."

"Unfortunately, Herr von Thorwart, a god-parent's wishes are superseded by the husband's wishes under the law, and I wish her to come here and help us through rehearsals of the last two Acts, and sing in the premiere if it comes to that."

"And the financial officer of the theater's wishes supersede even the husband's wishes. I won't pay for an understudy."

"Fine, then. She will work *gratis*. I am expecting Mademoiselle Gottlieb to recover her powers of speech momentarily. She has had a terrible illness, but she is on the mend. Dr. Mesmer, who is on a visit from France, treats her, and he assures me it is only a matter of hours before she is fully restored to herself."

Thorwart's eyebrows jerk up and his pale eyes narrow on Mozart.

"Mesmer?"

"Oh, did I say *Mesmer*? Ha-ha, how silly of me, just a slip of the tongue; Mesmer's permanently exiled, isn't he? I meant the famous Dr. *Egon Mentzer* from Lyon; I really can't imagine…"

"Mozart, will you stop babbling? You may bring my god-daughter to rehearsals, and she may sing the entire run, for all I care. I hope she proves to be more reliable than this Gottlieb girl, who gives us nothing but trouble. I'm thinking seriously of dismissing both her and her mother for failure to honor her contract. She has missed three performances of the damned play in the German theater, and she has your Italian cast in an uproar. I don't appreciate the mother being so sullen and secretive. It's all very suspicious."

"The girl is gifted, and she's only a child. Surely you don't blame her for her mother's behavior."

"This is a business I'm running here, Mozart, not an orphan asylum. You got what you wanted; now go away. I'll deduct Constanze's fee from yours."

"I expected you would. I would be so grateful if you referred to my wife as Frau von Mozart, as befits a gentleman speaking of a young matron. In exchange I will not refer to your wife by her given name either. How's that?"

"Get out."

"No, my lord Count, you shall not have her, you shall not have her!"

"What's that?"

"Quote from Beaumarchais. From the aria found in the hanged man's pocket. Thought it was apropos. How's this one? *Non più andrai, farfallone amoroso, notte e giorno d'intorno girando!*"

"Get out."

Mozart passes out into the corridor and into the theater to tune his clavier, to write some staging notes for his Act IV staging rehearsal.

In the hours that follow, Mozart's beloved wife Constanze sings the tiny but charming role of Barbarina, her light, pure soprano floating effortlessly to a shimmering pianissimo A-flat in the arietta. Shortly thereafter, Signor Mandini, singing the role of Count Almaviva, kneels to Signora Laschi in the role of the base-born Sevillian girl who is now Countess Almaviva. No revolutions break out in the city; no angry mobs pound upon the palace doors. Count Rosenberg, in his private box, seems not to notice how scandalously subversive this moment is. Indeed he is not listening: he is mopping his face with a handkerchief and staring into space. The composer notes that Mrs. Bussani's confidence to Da Ponte about this moment was incorrect, and therefore absolutely nobody can be eliminated from the list of conspirators trying to wreck his show. Count Thorwart, looking sleek and pleased with himself as if he had written the play, twinkles his fingers discreetly to Constanze in the final stretto as the finale of Mozart's scandalous play bubbles to its close.

✌ Scene 10 ✍

Mozart's bedroom, April 24, night

Mozart and Constanze: Duettino di rivelazioni

"*Merde! Kaka!* I'm not having a good time at all! I just hate being patronized by those damn Italians! You'd think people would at least be grateful that I could learn the beastly role in 15 minutes, step in and sing the silly recitatives they can't even remember after weeks of drill!"

"*Chérie, du calme, quelle espèce de passion!*"

"*M'enfin*, I know I'm a matron and I stopped looking like a little girl a while ago, but honestly, darling! And that fat Nancy Storace with the cow's eyes you think so much of, well! The woman never misses a chance to remind me that she is the international diva and I am the dilettante, and that my voice is rather pretty but my stage manner lacks this or that, and why don't I try this bit of staging and this pose and this *gestique* that she used with such great success while singing for the Helsinki Grand Opera … I could just kill the bitch!"

"She's just jealous. Storace has ambitions to take over your role, sweetheart."

"Go on! She wants to sing Barbarina?"

"No, loviekin doviekin, she wants to sleep with me."

"Ah, ha. *Und es war Licht.*"

"But darlingdear, I'm otherwise occupied. You sound so girlishly lovely in the little air; you're charming onstage; your eyes are black and comely; you're smarter than all of them put together, which is not saying a whole lot, I suppose … and heaven be continually praised, you're married to me. Forever. Not subject to revision, derision or division."

"If you insist, dumpling, I shall abide by the terms of my contract, letter and spirit. You know, I'm not all that wild to be onstage as I
once was; and I really don't enjoy the life, the back-stabbing, the petti-
ness, the creeping anxiety. I'd rather stay home and keep the oven warm."
"Ah. Are you pregnant then?"

"Yes, dearie, I am. Let's pray hard for this one."

"And – your operatic ambitions are once more deferred?"

"*Per sempre*. Let Ouisia and Josepha and Sophie be in show business; I hate
everybody else in it! Except Benucci; he's a lamb, and his mind is fixed firmly
on his craft. So if you run off with Storace I'll run off with him."

"Let's save the coach fares and let them run off with each other."

❧ Scene 11 ❧

Mozart's house, April 25, 7:00 A.M.
Recitativo, Mozart, Constanze and Da Ponte

"Bubikins, you can't imagine what! They've found *another* dead man from the theater! Last night! Everyone on the street says it's murder."

"Another man hanging at the theater? Oh Dear God! My big fat Egyptian goose is cooked. Who is it?"

"No, not *in* the theater, a man *from* the theater. They found him floating in the Wien last night, but not drowned; they say he was strangled by a wire. It's Herr von Drossel, the chief usher."

"Oh woe, woe, double woe is me! Oh, ever so much worse than woe is me! Stanzerl, did I not tell you, that man told me he was busy eavesdropping in the passage the night of the Haegelin murder? That he was one of the sizeable throng crowding the passage the night of the Haegelin murder? That he heard Rosenberg and Haegelin screaming at each other? You say Drossel was strangled by a wire? I wonder if Drossel went to the police and – or more likely went to Rosenberg and demanded – *ach*, is it really Rosenberg?"

"There's a knock; we have company. Put this on. It might be the police or somebody. Marianne, who is it?"

"It's Da Ponte; I'd know that voice anywhere. Has he escaped from his dungeon cell?"

Da Ponte enters the Mozart bedchamber, followed by Marianne, trying to stop him, or take his cane, hat and coat. There are limp bits of straw in his hair; and a distinct aroma of stale garments, mildew and damp stone hovers around him.

"*Carissimi*, lovely to see you! Here I am, free of chains and my durance vile, as of fifteen minutes ago! I came right over, I'm panting to take you to breakfast and coffee. My dear Stanzina, you look good enough to eat, in your negligee, such naughty brown raisins of eyes as you have; surely you are the most delectable matron in the city. Can I get into bed with you right now? And you, Signor, look like a rooster ruffling his plumage after treading his hen … I hope I haven't busted you; no, wait – I hope I have; what fun!

"Where's the best Kaffeehaus in this district? Better yet, where's the best spot to be seen by everybody? I must announce my liberation to the world. Yes, I'll give you a minute, but hurry it up, no quickies!"

❧ Scene 12 ❧

A Kaffeehaus, April 25, 7:30 A.M.
Mozart, Constanze, Da Ponte: Trio buffo

"Now is the time for drinking, now the time to beat the earth with unfettered foot! Ah, my dears, the mere aroma of coffee induces in my parched soul an ecstasy beyond ecstasy. I knew they wouldn't keep a blameless man in the clink for long. This is Vienna! Oh, may God rain blessings down on happy Austria and her enlightened Monarch! May He bless this wonderful establishment in which we now sit, freely discussing the news of the day as if the dank shadow of the dungeon had not just passed over us!"

"I think being chained in that dungeon while another man from the theater met his death was extremely clever of you."

"Ah, my dearest friend, always alert to matters of my personal welfare, aren't you? The convenience to yourself never occurred to you, I am sure. But, all forgiven, water under the bridge; we are all together again. Ah, what fine coffee; what excellent cream!"

"And try this Linzer thing; you may need to pardon me once again."

"Darlings, I proclaim that we are, in spite of occasional backward slidings, living in a wondrous time. We teeter on the precipice, my friend. Which way will fate tip us? To mount on shining wing upward into a golden age of Humanism? Or to tumble backward to the dungeons, oubliettes and seignorial *bastinados* of the feudal era?

"Perhaps we might even soar as far as a republic, who knows? So much progress, so much that is new and terrifying and precarious in this brave new world, that has such pastries in it, as Shakespeare would have said, had he tasted this one. How did it all begin, this precipitate explosion of wisdom and progress? What is the wellspring, the fountainhead, the progenitor of the Enlightenment? Can you tell me, in a word, a single word?"

"Philosophes? Mercantilism? Industry?"

"More elemental even than those. In a word … *coffee*! Why coffee, you may ask … ah, no, I see you agree with me entirely. Coffee, *Kaffee*, *café*, the one beverage available to the general populace that actually makes them *smarter*! Enlivening the brain, lubricating the logical apparatus, making room in the imagination for formerly unthinkable ideas! The ordinary man drinks his coffee and begins to think his thoughts – to ask his questions, talk to his neighbor. Can progress be far behind? Is it any wonder that so many princes have tried to suppress this divine drink? Princes always fear people who ask questions and talk to their neighbors. Notice, if you please, that princes are happy to provide their subjects with alcohol, which dulls the mind and turns men into oxen, who bear the yoke of servitude without complaint."

"And, Renzo, don't forget the noble coffeehouse, with its debates, its pamphlets and gazettes!" *cries Mozart.* "Here where we sit in a new agora, the new academe, the coffee on one side, the gazettes on the other, and in between – humanity drinking the magical brew and discussing – politics! Law! Science! We witness the birth of a true civil society! Oh, wondrous time, when mankind wakes up and smells the coffee! Who knows what great leaps forward civilization will make!"

"From what I can see," *giggles Constanze, looking up from a gazette,* "three-quarters of these writers and thinkers seem to be debating the dangerous and provocative over-exposure of housemaids' bosoms."

"Unfortunately, my dear," *says Da Ponte,* "your minimally educated Viennese journalists, beaned up though they be, never discuss anything remotely serious! Have you read – can you possibly have read – all the pamphlets that came out this month professing moral outrage at the daring décolletage now in fashion with Viennese housemaids? Those lush and lingering descriptions of creamy englobed housemaids' bosoms, so scantily clad that their pink-tipped buds peep boldly from under their lace?

"These thunderings of moral fury have been so lavishly prurient that our good Nymphs of the Evening, realizing they were missing a bet, all started dressing up as housemaids! They even carry featherdusters! They're raking in the dough!"

"Good on them," *says Constanze.* "Why should they not enjoy the fruits of the Enlightenment?"

"But this sort of yellow journalism, my girl, does not pass as enlightened discourse, social criticism, or even graffitti, as far as I am concerned. Is Vienna a serious town? Are people discussing Adam Smith, or Schiller; are they writing essays on Kant? No, they are sniggering about bosoms, or hissing about scandals in the theater! I am beginning to despise the intellectual shallowness of this so-called enlightened city!"

"You have, as usual," *says Mozart,* "debated yourself around to the backside of your original argument and are now rogering it. But getting back to your present happy situation. Did they let you out directly after they found that poor Drossel in the river?"

"No. Who, in the river?"

"The head usher of the Burgtheater. Strangled with a wire. Dead, floating in the Wien."

"But why should they even connect my re-entry into society and the sad death of what's-his-name, as I see you have already done? His Imperial Majesty, having been at long last informed that I was unjustly detained, decreed my immediate release at dawn this morning. Before breakfast, thank God. His Majesty may be testy and a miser and a fashion disaster, but he is loyal to those humble beings who do him good and loyal service."

"I connect the events for the following reasons, Lorenzo. Because, your sudden freedom smells funny to me. Because, Monsieur *mouche* von Drossel, may angels waft him through the skies, confided in me for a small fee, that he had overheard a violent argument between H.E. Count Rosenberg and Haegelin in the Spectacles Office late on the night before Haegelin's body appeared in the theater. Because, it's highly possible that Drossel tried to shop this information around to the police, or the Emperor – or wait! even more likely – Drossel went to H.E. and made him an offer to rent his silence in the matter of the shoutfest, and any pertinence it might have to the subsequent death of one of the shouters. Because, perhaps the Count could have killed Drossel and then ordered that you be released, so they could re-arrest you for the murder."

"Amadé, that is just so Baroque. You think H.E. had a little tiff with Haegelin, murdered him and hanged him in the … then he murdered whosis and is trying to frame me for both murders, one of which is a suicide? *Che pazzeria!*"

"Perhaps not, Renzo. Drossel hinted to me that H.E. and the censor were arguing about the little Gottlieb. Now I think of it, I *know* they were arguing about her and – my God, it has to be – the *droit du seigneur!*"

"You mean Haegelin caught the count boffing the Infant Phenomenon and bawled him out? Or vice versa, even better!"

"No, Haegelin caught the count."

"How do you know?"

"The little Gottlieb has recovered her powers of speech and spilled the beans."

"So! Our dear Count Orsini-Rosenberg has deserted his hordes of whores and housemaids and focused his attentions on little girls? Got a touch of the French disease, has he?"

"How swiftly your mind leaps forward … but perhaps it has traveled this road before?"

"Darling, I don't mess with children. I like some bosomage on a woman. However, as one can count upon the sun's arising in the morning, you can count on the nobility, in all times and places, to do what they have always done. Want, want, want. Take, take, take. But taking an under-age actress's maidenhead is not exactly a criminal offense. Actresses usually have a few maidenheads to spare."

"But soon after all his wanting and taking and shouting about it with Haegelin, Haegelin's remains ended up as the counterpoise for the Fallbeil curtain!"

"Proves my point. Rosenberg is many things, but he's not a practical joker."

"My love, you suspect Rosenberg," *murmurs Constanze, her nose still in the gazette,* "because you despise Rosenberg for having violated a child. And because you find him despicable you assume that he is a murderer and the one blocking your play. I agree with Renzo, it's completely illogical: it's his own production, backed by his own Emperor, in his own theater, which is not the venue he would choose for his personal shenanigans."

"He's still guilty as sin if you ask me," *says Mozart,* "and he proclaims his guilt by insisting on Haegelin's being a suicide in the teeth of the evidence."

"The question remains, if it's really truly a murder, why did he, or anyone, hang the body in the theater?" *asks Constanze.*

"Perhaps he hired Casti or Bussani to do it," *says Da Ponte.* "I'd like to think so."

"You just want them out of your way, Renzo; and I don't blame you. But it would be so out of character for them; Casti is a cringing toady. Bussani is a small-time snitch and a singer, not a murderer, although his intonation would kill all nine Muses at one sitting. God knows they want *you* out of *their* way, but the porn and the poison is much more their style."

"With how much ease do we believe what we wish!" *murmurs Constanze from behind a gazette.*

"Hopla! Time to go. I must meet my *friseur.* We are going to rehearse something or other today, and heaven knows what will happen, but the famous composer is going to look elegant. Would you like to freshen up *chez nous,* Renzo? Get some of the straw out from under your collar?"

"Yes, my dears. *Andiamo,* let's go. *Garçon,* the bill! My treat, as I promised. After you, dear Madame. I do hate all this denouncing and snitchery and bitchery; I really do. I am and have always been a man of peace, as you well know. *Arrrrgh!*"

Da Ponte, having gained the street, suddenly leaps into the path of a large pale man, spins his cane in his hands, grasps the shod end and smashes the obsidian handle into the man's mouth. Blood and bits of teeth and gum fly everywhere, and the big man drops like a stunned ox. Constanze shrieks. Mozart drags her behind a vendor's booth. The vendors and passersby also shriek and somebody yells for the police.

"Diguri!" *howls Da Ponte, beating the prostrate man about the head and shoulders with the cane.* "Now you know how it feels!"

"No, no, *sono innocente, lo giuro* – I'm innocent, I swear – it wasn't me! I didn't do it!" *gurgles Diguri, rolling into a ball in the dust and spitting more teeth.*

"Stand up and let me extract the molars, you fetid yelping mongrel!"

"It wasn't my idea: the others … ow, ow!"

"What others, what others, what others? I'll kill them all with my bare hands!" *yowls Da Ponte, gasping for breath, staggering and leaning heavily on the bloody cane head as he aims feeble kicks at the softer portions of Diguri's anatomy.*

Two police officers round the corner at the trot. They restrain Da Ponte, who promptly sits down in the dust, smiles pinkly at them and blows them a kiss.

"Oh, welcome, dear hosts and companions of hours only recently past! Thank heaven you've come, and in the nick too! Seize this scoundrel, if you please. Bind him fast! He tried to poison me last summer, then he denounced me to you and used his own bottle of poison as proof that I was up to no good! Drag him off! Wrap him in chains! Staple him to the wall! Shave his head! Feed him on hard crusts that will break his gums and cause his guts to seize up and never produce shit again!

"Yes, of course, I too will accompany you to the *Polizeihaus*, but the manacles are not strictly … *che cos'e?* You're arresting *me*, not *him*? But he's the *guilty party*, can't you dumb geese see that? Well, seeing as you are so pressing, I won't resist. It's back to my home away from home! Mozart, carry on as best you can. As you see I have vital business in the area of social justice and civil order. I will join you as I may. *Addio!*"

The Mozarts emerge, trembling, from behind the vendor's stall and stare after the retreating Da Ponte and his police escort. The large pale man has vanished, but bloody bits of him still lie in the dust under their feet. The composer is as pale as flour. His hand presses against his heart; his wife allows him to lean on her a little.

"Let's go home, Stanzi, I need to close the door and lock it and beat my head against it."

"We're almost there, love; just breathe slowly; here we are, here's the key, here's the stair, here's the door; do what you must."

"Oh God, Stanzerl, I feel so faint. There was so much blood. I know as a good Freemason I am supposed to maintain calm in the face of death, but I have seen too much death and near-death lately. And the violence – it makes me want to puke. I didn't know Da Ponte had it in him, physically or temperamentally, to hit a man so hard and so often. He called that man Diguri. That's the name of the rival who supposedly poisoned him and evidently planted the poison bottle in Da Ponte's apartment. Strange that this Diguri would turn up the very morning Da Ponte was released from prison."

"Even stranger that he should turn up the morning *after another murder is committed.*"

"Oh … yes, of course. Do you think that great oaf did the Burgtheater murder?"

"Which one? I don't know about the first murder; we seem to be calling it a murder now, don't we? I suppose he could have. All sorts of people seem to have been lurking backstage that evening with mayhem on their minds; why not this man too?"

"Da Ponte wasn't."

"Do we really know that? Did you ever ask him? Maybe we should make a list of who was there or could have been there, and what prompted them to be there, and what might incite them to murder."

"Oh yes, let's. A list of lurkers seems more productive than hitting my head on the door. Let's go have our hair done and make lists all the while. Starting with Counts Rosenberg and Gulas."

✑ Finale ✑

Mozart's home, then the Spectacles Office, Burgtheater,
April 25, 10:00 A.M.

Mozart, Constanze, Stephen Storace, then Thorwart

Before the list has grown very long, however, the door undergoes its threatened drubbing,
but not by the agency of the famous composer. A heavy and exigent knock brings Mozart, hair
half-done and his small person en deshabille, *rushing to rescue it. On the other side of the*
door is his British student and assistant music director, Michael Storace.

"Storace! Why are you are knocking like Death on my door? And all pale
and upset as well! Is your sister in some vocal difficulty, God forbid? Or did you
just discover parallel fifths in your clarinet sonata?"

"Maestro, forgive me, but the rumor is they have dug up Haegelin's remains, on orders from His Excellency's office! And the coroner's verdict has
been officially changed – to murder! They are postponing all theater activities
until after the funeral, since he now may rest in consecrated ground; and everyone involved in the *Figaro* production is compelled to go. Also, Monsieur Deputy Thorwart wants to see you in the Spectacles Office most urgently, within
the hour."

"Murder! Thorwart? His Excellency's office? Thank you, Storace; I'll just
be a minute ... but really, why do I bother to come like a lapdog when they
snap their fingers at me? By the pricking of my thumbs, Da Ponte is in worse
danger than ever, and I've lost another day's rehearsal, and *Figaro* is doomed!"

Twenty minutes later, Mozart presents himself at the Spectacles Office door – suited,
droop-stockinged, untidily cravatted, and half-coiffed by Mozart's very aggravated personal

friseur. He enters Thorwart's office without being announced or knocking first.

"You wanted to see me, Monsieur?" *asks the composer, omitting the deferential bow and formal greeting to his Godfather-in-law.*

"You have heard," *says Thorwart,* "what has transpired this morning? Shut up and listen to me, Mozart. I am going to get to the bottom of these shocking affairs once and for all. Two murders in one week! Yesterday His Excellency strongly hinted to me that he would like me to take the investigation and resolution of this scandal into my own hands, and today I am resolved to do so. No sooner was that unsavory person Da Ponte released from prison last night, than a second murder occurred. The police found our own esteemed head usher, Herr Drossel, floating in the Wien. Evidently he had been garotted with a wire. He had several hundred Gulden on his person, so this was not a robbery but a vicious murder, a vendetta."

"Surely you don't connect…"

"On my own initiative," *Thorwart smirks and preens,* "I have had poor Herr Haegelin's body disinterred, in order to ascertain whether, in all the commotion at the theater, he had been too hastily ruled a suicide. It had pained me terribly to see such a loyal public servant buried in the prison graveyard, while these Italian charlatans and assassins walk free. Well, my suspicions have proved correct. It seems as if the coroner was entirely wrong in his earlier judgment; or perhaps he was persuaded or bribed to overlook the evidence. He now concurs that the poor man was approached from behind and his windpipe crushed *by a wire.* Yes, we now have two victims killed by the same cowardly method; obviously the murderer is the same vile scoundrel in both cases! Haegelin's remains will be properly buried with all the obsequies, in a proper grave, by noon today. I have ordered Da Ponte to be returned to prison."

"You sit there and tell me that Da Ponte killed Fritz Drossel *and* Haegelin? For God's sake, man, he was in a dungeon four hours ago!"

"You are mistaken, sir. The police log clearly states he was released yesterday evening."

"What police log? I have seen the man at my doorstep at seven! In the *morning*! He told me he had come straight to my house from jail! He had straw in his hair! And I was with him when he was arrested again: for brawling!"

"The brawling was coincidental, except insofar as it substantiates the irredeemable baseness of his character. I always suspected him in the first murder, after he made that unconscionable scene in Haegelin's office. I was pleased when I heard he was detained."

"Then you never believed it was sui-"

"Don't interrupt me. So it goes without saying he is guilty of the second slaying. What could be more obvious?"

"Did His Excellency *really* command Haegelin's disinterment?"

"As I told you, he handed these affairs over to me, and I am proceeding on my own initiative. I would not involve His Excellency in such sordid matters. He has not been feeling well during this whole sordid affair."

"He's about to take a turn for the worse, I'd bet on it."

"What did you say?"

"Oh, nothing. So, why are you telling me all this?"

"Well, Mozart, there is more Italian chicanery going on around here. I don't trust that Casti; I know Da Ponte is a cold-blooded villain, and frankly, your troupe of Italian singers are behaving very strangely. I gathered them together, *sans* the little Gottlieb and my god-daughter, here in this office; I announced to them that poor Haegelin had been disinterred and officially cleared of the crime of suicide; I told them that their attendance at his funeral was obligatory. During my speech, Madame Mandini fainted. Madame Bussani slapped her husband. Madame Laschi ran sobbing from the room. Signor Mandini did not go to the aid of his wife but stood off to one side cursing rather loudly. Can't singers learn to modulate their voices in small rooms?"

"You don't trust Casti? *Casti?* How did he get into my troupe? What role is he singing, exactly?"

"He's an Italian, is he not? An Italian upon whose every feature the moral rot announces itself. These unsavory foreign people, one never knows what they are saying, and when they do speak in a proper language they always mean something else. They are subversive, immoral and dishonest, and I hold you responsible for the whole Transalpine lot of them. They are a criminal race."

"But…"

"Your assignment is to discover what in God's name they are doing. One or more of them could be in league with Casti or Da Ponte. Casti has too much influence on H.E., and I am convinced he is deeply involved in this scandal, but of course I cannot say so. I believe H.E. is shielding him out of some misguided sense of loyalty, but I mean to ferret him out and send him packing back to his loathsome country. He's a troublemaker; they are all troublemakers, and so are you. I don't want you at court. I don't want my god-daughter mixed up with such people as you befriend. I suspect that Da Ponte's murders of people at court may be part of a larger Italian anarchist plot against our King and Kaiser."

"What? *What?* Do you just make this garbage up? Do you not realize that it's Gulas who invents these International Conspiracy fairy tales? He sees plots everywhere."

"Count Gulas to you. The Emperor believes him."

"He's playing on His Majesty's fears!"

"His Majesty has no fears."

"Right. But remember, please, that His Majesty also trusts Da Ponte. They are very friendly. He knows that Da Ponte could not possibly be a political agitator. My God, man, he's just a free spirit, a free talker, just a scattershot child of the Enlightenment, who writes poetry and walks with a cane!"

"Mozart, let me put it frankly. I believe that your cocky attitude, your *louche* Jewish and Italian friends, your unseemly behavior with such Bohemians as Baroness Waldstätten, and your impudent staging of *Figaro* are all consciously contrived to promote unrest in the city and undermine the authority of the Monarchy."

"*Show* me the Monarchy in Figaro! Show me *one monarch*! Look under the beds, in the closets, among the geraniums in the garden! Not one lousy monarch! But there's a count, Count! A count, behaving like all Counts or Cunts, of whose tom-Counting after other men's wives I do not approve! Do you hear me, sir?"

"It is well known that several members of your cast are involved in intrigues."

"Oh, do you *think* so? Surely not opera singers? In an opera house?"

"In addition to the melodramas of Mandinis and Bussanis and that hysterical Laschi woman, I must tell you that official people have come to me and said that Casti and Da Ponte are in league in some pornography publishing scheme!"

"They are bitter enemies, Thorwart!"

"Enemies may have common cause and ally themselves if it profits them. Shut up and listen.

"Madame Storace, an Englishwoman of whom I am very fond in spite of her Italian antecedents, has the idea that you are some sort of great composer. I don't see it myself, but I withhold judgment for now. Perhaps, if you do the tasks I am going to assign to you, and this matter is properly cleared up, and these criminals brought to justice, I can arrange for her to take you to London, where she and her brother could sponsor you and get you all the best introductions."

"*She* suggested this to *you*? Goddamn and more than Goddamn! Never a thought but for my personal welfare, as Renzo would say."

"Shut up. I'd love to throw you out of the country right now, but your first task, Mozart, will be to observe your cast at the funeral, which you will attend, and then to meet with any of the singers who behave oddly, on the pretext of giving them a little musical brush-up. Your Italian is suspiciously good; you will interrogate them on the subject of the murders and the pornography and any possible plots against the Crown, and report their confessions to me."

"You want me to help you concoct a totally specious case against Casti, who is in the employ of His Excellency? Or perhaps my own friend and colleague the *abbé*? Or against my own singers? Or myself? Why does His Ex … ah … hmmm. So, where's your regular *mouche*, anyhow? Why isn't he taking on this job?"

"None of your business. He got in some trouble with the police if you want to know."

"Is my job description the same as his? Do I get to denounce people right and left? No matter how high or mighty? No matter what the offense? *Carte blanche*?"

Mozart stops in mid-rant and stares, open-mouthed, at Thorwart.

Beat.

Mozart regains his power of speech and asks:

"It's you! This isn't the first time you have issued orders in His Excellency's name, is it? I have a growing feeling that you signed His Excellency's name to the memos sent to the late censor commanding him to mutilate my play. You did it, didn't you? You decided to use the power of the Chancellor's office to butcher *Figaro* so badly that I would have to withdraw it from the theater and pursue my career in another country. Am I right?"

"Your play is too long. People like to go to dinner or the salons after the opera. They want to be out by nine. Your opera drones on and on."

Mozart shrieks, tears the coiffed side of his hair, leaps across the room and bangs both hands on the desk.

"*You're* the butcher! Jesus Christ with a toothache, man! Give me one reason why I should I do spying – or anything – for you!"

"Take your hands off my desk. To retain some faint hope of *Figaro's* playing in the Burgtheater, I suppose." *Thorwart pulls out his watch, opens and studies it.*

"You would do this to me?" *Mozart in soprano range.* "Are you that determined to ruin my career? Do you want my little family to go hungry? Do you truly want us to have to fly to England, and beg in the streets of London for bread? Thorwart, for the love of God, what is *wrong* with you?"

"St. Petersburg is another possibility. Do as you are bid, *monsieur.*"

The two men glare at each other for several seconds. Mozart blinks first. Then, suddenly, he grins. He bows and scrapes. Quite low. Hiding the grin. He clicks his heels, Prussian style.

"Oh, right away, Dear Sir. In fact I am all eagerness. I'm quite sure all the singers will break down and confess that they murdered Haegelin for reasons of unrequited love or because their favorite *secco recitativo* was cut out at the last minute. I'll report every sob and sigh, and every last bitchy remark about other singers' sour intonation or foul breath; every backstage flirtation, every complaint about cold drafts in their dressing rooms, every incipient illness and unflattering costume! And get right back to you, Sir! I'm on it! Consider it done! Good day!"

Mozart bolts from the office, holding his laughter until he is safely outside the building.

"Well, well, wheels within wheels, plots within plots! I believe Thorwart has laid a clever trap, in which he might very possibly catch – his own boss! He's working overtime to expose that which His Excellency is working overtime to cover up, and if he succeeds he'll be dismissed! Hooray! Rosenberg protects his mangy pet Casti (or somebody else), while Dear Godfather toils to pin the crime on Casti (or somebody else)! H.E. will be stricken when he finds out that the coroner's suicide decision has been changed back to murder. But wait! There are two murders now ... done by whom? Or two whoms?

"*Were* the two murders really done the same way? I don't trust Thorwart's tale about two wires and two crushed voiceboxes. I need to see for myself ... but how? It seems that I am a *mouche* now; perhaps I can invoke the power of the Spectacles Office and demand to examine the bodies. Ugh!

"Pfui, I don't want to be a snitch. There's this play to put up, and the horn trio to rehearse and ... damn Thorwart! He's given me more than enough cause to slay him outright, but murder is so done these days. So willy-nilly, I might as well help him proceed with his efforts to ruin himself. Rosenberg may be forced to dismiss him for acting on his own and digging up the censor ... unless ... wait ... unless Thorwart is actually out to ruin H.E. and take the Chancellorship for himself! But that would make Thorwart the murderer of Drossel ... no, no, I can't go on imagining crazy scenarios like this. My mind is in knots. Where is the truth in this affair?

"At least Dear Godfather's cutting-my-opera-to-the-bone strategy has stopped for the moment; Johnny Thor-fart has been so busy playing policeman that he hasn't tried to remove the middle acts, or the finales, or Benucci's airs, for two whole days running. *Figaro* may have escaped mutilation or murder, or somebody wants me to think so ... somebody or, of course, somebody else.

"But there's still the plot against Renzo! Casti and Bussani are the ones hell-bent on ruining Da Ponte, and I need Da Ponte! If I lose Da Ponte I'm crippled; no Don Juan opera, no more fleet and clever librettos, and no more personal access to Caesar. Maybe I *should* tattle on these two to His Majesty! But what if I'm wrong? Catastrophe! Storace could be right: I belong in London, and she's wheedling Thorwart to get me there for my own good. I don't want to be in her power; she wants too much! Well, off to collect the wife of my bosom, attend this mandatory funeral, and afterward perhaps pay a visit to the victims' gravesite in my new official capacity as a secret agent. And this evening I get to play at conundrums with the singers and listen to their endless tales of love, loss, and love again."

Act III

☙ Scene 1 ❧

A chapel on the outskirts of the city,
April 26, 8:00 A.M.

All participants, with exceptions

In addition to the family members and Baron van Swieten, the entire Italian troupe, several playwrights, actors, and a smattering of Burgtheater clerical staff have also been drafted to attend. Mozart and Constanze place themselves in an alcove, where they have a good view of the company of mourners. Nanette Gottlieb is not among them. Frau Gottlieb, however, is in attendance; skulking like the shadow of Death in a dark corner.

From a group consisting of the poets and playwrights who had suffered under Haegelin's blue pencil, Mozart can hear a steady, low hiss and hum of irreverent jokes, snorts and muffled guffaws.

"Did you kill him, Hans?"

"Yes, I did."

"No, you didn't; *I* did!"

"No, it was me; I swear!"

"Is it true he appeared as a spook and censored the eulogies?"

"You mean he actually had some sort of a life that needed censoring?"

"Well, actually the priest had to slip in some made-up bits … hangings, duels, crimes, assignations…"

"Well," *whispers Constanze, keen-eyed in her role as special deputy mouche,* "the singers are all dramatizing themselves as usual. Kelly is sniggering behind his hankie. Madame Mandini is sobbing uncontrollably, and her husband is not stealing his manly arm around her as a solicitous spouse should."

"Check. Interview her. Interview him."

"La Laschi is playing the Tragedy Queen."

"Check. Interview her."

"The Bussanis are standing well away from each other."

"I need to speak with her. Save him for later. If at all."

"Storace turns her cow-like eyes upward to God, praying fervently, no doubt, that she will soon have a tame composer to take back home to England in her hat box."

"Leave her out. I'm so annoyed with her."

"And the redoubtable Frau Gottlieb, as hard and cold as a marble statue: she could do murder, sell her daughter and finish a row of knitting in the same minute."

"Well observed, well analyzed, wifekin mine. Well, *nunc dimittis servum tuum Domine, secundum verbum tuum in pace* ... let's go home."

❧ **Scene 2** ❧

Mozart's house, April 26, 10:00 A.M.

Mozart, Constanze, Rosinante, grave-diggers, then
Casti: Soliloquy, duettino

Mozart, it may be recalled, is one of the few employees of the Burgtheater who had a good, long look at the marks on poor Haegelin's throat. Despite his need to forget them, he remembers them very well, having seen them often before his eyes in the still watches of the night. His impressions of those marks have been interpreted by Baron van Swieten as those of a murder by garrotting. The composer is inspired to spend an hour breathing in the fresh air of the countryside surrounding Vienna, in the hope of violating a fresh grave and examining the alleged wire marks on Herr Drossel's dead neck.

"Stanzerl, sweetie, have you seen my riding britches?"

"Under the bed, dear."

"Ah, yes. I'm going to hack out on Rosinante to the New Graveyard."

"Now? Aren't you rehearsing the horn trio?"

"I'll be back in time. I am thinking of preceding the municipal funeral cart out to the cemetery to do a bit of spying. I really need to see how Drossel was killed…"

"To judge whether the *mode d'emploi* really is the same as that in the Haegelin murder?"

"Exactly. Dear Godfather Thorwart swears they are exactly the same, all the better to condemn Lorenzo or some other handy Italian; but I don't trust anything he says. I need some hard evidence that there is a murderer afoot! So your husband will trot out there and have a peek at one, or both. Then I'll need a bath, a good, long one; then some lunch; then the horn trio, followed by musical brush-ups with the cast."

"That's a nice, full day."

"Dear Godfather commands me to snoop, so snoop I shall. I'll bribe the grave-diggers to let me do it. Just a few rips in the shrouds, breathing through the mouth, holding down the gorge…"

"Let me send Marianne to rouse the stableman."

"Have you seen my gaiters?"

"Try under the bed again."

✌ Scene 3 ✌

The countryside, south of the city,
9:30 A.M.

Within the hour Mozart is up on his comfy old nag, ambling through the south gate of the town, toward the cemetery. Apple orchards are in bloom, birds sing in every bough, and wild roses peep out of the hedges. He confides in his good beast as they go.

"Country air: clears the head, does it not, Rosinante, old sweetheart? The old keenness returns. I'm glad Caesar banned burials within the city precincts; it was getting so unsanitary. Suburban cemeteries work so much better. But, I ask you! Burial in rough hempen sacks to save on coffin wood, and no grave-markers allowed? The names of dear departeds scrawled on the wall like so many graffiti; multiple bodies dumped helter-skelter into a common grave; is this civilized?

"Angry pamphlets about the graveyards are churned out from every quarter. Common and noble, voices are raised in protest; all of which makes Caesar angry. Well, His Majesty abolished censorship of journals and pamphlets, so what did he expect, continual hymns of praise? He is so mulish, but even he must know this sort of pennypinching turns his subjects against him. Such a strange man. He instituted modern agricultural practices, and he went into the fields and plowed with the peasants; how they loved that … he opened up the royal parks to the general public, ditto. But treating the dear departed like so much garbage? *Casus belli.* Don't repeat this conversation to anybody, understand? I knew I could count on your discretion."

After which, Mozart holds his tongue and spends the rest of the trip composing a new set of party dances for the annual Hoftheater costume ball at Galitzin's. He arrives at St. Mark's

Cemetery well in advance of the procession, and passes on.

"No sense being observed by all the theater folk to whom Drossel endeared himself over the years by ratting on them," *Mozart confides to the horse. The horse nods in agreement.*

"I see that the grave of the day is already dug, so we'll just walk on a mile further, then circle back. If we time it right I can sneak a look at the Drossel neck in the interval after the mourners leave but before the quicklime – or more bodies – fall on top of him."

The composer returns to composing as the pastures and farmsteads slide by; after a while he checks his enamelled gold watch, a gift of Marie Antoinette, and swings the horse around.

"Whoa, calm down, darling, we're not going home just yet. What a civil servant's mentality you have! You could at least pretend you are enjoying our excursion."

Mozart is in luck. He can see the mourners – not that many – leaving the cemetery and straggling back toward the city. The grave-diggers are sitting on the steps of their hut, forti-fying themselves for the task ahead by passing a bottle. The composer turns his reluctant but acquiescent steed off the road.

"Halloo, good fellows! Missed the funeral; come to pay my respects; could you mind the horse? Here you go, get yourselves a refill."

Mozart approaches the raw hole. Bodies in sacks, and heaven be praised, only three: Haegelin (easily distinguished by the ripe aroma, the result of having spent four days under-ground in the prison bone-yard), somebody short – perhaps a child – and the tall, lanky form of the late Head Usher, Fritz Drossel.

"Phew, I'll do him second," *the composer tells himself.*

Mozart glances back at the laborers, who are examining his horse, laughing and debating its market value. The coast is as clear as it is going to get.

"Stay calm, Amadé; you're a Freemason; death is your friend…" *He jumps into the pit. Struggling for balance on the heaving floor of flesh, taking a few oral deep breaths, he rips the loosely stitched seam of the linen shroud and peers at the dead face of Fritz Drossel.*

"Sunken eyes, yes. And the neck – voicebox broken and collapsed; another horizontal thin red line – thinner – it's a wire-wound cello G-string or I am a noodle! Somebody, the same somebody too, seems to be working his way up the circle of fifths. Who's going to get the D-string, I wonder? Oops, another hearse arriving…"

Mozart scrambles out of the grave, takes one look at the vehicle that has just pulled up at the cemetery gate, gasps, and jumps back down on top of the corpses.

"Damn me if that isn't Count Rosenberg's coach! What is he doing here after the funeral is over? Wait, that's not Rosenberg getting out; it's – oh, shit, it's Casti! And – shit again, that fat, newly toothless Italian Diguri! Stranger and stranger! And decidedly dangerous! Maybe I'm the one getting the D-string! Death in D minor…"

A howling orchestral tutti ff D-minor chord – then its dominant … heartbeats and goosebumps – syncops … "I'm standing in my own grave!" *mutters the composer as the music plays in his head.*

Shuddering as the flutes and violins crawl up and down his spine, the composer crouches by the rim of the grave and watches Casti speaking urgently to Diguri. He cannot hear a word they are saying, but he does not have to; they are Italians. They mime everything. Diguri is going away, south, probably to Italy, and not coming back, understood? Yes, understood. Here are your safe-passages, letters of introduction … Casti hands the hulking man a packet of papers and a large purse and bids him go. They do not embrace. Diguri limps off down the road without looking back.

Casti then calls the workmen to him. He tosses another purse to the gravediggers. They abandon Mozart's horse, divide its contents among themselves, gather up their shovels and carts and move toward the quicklime pit. Casti approaches the grave. He looms above Mozart like a blasted tree, silhouetted against the pale azure sky. Mozart, despairing of hiding himself anywhere except under a week's worth of dead bodies, pops up suddenly, like Punchinello.

"Ah, Gesu!" yells Casti, almost collapsing with horror.

"Good morning, Signor Poeta. It's me, Mozart. Still alive."

"Maestro. I thought for a second it was … what in God's name are you doing down there?"

"Well, Signor, it's complicated. I'm not supposed to say, really, but just between us … I am here on – on *top secret Freemasonry business*. The nature of my mission is this … Herr von Drossel was newly initiated into my lodge, you see, and he needs to be buried with the proper 'ancient rituals' and with the proper Masonic insignia. Don't tell anybody, but it's part of our sworn and sacred duty to attend our dead in this way. This token…"

Mozart reaches underneath his redingote and yanks the gold Masonic key off his fob. It is a very pretty bauble, but a Mason can part with baubles if he needs to, and Mozart needs to.

"I have been charged by the brotherhood to lay this mystical insignia on his chest, and the ritual will be accompanied by ... by certain top secret words. I couldn't do this in public at the funeral, you know. Please excuse me for just one moment – no peeking, now – and I'll join you topside."

Mozart, wincing, lays the gold ornament on the breast of the poor strangled snitch Drossel, who had never dreamed of being a Mason in his entire life.

"Pumpa pumpelichnaya, forkanorkila, schnippke, schnappke, George Washington Esterhazlimka Bouloumitsa," *he chants.*

Mozart scrambles out of the grave. Casti, who has also spent the past several minutes thinking fast, is now eyeing the composer with suspicion. Mozart stands up, brushes off his clothes, assumes a contraposto, settles one hand on his hip – and opens his mouth.

"By the way, Monsieur Casti, what are *you* doing here? Are you also acting, perchance, under orders to bestow a parting token upon some – departing soul?"

"I don't know what you mean, Mozart; you speak in riddles, as always."

"I'll be plainer. Who was that man you just paid off? Is he not a notorious smut-monger, and the man who tried to poison Da Ponte? What's more, why did such a thug arrive here in his Excellency's coach?"

"He- I- I am going further eastward to do an errand for his Excellency."

"How far east might you be going? Turkey? Wallachia? Albania? Do you always give lifts and gifts to criminals?" *Mozart struts up to his rival until he stands almost chest to chest with him.*

"If you will excuse me, maestro, I must attend His Excellency's business. Good evening." *Casti backs away several paces, then turns and scuttles for the coach. Mozart smooths his hair back, adjusts his waistcoat and smiles.*

"Well, dear Frau Gottlieb, my mentoress, queen of the Star-flaming Dragonladies, thank you so much. Accusing one's accuser really works out well. But why are Casti and Diguri out here, going south and east to destinations unknown or totally fictitious? Does this mean ... anything? Are those two involved in the murders ... but why? What? Whom? Which? Whereby? Whence? And again for Heaven's sake, Why? I don't know what it means."

Mozart stands a while by the open grave, staring into it and thinking hard.

"Excuse me, my Lord; we have to pour the lime in now."

"I'm not a prince; I'm just a man, really. But can you please tell me something?"

"What's that?" asks the gravedigger.

"What did the Italian pay you for?"

"Extra lime to be thrown on the tall one there."

"Thanks; get something to go with your wine."

"More wine, most likely."

"Good idea. Good evening to you."

Mozart catches up his nag, who has been grazing unsupervised among – or upon – the dead. The composer scrambles aboard and rides with a slack rein and expression, as the good old fellow marches homeward with a new spring in his step, and his ears pricked toward the stable.

❧ Scene 4 ❧

Mozart's house, April 26, 2:00 P.M.

Mozart and Signora Mandini: Duetto capriccioso

"Maestro, I am so upset with all the turmoil in the theater – I know we have been over this before, but I cannot seem to remember what I'm supposed to be expressing in the aria."

"But *cara Madama*, you are doing so splendidly. You sing the roulades so smoothly and accurately, and hit the high notes with such daring and precision. Take heart; I will help you in any way I can."

"It's the first section, Maestro. Is it fast; is it slow? I am so unclear on the affect!"

"Nothing easier, dear lady. Just think of goats. Goats, on their hind-hooves, dancing the minuet. Perhaps they are wearing perukes. Certainly with lace cravats and cuffs – and velvet coats. Coats wearing goats. Goats behaving toward other goats in a genteel and civilized manner, their little front-hooves gloved in cloven kid – ugh, not kid, velvet – gloves, treading a courtly measure at a ball. Usually one thinks of goats as being ruled by their passions, you know, but compared with mankind…"

"It's so true, Maestro; even goats are better than – than – oh, oh, oh!"

"Please, Madame, do not weep; whatever is the matter?"

"Men are such beasts! I am so glad he is dead!"

"Which one – I mean, who?"

"All of them! Haegelin especially. Laschi was so busy seducing my husband, and I wanted vendetta! Haegelin made such generous offers … to … well, to make things difficult for Laschi. She is a lascivious bitch; she doesn't care who she does it with. She enticed my husband just to make me upset, so I would miss my high notes, which are a damn sight better than hers – no matter what they say."

"Madame, please, take advantage of my handkerchief. Fresh this morning."

"I became his mistress. Yes, even Haegelin was a man, and much worse than a goat, let me tell you. I discovered – I will not say how – yes, I will so – I discovered that he was really in love with Laschi all along, and that she had spurned him and mocked him to his face and behind his back as well. Maestro, he kept calling out her name instead of mine when we were having intercourse."

"Oh dear, Madame, even the most dissipated goat would never do that."

"I was angry. I threatened to kill him. I shadowed him around town."

"What, you too? *Quelle procession!*"

"I would happily have killed him, if Signor Da Ponte had not done it first."

"We don't really know that Signor Da Ponte killed him at all, now, do we? It could have been anybody. Evidently."

"What about Laschi; could she have done it? That bitch gets all the breaks; she always has. She took my husband, she took my lover, she took the dressing room nearest to the stage, and she always gets better parts than me. She barges her way downstage center and bellows in that horrible squalling voice of hers, just a little bit flat all the time – surely you have noticed? Why does she always get to play heroines while I am always cast as someone's *mother*? I'm younger than Laschi by several years! And thinner!"

"Madame, please. We cannot blame La Laschi for all our misfortunes. And Marcellina is such a *sympathetic* mother role … at least in Acts Three and Four! You see, in this character, how a person can change for the better in the course of a day. Take heart; if you hated Haegelin so much, then you are well rid of him and you can start fresh with – with somebody else. Now let's work on the aria, shall we?"

"No, No, Maestro, you don't understand – I *loved* him! He was so timid, so maidenly, so submissive with me. I'm sure he had never been with women before, except in his revolting fantasies of Laschi. He begged me to chastise him, you know, to strike him on the ass with a birch rod or a hairbrush, and pretend to be his mother … and tell him he was a naughty boy. Oh, God, *always* playing mothers! But scolding him and whipping him was the only way he – and then he could – anyway, what a damn relief for me, after my husband, who is such a coarse, selfish, overbearing beast in bed, for the few seconds it takes him … but jealous, always so jealous. You know, perhaps Mandini killed him, have you thought of that? He thinks he is the only cock on the dung heap. Where was he that night; does anybody know? I can tell you for certain that he wasn't at home!"

"Your husband? Are you accusing your husband?"

"Well, no, not exactly."

"Are there any other cast members you would like to accuse?"

"Laschi."

"So, Madame, *incomminciamo*, "Il capro e la capretta," The goat and the goatess, who always treat each other nicely, and the little velvet gloves … lovely, lovely, all skipping and dancing the minuet. You have the affect exactly. Goats … in coats … and waistgoats … perukes on their horns…"

ᶜ᷉ᵒ Scene 5 ᶜ᷉ᵒ

Mozart's house,
The same day, 3:00 P.M.

Mozart and Signor Mandini

"Now, Mozart," *booms Mandini*, "tell me again, who is it I'm supposed to be in love with?"

"In the show or in real life?" *chirps Mozart.* "Sorry, Mandini."

"What for? Now let me get this straight: I'm married to Laschi but I am chasing after Storace who is about to be married to Benucci."

"The count is married to the countess, but he's chasing Susanna, who's about to be married to Figaro."

"But I'm really married to Marcellina."

"Well, yes, in real life Marcellina actually is Signora Mandini, isn't she?"

"So why again do I get so angry when Storace tells Benucci that he's already won his case?"

"Well, because you're the presiding judge *in* the case; you remember? And you have a vested interest in the outcome. Remember, Marcellina is suing Figaro for the breach of a marriage contract, and you have already decided to find for Marcellina, which means Figaro will have to marry *her* unless he pays her the money he doesn't have, so he won't get to marry Susanna, so Susanna's available for you. Do you follow?"

"But – dammit, the woman is his mother!"

"That's the funny bit, Mandini."

"Not to me, it's not. I mean, I don't like it when my wife looks around at other men."

"She's just play-acting with Benucci, though, isn't she?"

"Philandering is for men only, don't you think?"

"Oh, Mandini, this is so sudden! Do you fancy me, then? Is it my music? My fashion sense? My limited ability to advance your career? Tell me, darling, I beg you."

"It's nothing like that, Mozart; what do you take me for? A queer? I only meant that women shouldn't stray."

"I know what you *meant*; but consider how hard it is for a regular manly man to stray without there being a woman involved somewhere. So, naturally, I just leapt to the conclusion that women didn't interest you. Sorry ... unless you really do love me after all."

"Will you stop that! For your information, I meant that I don't like my wife making eyes at Haegelin; that's all. I'd like to kill the bastard."

"Relax; he's already dead, remember?"

"Well, if he were alive I'd kill him. I went to the theater after the show the night he died to have it out with him."

"Not you too! Was *everybody* in the theater that night?"

"Why, were you there?"

"No, Mandini, I was having an assignation with a lovely soprano."

"Not my wife!"

"No, you ox, *my* wife."

"You sly dog you!"

"So, Mandini! Did you kill him then?"

"Of course not. I couldn't find him."

"Did you notice anything strange going on in the theater, or – in the office hallway?"

"Well, to tell you the truth, I bumped into – into an old acquaintance, and we went into one of the boxes in the house and had a bit of a chat."

"And from that excellent vantage point did you happen to notice any unusual events, like Haegelin hanging himself or being hanged willingly, or against his will, in the stage house?"

"Maestro, I wasn't paying all that much attention; I was occupied with a lovely soprano."

"Your wife?"

"Possibly."

"What was she doing there?"

"Who?"

"If you must know, Mandini, I think you are holding back something. I begin to suspect that either you or your wife had a hand in murdering Herr Haegelin."

"You don't say! It was probably her, then. I was with Laschi, and we were too busy fucking up a storm to notice who killed him, so put that up your asshole and fart it back out."

"Aren't those boxes always locked?"

"Oh, I pay Drossel to keep one open just for me."

"Will- will anyone vouch for you?"

"What's wrong with Drossel vouching for me?"

"He's dead too, remember? Maybe he told the Spectacles Office or the Emperor about your assignation before he died. He was a spy, you know. Will Laschi vouch for you?"

"Why does anyone have to vouch for me? Why does anybody have to know? Why can't we keep it *entre nous?*"

"Only if you can prove you didn't murder your rival."

"Who's that?"

"Herr Haegelin? The other dead person?"

"Oh. Kind of a stick, wasn't he? Can't think what my wife would see in him."

"Well, he was quite intelligent."

"Lot of good that does a man."

"Evidently." *Mozart tugs great tufts of his hair loose from his pouffe and yanks them straight up so that he resembles a donkey.* "Let's at least go through your accompaniato and your aria, Mandini. You may think of Haegelin ravishing your wife with his keen and swordlike wits while you do."

"Hai già vinta la causa?"

While he plays the accompaniato *Mozart muses:* "Can anybody, even a singer, really be this dumb? Is he feigning imbecility? Anyway, how smart does a murderer have to be?"

✌ Scene 6 ❧

The same, 4:00 P.M.

Mozart and Signora Laschi

"My dear Madame, may I have another word with you about ... about the second act?"

"What is it-a now, Maestro? Have you, at last, relented in the matter of-a the high C's?"

"No, Madame, the high C's will stay as they are. Storace will sing them and you will conserve your energies for the third act recitative and aria, which are the musical and dramatic centerpiece of the entire opera; all eyes and ears will be riveted to you; you must be in perfect form for this air, need I remind you?"

"So you won't-a relent and let me substitute Salieri's air?"

"*No*, dammit, I *won't*! This is a goddam Premiere, you blinking idiot! In the Palermo production, on the Russian tour, in the London revival, you can sing any damn ditty you want. You can yodel and do barnyard imitations for all I ... ah, please excuse me, Madame, I lost control. My anxieties over the show and ... other matters seem to be fraying my nerves."

"Maestro, I am an artist and I am-a the *prima donna*, and I am not accustomed-a to being spoken-a to in that-a way. This time I forgive you, because I know you are a provincial-a booby with-a no manners, but I warn you; do not try La Laschi a second time."

"Thank you, Madame; there will be no second time, I assure you. Now, in the second act finale ... it is about your husband's ... I mean Count Almaviva's jealousy, and his threats to kill his supposed rival, Cherubino. I am wondering if you could alternately express fear and indignation during that episode. It will make the count look more ridiculous, and play up the irony of your situation, don't you see?"

"No."

"Well, for instance, right here, where you sing '*voi sapete*,' 'you know' … right before he sings '*non so niente*,' I know nothing,' what do you think she means?"

"She is protesting-a her innocence, I suppose."

"Well, yes, of course, but I believe our distinguished librettist also meant that … she is about to remind him how often *he* has strayed and how she knows he is even now attempting to do it again. Do you see? She is calling him to account, and he interrupts and shouts her down, denying it all. He's a bully; that's how he defends himself against the truth."

"Oh."

"We are all of us human and fallible, and we all have our secret shames and sins. At our best we admit them and beg pardon – at least we do when we are caught … but the count spends two more acts denying the truth before he kneels to the countess. Do you see how you set him up for his moment of repentance, right here in this duet?"

"No."

"Madame?"

"I don't-a like singing ensembles. The others get in-a my way. Mandini is always-a taking-a the down-center spot."

"Madame, I must tell you at this point it is possible that he may not take it ever again. Perhaps you have heard that Signor Mandini is under suspicion of murder? He was seen in a box in the house after strike, where no one is permitted to be. The theater administration and the police know he was there."

Beat.

"Madame? Does not Mandini's possible arrest and withdrawal from the cast please you? Downstage center will soon become vacant and available for you."

"Was he alone?"

"When?"

"When-a the people saw him in the house."

"It is said he was with a woman."

"Was the woman identified?"

"Ah, well. Mandini was closely questioned, by agents of the law, you know; and he said it was, well, you."

"Oh."

"I got the general idea that he was hoping you would vouch for him in the matter of his innocence in the murder case. Otherwise occupied, reliable witness, and so on. Were you with him that night, and can you attest that Mandini is innocent of the crime?"

Beat.

"Madame, did you comprehend my question?"

"Yes."

"Then, you will corroborate his testimony?"

"No."

"Are you quite sure you cannot vouch for Mandini?"

"Yes. Quite-a sure."

"Then, Madame, we must all go on as best we can."

"I suppose so."

❧ Scene 7 ❧

The same, 5:00 P.M.

Mozart and Signora Bussani

"Now, my dear little Cherubino, are we ready to put the final polish on your airs today?"

"Yes, *caro maestro*, and – may I ask – if I might put some *abellimenti* into the *da capo* of my *arietta*? Just simple ones, to show the child's growing excitement and happiness?"

Madame Bussani's cheeks flush rosy with embarrassment at her own audacity, making her look even younger than her eighteen years. She is tiny, girlish and smiling shyly, as she meets Mozart's eyes for a brief instant.

"Of course, you may, my dear, as long as they portray the boy's yearnings for love and not your yearnings to show off your voice, lovely as it is. Do you remember what it was like to be that young, and yearning so desperately to be loved?"

The soprano's eyes widen and moisten. She looks at the sheet of music in her hand and murmurs, "Voi, che sapete…"

"Yes," *says Mozart.* "The poor little lad is driven hither and thither by his awakening passions. He loves all woman-kind, but his true love is the wife of another man. He is helpless before her, yet he is bold enough to write this little air and to sing it to her in her boudoir. She is so amused, so touched – and so lonely, since the count has abandoned her – that she encourages, nay, she *needs* his boyish attentions. Perhaps, too, in some dark corner of her heart, she wants to get a little bit even with Almaviva, do you not think?"

The soprano looks full at Mozart now, tears coursing down her face. Sobs follow. Then,

a few hiccups and a nervous giggle. Then she squares her shoulders and speaks without hes-
itation.

"I went to the police. I told them they were my husband's dirty pictures. He and another man, a big fat Italian man, took the pictures and the plates and some other things from the house. I think the fat man makes or trades in such pictures. I heard them say they were going to plant them in somebody's rooms and then rat on him for publishing illegal material. At first I was glad those pictures left my house. My husband made me look at them all the time and then do what they depicted, and I did not like to do those things. Then the day after the *abbé* Da Ponte was arrested, my housemaid told me that they had found the pictures and the plates and other things in the *abbé*'s flat. Then I knew for certain that my husband … well, I knew that he had framed the *abbé*. So I denounced him. I do not understand why the fat man was helping my husband, but if I ever find out I will denounce him too! The *abbé* has been very kind to me. He is a tender man."

"He is my friend," *whispers Mozart.*

"So when I went to the police I didn't stop to think that my friendship with the *abbé* was the cause of my husband's actions. My only thought was that he had tried to frame Da Ponte and I told them at the police house who the pictures belonged to, and that they should let *Abbé* Da Ponte go free, that my husband was trying to ruin the *abbé* for some personal vendetta, even though he was singing in Da Ponte's show. And they let him go, for a few hours, but then they detained him again. So it was all for nothing that I denounced my husband, and I am so unhappy, because the police told my husband he was dismissed as a *mouche* because he had planted those pictures and lied about them. Then for good measure they told him it was I who had denounced him. So I have betrayed my husband twice and for nothing, and it's all my fault."

"That was really rotten of them to rat you out to your husband. Denouncing people gets to be a habit, I suppose. Is your husband treating you ill?"

"He does not beat me, but he also does not speak to me or touch me. I would rather he did beat me; I would stand like a lamb and let him do it, and then we could have peace. Because of course…"

"Of course. It is ended. It was so brave of you to go and say that an inno-cent person was falsely detained, even if he was re-detained afterward. Do you know the day and hour of Da Ponte's release from prison, my dear?"

"Yesterday, very early in the morning, I think."

"You are not sure?"

"Yes, it *was* yesterday. My housemaid told me when she came in at six. I was so frightened and upset thinking what might happen to him. I am so fond of him."

"Yes, Madame."

"He talked to me so prettily, of life, of poetry, of love. Now I have no one like that to talk to, someone who listens so intently. 'If there is no one to hear me, I shall talk of love all by myself...'"

"And so, my dear, let us cheer up and hope for better days. Think of young love and its joys and wounds. Let's rush and tumble through your first air *alla breve*, and you may talk of love to the mountains and the echoes and the flowers and the streams, and I will listen, not as intently as *Abbé* Da Ponte did, but as intently as I can."

✧ Scene 8 ✧

The Polizeihaus, April 27, 8:00 A.M.
Mozart, Da Ponte, guards

Mozart is let in by the guards, who withdraw. They have decided that since the pair is so harmless and since they tend to speak in a barbaric and incomprehensible tongue, they do not need to attend, but can safely lounge outside and take a few nips during this second interview.

Mozart is in considerable disarray and distress. He greets Da Ponte with a handshake in the English fashion, then paces nervously around the perimeter of the room, winding his watch. Da Ponte lounges on his pallet as elegantly as a leopard, but his black silk suit, having served through two separate incarcerations and a street brawl, is much the worse for wear.

"Darling, it's lovely that you can attend one of my at-home days. Please do sit down and the housemaid will come by shortly and serve us coffee and a nice *Kügel*."

"How are they treating you, really? Are they going to let you out?"

"Oh, I think not. I am given to understand that I did some murder while I was locked up in this charming apartment, and it is this murder, not the bashing in of my friend Signor Diguri's teeth, the one act of violence of which I am truly guilty, accomplished on that bright morn when I so briefly enjoyed my freedom, that has brought me here once more."

"Thorwart told me that they let you out the day before the second murder. I suppose it's much more convenient for him to think so."

"*Second* murder? There actually is a *first* murder?"

"Yes, officially, now, there is. They dug up Haegelin, and the coroner changed his opinion from suicide to murder; then they re-buried him very quickly in consecrated dirt, or actually consecrated quick-lime, as it turns out.

It appears both he and Drossel – the second victim, remember him? – were killed by a wire garotte, from behind. I can personally attest to the truth of this, having compared the injuries to both their necks and both their voiceboxes."

"You compared both their – what in God's name are you doing in your free time, Amadé?"

"Oh, do you mean what am I doing, besides putting up that little skit at the Burgtheater? Desecrating graves, composing a piano concerto and a viola-clarinet trio, and extorting a deluge of lurid sexual confessions from the cast of *Figaro*, who are all sleeping with each other. You?"

"Lots of pacing up and down. What do you mean, you're desecrating graves?"

"I'm a spy now. Spies do that sort of thing. How did I metamorphose from a musician into a spy, you may ask?"

"I may ask. I do ask."

"Listen and learn." *Mozart is pacing again, picking at his clothes and running his hands through his hair.*

"Dear Godfather Thorwart, chief financial officer of the theater, has started his own private investigation into this affair. He is pursuing an imaginary Italian International Anarchist plot, with you at its head, and Casti as your loyal deputy, and Haegelin and Drossel your hapless victims."

"Wha-a-a-t?"

"You obviously did the murders in an excess of Transalpine viciousness, the enormity of which prompted Thorwart to order the coroner to disinter Haegelin for an encore appearance. Then Old Thor-fart press-ganged me into his posse and told me to nose out the murderer, who would be, he hopes, you. Did you do it?"

"Absolutely not!"

"I didn't think so. Here's why I don't think so: Dear Godfather does not know that I got a very good look at Haegelin's garotted neck the afternoon he was cut down from the flies. He does not know that I stumbled upon the murder weapon in Rosenberg's office, and that H.E. attempted to snatch it from me when he saw that I had it in my hand. *Even I did not know this until I said it just now!*

"Thorwart also does not know that I examined the dead Herr Drossel's neck while kneeling next to his, and *on somebody else's* —probably Haegelin's — mortal remains in the grave pit; and that I observed that the two wounds were exactly the same, only Drossel's was made with a thinner wire. So I have discovered one murderer, and two weapons — one cello C-string now in my possession, the other which exists only as the marks of a cello G-string on the Drossel throat; ergo, I have a strong suspicion that Chancellor Count F.X.J.W. O-R or his proxy has done both vile deeds, and a dead-certainty that my friend Da Ponte has not."

"Mozart, I need a drink. *Garçon*! Damn, none available. I cannot believe you did this spying operation! Or that Rosenberg did a murder, much less two."

"Me neither, as much as I would like to."

"Are you taking this to Caesar?"

"How can I? The two victims are deliquescing under the sod, I found a moldering cello string in an opera theater, and from these clues I fantasize that the man who was once my fan and patron, and who currently has the power of life and death over *Figaro*, has perhaps killed two people and will happily squash me like a bug if I denounce him with this ridiculous evidence."

"So. You want me to die: either in here, or waist-deep in the Danube, is that it? Are you abandoning me, then?"

"No, no, I absolutely *am not*! I'm just re-grouping here; please observe, I'm holding my head and tearing out what hair I have not already uprooted. Look, Renzo, I need you. I want you. I love you. We have operas to create: *Don Juan* and more. I have to get you out and in the clear. But how?"

"Any good news at all? I am feeling even lower than before, if that is humanly possible."

"Well, yes, there is. She betrayed her husband to the police to set you free."
"She?"

"Signora Bussani. She came here to the prison and told the cops that her cuckolded husband had planted contraband in your flat. So they fired him, and just for the fun of it, they told him his own wife had ratted him out."

Da Ponte draws a shuddering breath. His dark eyes widen, glistening with tears. He stares at the composer as his face crumples and those tears run unheeded down his gaunt cheeks. He begins to sob quietly.

"She's true, dear Renzl. She is also in trouble, obviously. She was totally wrong about who was plotting to cut '*Contessa, perdona,*' though. It never was Rosenberg; it was Thorwart, trying to wreck my career in Vienna, and my marriage as well. But Thorwart has other fish to fry now, like playing policeman and solving the murders, and just maybe trying to bring down Rosenberg. So we can also rejoice that the death-by-a-thousand-cuts plot is on stand-by."

"I love her. *I love her.* We'll run away."

"But how La Bussani, or her husband, got wind of Thorwart's plot in the first place is beyond me…"

"*I love her.*"

"I think our Chancellor of Spectacles is still working to cover up the murders. Haegelin was a witness to his crime of procuring and paying for a prostitute, and so was Drossel; and they're both dead. The child is the last witness alive who can corroborate Drossel's story and accuse Count Rosenberg."

"She is! I'd forgotten! That adorable, sweet child! She may have actually seen the murder! She must tell all! That's solid proof! I'm free! He's guilty! The Emperor must hear about this!"

"She won't do it."

"Why not, in God's name?"

"For the same reason I won't do it. First, she never mentioned a murder in her story. Second, if she did mention one, nobody would believe her. Third, her career would be over. Not she, not anybody in the theater wants to rat on Chancellor Rosenberg, even if he killed a thousand censors in full view of the audience during a Saturday matinee."

"*E vero, e vero.*"

"Besides, Renzo, the child finds it almost impossible to talk about what was done to her, much less serve as a witness in a trial. Think of Donna Anna in the Don Juan play. A rape, a death … maybe … she doesn't just chat about it. She didn't even remember at first!"

"I am doomed. I'm going to die in this room. Please, Amadé, I mean it: you have got to get me out of here! I'm not a strong man, I can't chew my bread, my bones are brittle…"

"Yet you are such a vigorous lover of young women. How do you manage it?"

"I employ a bodily part, darling, that does not contain a bone, brittle or no.

Do *not* start with me now! I am through with all women except this last one! *I love her! I must see her!* Now listen to me, I am serious, and I am begging you! Get me out of this damn prison and we'll all go to Prague or London together! I implore you; I am on my knees before you!"

"I'll do it; I swear I will get you out of here even if it kills me, or if I have to murder *Figaro!*"

"Just help me up here ... we'll move the production somewhere else. At least the show won't die, my dear. *Figaro* is immortal!"

⤳ Finale ⤳

The Burgtheater, April 27, 2:00 P.M.

Le Nozze di Figaro, piano dress
All participants, with exceptions

The cast, crew and other interested persons attached to the theater have assembled for the piano run-through of the opera Le Nozze di Figaro. The fabulous singing Weber girls – the magnificent Aloysia, the fiery Josepha, the future Queen of the Night, and the scatterbrained but still talented Sophia – have gathered to cheer on their sister Constanze, who is covering – and perhaps even premiering – the role of Barbarina. Their mother Caecilia is with them, having only recently decided that her son-in-law is not a scoundrel, thus abandoning the Thorwart faction even as Mozart has (unwillingly) joined it as its chief spy.

Salieri and the other official court composers stand together talking among themselves. Still missing from the throng are Mademoiselle Gottlieb the ingénue, and her mother. The librettist of the new work, Abbé Da Ponte, is absent, because he is currently languishing in prison. Also missing are the Imperial censor and the head usher, who are dead.

Certain leading members of the cast appear to be in states of agitation. However, their pale faces and dilated eyes, nervous glances and spasmodic gestures are as nothing in comparison with the physiognomy of His Excellency, Count Orsini-Rosenberg, Grand Chancellor of Spectacles, who enters the house on the arm of – not his loyal deputy Johann von Thorwart, but his tame poet Giambattista Casti, who is smirking in the composer's direction as if to say "You see where your behavior has gotten you? You are on your way out." His Excellency's ashen complexion glistens with a film of sweat; his tread is unsure and stiff, as if the count was trying with all his will to keep his knees from buckling.

Mozart gazes at Rosenberg, hears the three muffled trombones again, then ducks his pouffe to hide a secret smile.

"Haegelin has arisen from the dead," *murmurs the composer to his wife, who stands beside him, prettily costumed as a Spanish maiden* … "hauled out of the sepulcher by Thorwart to accuse the Grand Chancellor! *Pentiti!* Yes, the net of his own guilt closes in on H.E., or I am an Albanian. Serves him right!"

"The count," *Constanze observes,* "looks as if he is about to faint. But if you think that the Chancellor is making a spectacle of himself, join the crowd and look the other way, upstage left; but don't look too hard."

The composer does as advised, and beholds his prima donna Madame Storace, costumed as Susanna, except … except…

"Oh, my God, we're doomed! A coup de théâtre, perhaps two coups de théâtre, is about to strike. Can no one avert this double calamity? Or their eyes? I'll ask H.E., no, I'll ask Thorwart … come with me, I beg, don't leave me alone with Thorwart or I'll throttle him…"

Mozart, holding his wife's hand, humbles himself before Thorwart and asks for a five-minute delay to give an all-important note to Madame Storace. Thorwart glares at the composer with open contempt.

"Too many notes! Don't take all day with her, Mozart. People are watching you," *hisses Thorwart. Mozart lets go of his wife's hand, which he had just squeezed entirely too hard, and scampers in the direction of his prima donna.*

"Madame Storace, may I see you briefly in the alley?"

Storace, Mozart and then Mandini: Recitativo

"My dear Mozart, how does my costume seem now, without the *paniers*? Is this a better simulation of the local housemaids?"

" I-I- Madame, what has happened to the lace of your shift? It seems to have descended to dizzying depths…"

"But, Maestro *carino*, do you not want me to behave provocatively in this duet? Does Susanna not preen before Almaviva and stupefy him by consenting to fulfill his every carnal wish? Should there not be a certain amount of the legendary Storace bosom unveiled for him to see?"

"Heaven knows there is an amount for him to see – there is quite enough to strike him blind … but I feel that your modesty is in – a-a- precarious situation here. Bob one curtsey and the buns are out of the basket."

"But Maestro, I did *research* for this role! I went into the street, I observed ever so many genuine housemaids myself, and I adjusted my costume to look just like theirs. Does this not please you at all?"

Mozart lets out a hysterical shriek of laughter before clapping his fist into his mouth, biting it hard, and pulling his face into an expression of deepest gravity.

"I fear, Madame, that the ladies you observed may not have been, ah, genuine housemaids, but Nymphs of the Night, you know, costumed as saucy housemaids. It's a fad here right now ... so perhaps some compromise can be reached in regard to..."

"Don't you like them, dear Mozart? Oh God, don't you desire me at all?

"What? I adore them, both of them; I really do. I'm fond of you too, but I feel it is best always to maintain a professional – which means a cordial but yes, yes, impersonal ... it's not only that your brother is my student and your mother is backstage ... and so's my wife ... oh, all right, I'll kiss them since they're under my nose, but just once, and don't ask me again; I have other things on my mind, or will have presently. Now please, promise me you'll hike up your lace, go onstage and present them just this way to Mandini, will you?"

"Mandini is such an oaf, all groping hands and swelling ego and blustering barking baritone. Help me, Maestro; I need to find a proxy to help get me in a naughty mood and to endure his hairy paws fondling me. Oooh. Thanks a lot, Maestro; you've done me a huge favor."

"Ah! Ho! Hah! Wait a bit, my dear."

"*Ancora*, Maestro?"

"What did you say back then? Before 'Thanks a lot'?"

"Mandini? Oaf? Hairy paws?"

"Ahhhhhh, ha. You've just reminded me of something. If you don't mind a last-minute note, I'd like you to try a certain bit onstage in the opening duet of Act Three. Something from Shakespeare, to raise the tone of your character far above the tired old pert housemaid *cliché*. That's so 1784. Call Mandini over here too, will you? Yes, *buon giorno* dear Mandini, I want to give you a really clever piece of business I just thought up for "Crudel perche?." You, at any rate, might enjoy it."

"Oh, but Maestro, can I not do my usual things? Leering, stroking the chin, winking at the audience, tugging my nose and rubbing my hands together?"

"Time-tested as those bits are, I beg you to save them for a later time, the Act Four finale, say. Try this on instead. You, Madame Storace, are not to play the Naughty Nymph after all. Instead you are to be a chaste Susanna, guarding her virtue as best you can. You are a frightened Susanna, maidenly, even. You are so desperate that your own marriage take place that you force yourself to endure, ah, a certain amount of ill treatment. Let us see your revulsion and terror. That way you make Susanna a more three-dimensional character. Think of *Measure for Measure*. Can you do it just once, so that I may see how it reads?"

"Well, since it's you who ask, Maestro … all right, just this once. No pinching, Mandini, and I mean it."

"And you, as Almaviva. You are so amorous and selfish that you do not even notice how much you disgust her. I want you to pass your hands over her body as you would do to a horse at the fair. Then you must take her on your lap … yes, of course you can sing sitting down; you will be the first one ever; think of the sensation it will cause! And then run your hand up Susanna's calf and under her skirt."

"Ugh!"

"Madame, *du calme*. Just continue to sing the music and poetry provided, while making exactly the expression you are making now. Mandini, I rely on your good behavior here. The hand must stop two inches above the knee. You are not allowed to do anything that will make her miss her cues. All right, let's begin the show!"

Mozart takes his place at the clavier, and the piano run begins. The singers have settled down to work and acquit themselves brilliantly. The audience of friends and family sits enthralled, ravished, stunned, transported, through two acts, praising the composer to the skies as he re-tunes his instrument during the second break.

Act Three begins with the sulky mutterings of Count Almaviva, who is trying to think through the peculiar things that have been happening to him in the previous acts. He sings his tantrum aria. Susanna enters. She tells him she is at last willing to give herself to him; she and the count embark on the duet, "Cruel girl, why have you made me suffer so long?"

At the modulation to A Major, Mandini as Almaviva booms "I feel my heart filling with joy," and makes a grab for Susanna's bosom. Storace as Susanna shudders under the insult of it, but stands her ground, big-eyed with terror. "What an actress!" thinks Mozart. "What a bosom!"

At measure 29 Almaviva sits in an armchair hauls Susanna into his lap. He runs his hands over her breast and torso, and suddenly insinuates his right hand under her skirt, as Susanna freezes in horror.

At measure 42 His Excellency Count Rosenberg bursts out of his parterre seat, which closes with a loud snap. All heads turn to watch the Grand Chancellor of Spectacles stagger up the aisle and out of the theater, followed by his deputy and Casti. He does not, as Mozart hopes, cry "give me some light," but his precipitous, crashing exit is proof enough to the composer that Count Rosenberg is certainly guilty of rape and almost certainly guilty of murder. And that the count knows that the composer knows that he is guilty. Mozart continues cueing the singers and rattling on the keyboard.

During the next little bit of dialog between Susanna and her betrothed Figaro, Count Thorwart re-enters and comes marching down the side aisle and strikes Mozart on the shoulder.

"You there. This duet must be cut."

"You're disturbing my rehearsal," *snaps Mozart.*

"We cannot have this. Those filthy antics onstage have outraged His Excellency. This scene gives some indication to the audience that these two are – are arranging an assignation."

"Indeed *all* the indications lead anyone who has eyes and ears attached to a functioning brain to conclude that *that is exactly what they are doing!*"

"We cannot allow such shameful proceedings to be shown at the Court theater. It must come out."

"I would prefer to talk to His Excellency himself about it. It's not as if he has never heard this duet before. There might as well be no Third Act at all, or any Fourth Act either, without this duet."

"All right then, no third or fourth act!" *Thorwart grabs Mozart's short score from the rack and tears it top to bottom.* "These are the administration's orders. This rehearsal is cancelled. Now, Herr Mozart, you can petition me in writing to obtain my pardon and you may humbly beg to be permitted to perform your little play at a time determined by myself."

"Do you really think, Herr Thorwart, I need that score to lead this opera?" *Mozart shouts.* "I could do it in my sleep! I could do it dead! I demand to speak to His Excellency."

"You will make no demands in this theater, you arrogant little bumpkin!

You are dismissed, and this show is cancelled!"

Beat. General freeze in the theater.

"You. You can't mean that."

"Yes, I can. We'll put up *Barbiere* instead. No one will know the difference. Now get out."

Thorwart takes Mozart by the lapels, spins him round, kicks him in the derriere and walks away.

Act IV

❧ Scene 1 ❧

A private room in the Imperial palace,
April 27, 5 P.M.

Mozart and His Imperial Majesty, Joseph II

"Come now, Mozart; you must stop weeping. Or at least stop gasping like that; you sound as if you are being strangled. Please, try to contain yourself so that we can speak calmly and rationally. What are the facts in this case? How can I judge or mediate for you if you keep on like that?"

"Majesty, it's all just too much! I thought we were quit of all these censorship issues. First Haegelin, God rest him…"

"God does not rest suicides; they are sinners with no hope of redemption. They are buried in the potter's field with no obsequies. They are damned."

"But Your Majesty, Herr von Haegelin has been … Ah! … Oh! I … pardon me, your Majesty, suicides, damned, I know they are. Damn, damned, for all eternity. But this constant cutting and obstructing of my play, it is all too much! First the censor wanted a little insignificant recitative cut but never signed off on its removal. I would happily have fixed that somehow … but the *"si/no"* duet … I cannot! That I have to witness the dramatic structure of Act III crumbling because H.E. suddenly decides … he's seen that duet being staged several times before and never mentioned there was anything amiss! And when I defended my position to Herr von Thorwart, he told me that my play is cancelled and I have been dismissed from the theater! I appeal to you, I beg you, I kneel at your feet, I throw myself…"

"Now, now, dear fellow. You are young. You'll have other chances. Count

Rosenberg takes the interests of the theater and of the State very much to heart, you know. He has only today given me secret information that the Freemasons are involved with all this disturbance around your play. He has grave concerns."

Mozart, who has been wiping his eyes with his hankie and staring blankly at the moth holes and ink stains on the skirts of his Emperor's coat, starts, and meets Joseph's eyes with his own. And freezes in fear.

"He – he has, Majesty? I can hardly believe … Respectfully begging your pardon, I don't think the count's reasons for attacking my show have anything to do with … it's a diversionary … I think his reasons are personal. But I swear to you, Majesty, that the Freemasons would never…"

"Then *why* do they conduct their business in secret?" *shrieks the Emperor, turning red in the face.* "Why do they collude with Illuminati and the Asian Brotherhood and other anarchist factions? They have infiltrated my government even to the highest levels. Haegelin loathed the Freemasons. He was always deferential to Swieten, of course, but he voiced suspicions about many others, including Herr von Günther, my own secretary for international affairs."

"Forgive me…"

"Ah, if I recall, a lodge brother of yours. Don't try to tell me he was innocent. In addition to his Freemason connections, he was also a member of that – I can't even say the name – that International Jewish Anarchist Conspirator's cabal. Haegelin showed me hard proof that Günther was involved in provoking the Hungarian uprising, and that he was betraying me to Prussia and to their damned Masonic king. I commanded Pergen to put it about that the affair was all a hoax, but it was not. We have created a diversion. Now that they believe my attentions have turned elsewhere, I shall come upon them all unawares and crush their vile conspiracy."

"Surely, Majesty, the Viennese Freemasons are not capable … our ideals and hopes mirror your own: we espouse rationalism, science, equality under the law, civil society, modern commerce. We are all loyal…"

"I will *not* be made a fool of! You gullible little bourgeois Masons think you are the wave of the future, reading your learned books, piffling on about science and philosophy, playing your innocent little Enlightenment games! You have all been duped! Your very lodge is polluted by revolutionary propaganda in the guise of tolerance and humanism. You do not understand with what stealth and guile these Jew anarchists move, spreading their filth. These cursed Illuminati are cosmopolitan, as Jews all are. They have no national loyalties, and their stated aim is to rule the world. We have documents that prove they are trying to bring down every monarchy in Europe. Günther was their spy. Haegelin denounced Günther, and from that moment he was a marked man."

"Was it truly a murder, then, Your Majesty?"

"Whether murder or not, it is not your affair. Do not ever refer to what I just said or what I am about to say."

"No, Your Majesty."

"Restrict yourself to composing, Mozart. I will do the governing. Listen to me. I consider the loss of the British colonies in America the direct result of the machinations of Freemasonry. This same rabble is also active in France, and my dearest sister Antonia – the one who wanted to marry you when you were children – my sister, the Queen of France, writes that she fears greatly that the rumor of revolt is spreading everywhere in Paris. She has seen many things, Mozart, and is no longer as sweet and innocent as you.

"I say to you now, if revolution comes to France, there will be war with us. They will try form a republican government, and they will fail. They will turn on each other like rats, and terror will be unspeakable. The streets will reek with blood; the carnage will destroy the land and make it groan for the return of an Emperor!

"It does not lie with mobs and rabble and secret cabals to correct injustice and bring about a new order. It lies with Kings, Mozart. It lies with me. The common herd cannot govern. No! Never! They have not the weight of divine authority. Democracy cannot last, not in France nor in America."

"Your Majesty, why would the Freemasons or anyone go out of their way to ruin a harmless play like *Figaro*? One might think they would espouse its – its humanism."

"I myself espouse it. But *Figaro* is not the center of the world to anybody but you. It is pure coincidence that Haegelin was hidden in the theater. Would you be surprised to know that there was a recent attempt on my own life near the theater? I have denied it utterly but am convinced the Illuminati were behind it.

"I am hemmed in by enemies on every side, Mozart, and not only by the secret societies, who fancy they are preparing themselves to assume power, whether by guile or violence. I am opposed in my reforming projects by the Church, the guilds, and the Old Guard. They refuse to comply with my edicts, although I work for the common good. But I soldier on; I must hold firm the course of my own revolution, a Kingly, Caesarly revolution. It is a dark and dangerous course, but there must be no hesitating."

"Your Majesty, if I may say so, I believe Count Rosenberg has an animus toward my play and me, and some connection with…"

"You may *not* say so! No more about Haegelin or my Chancellor! This is a very dangerous accusation, Mozart. I told you never to speak of this, did I not?"

"Your Majesty, forgive me: I believe His Excellency's interference with my play stems from a-a- personal interest he shows in Mademoiselle Gottlieb."

"How splendid for her! The child is not only an exquisite actress, but a fine singer, so I am already doubling my money. If she also amuses my Chancellor, I'd say she was an absolute bargain, definitely worth keeping in the troupe, even if she isn't Italian. Let me just make a note to lower her wages. There. I'll let Rosenberg cover her salary instead."

"Your Majesty, I believe that if her family's circumstances were not so straitened, the girl would not have chosen to accept his protection."

"Why not? What's wrong with Rosenberg? Splendid fellow, man of position, connoisseur of the arts, able to open many doors for her!"

"But…"

"Mozart, she is an *actress*! Finding patronage is what theater people do! If it comes to that, it is what everyone does, including you. I will not have any more whining about this matter."

"But there have been two deaths associated with the theater, and I…"

"Exactly! And what about that second Burgtheater death, the demise of good Herr Drossel, whom I personally retained as a source of information, murdered and thrown in the river? Do you really think His Excellency murdered him for his paltry purse and tossed him into the Wien? It's unthinkable."

"I-I- think Herr Drossel may have extorted money from His Excel…"

"You over-step yourself, Monsieur. How dare you present me with this

warmed-over gossip? Can you prove these monstrous, slanderous denuncia-
tions of my Chancellor with actual evidence? Documents, two reliable witnesses, as the law dictates? If you can, do so immediately. And if you can, Monsieur
Mozart, I will allow your play to go up in my theater this week. If you cannot,
I guarantee you will have great difficulty getting *Figaro* or any other opera you
write considered for performance in the *Hoftheater* again. I would begin to consider emigrating to London or to Prague if I were you. I would be only too
happy to defray the expenses of your journey as a parting gift. Good evening."

As Mozart walks weeping through the antechamber, six buxom housemaids come to at-
tention, primping their hair and tugging at their lace to expose more décolletage. The composer
wipes his eyes and watches the little flurry among the ladies, and he laughs. The laugh has
no mirth in it.

ᕲ Scene 2 ᕲ

The streets of Vienna
Mozart and Von Born

Mozart totters through Michael Square and down a street, heedless of where he wanders, trying to gather his wits and courage and do something, anything, God knows what, to save his show. Figaro*! His* Figaro*! The best opera in the world, and everyone from Frederick the Great to his own cast seems hell-bent on keeping it from being played.* "Goddamn! Help, somebody, help!"

Mozart awakens from his trance and finds himself walking down Landskrongasse.

"Why, here's the Freemasons' house right in front of me again. Deserted, windows all dark. I guess they all saw the writing on the wall while I was busy putting up my play."

As the composer stands looking blankly up at his lodge, the door of the house opens and Ignatz von Born staggers out the front door and into the street. He is carrying what looks like a specimen case – and a valise.

"May I help you with your things, Monsieur Von Born?"

"Oh, it's you, Mozart. No, thank you, I am somewhat pressed for time and must learn to manage my luggage myself; now if you will excuse me…"

"Are you visiting another city, sir?"

"Don't ask me where I am going. I am leaving the country; my destination is yet to be determined. A good friend, well, your good friend too, Baron von Wetzlar, makes the arrangements."

"The good Wetzlar would tell you to travel lighter than this; those cases look so heavy. Master, I have had a terrifying interview with the Emperor. I have only the vaguest idea what he was speaking of. Is there going to be more trouble?"

"Yes. Our King and Kaiser believes that the Freemasons and Prussia are plotting against him. The provincial nobles profit by his misprision and so they feed His Majesty on tales of betrayal, even murder, at court; they want their feudal privileges returned, and the central government weakened. I have been denounced by one of them."

"I can guess which one, I think."

"Shhh. Goodbye, Mozart. I really love your music, especially the clavier concerti and the music for the funerals. But I smell catastrophe on the wind. I fear for our order, for the Enlightenment, and indeed for the Empire."

Von Born staggers down the street in the direction of Wetzlar's home.

Mozart waves at Von Born's back, turns, and totters blindly on. He is weeping again and wondering again if Gulas committed the murder, and how to prove that he did. His heart is pounding; he is trembling and beginning to feel faint.

The composer's breath comes in gasps; he leans against a wall, wiping his face. Through the haze of his tears and the haze of street dust, he sees not twenty paces ahead of him a glowing lantern of a nose, surrounded by a wizened little face and supported by a spidery leprechaun's body.

⤳ Scene 3 ⤳

Mozart and Michael Kelly

"Drat, it's Ochelli; nowhere to turn before he gets here; where is a nice dark doorway when you need one?"

"Maestro!" *trumpets the tenor with five paces still between them.* "What a fabulous scene in the theater! What a treat to see the Chancellor running from the building as if he had the flux, har-har. And there's something even better! Did you know that La Storace has denounced you to the Emperor?"

"Oh really, O'Kelly? Wait … what? Denounced me, you say?"

"Yes indeed, some morals charge or other. What were you two doing in the alley, tee-hee! Disrupting the orderly process of rehearsal, and so on. False witness and so on. Give her credit, though, La Storace also sued for clemency, on bended knee, with her lace slipping down past her nibs, they say – and offered to sponsor you, if you get me, har-har, in London! Who could refuse her, eh? Thorwart told me not to tell you, but just between us, they say the Emperor is considering packing you off. Isn't that hilarious? It makes me want to violate my contract, up stakes and become one of your traveling party. London is wonderful, they'll love you, and with Storace easing your entrée – into the *music world*, that is – we'll all be rich and famous! When do we go?"

"She *denounced* me directly to *His Majesty*?"

"But it's not certain you'll actually be exiled. Thorwart said he thinks you should go alone without your family, so he can keep a close eye on his god-daughter."

"That bastard!"

"It could swing either way, don't you think? I think our *prima* has seen the handwriting on the wall, with regard to *Figaro* at any rate. It will never play here, too many intrigues, too many enemies, too many murders, hahahahaha. But the show must go on, maestro, so why not in London?"

Mozart hears a heavy martial tread behind him. He spins about and stares wildly at three policemen marching up the street.

"Are they going to deport me right now?" *thinks the composer.* "Are they going to lift me up under the arms and drag me to the nearest border? With any luck they'll drag me northwards toward Bohemia, but they'll probably just take the shortest route…" *(E-flat, descending circle of fifths, melody above it sliding down by semitones, and Storace's voice sings, "L'alma mia mancando va…")*

The soldiers march past the two men, eyes front. Mozart leans against a wall and puts his hand over his thundering heart.

"Of course, maestro, if you think you can plead with Caesar to let us proceed, I'm with you one hundred and fifty proof. We can go on tour, you know, after our run in Austria. London, Prague, Petersburg, and then Paris! Think of what a *fur-r-r-rore* we could cause there."

Mozart, muttering to himself and clutching at his breast, turns and staggers back across the market square toward his house.

Turning the last corner, he crashes into van Swieten, who is leaning against a wall and wiping his face, in a manner that suggests he is going to join his young protégé Mozart in a heart attack à deux.

ᶜᵌ Scene 4 ᵋᵓ

Mozart and van Swieten

"My dear Baron, you look as if you had seen the Devil himself."

"Worse, Mozart. I have just been released from the Polizeihaus; the guards escorted me just here and marched off. I thought they were going to deport me. I was interrogated for several hours."

"Baron, you are shaking all over. I am too. Please, let's go sit and refresh ourselves a moment."

"No, Mozart, no! I will tell you what happened, since it concerns you, but only here, in the street."

"It concerns me? My dear friend, what could they possibly want to … Oh, dear … was it about … my play?"

"No, Mozart. Initially they quizzed me about my Berlin connections, particularly at the royal court. Then they brought up the whole Günther scandal again, even though it has officially been dismissed, and then they asked about – about our lodge … they were very pressing, they manhandled me, and I-I gave them information that should have remained secret. About some of our members, or rather, former members. I am so ashamed."

"This is terrible! The world is ending!"

"I have lost Caesar's favor, I fear. Do you have any idea how many administrative posts in this empire are filled with Freemasons? Enlightened, forward-thinking men with the good of the nation at heart … but His Majesty fears a shadow government, and the old nobles whisper to him that there is a plot afoot to overthrow all the monarchies of Europe. Starting with his."

"Baron, I am sure Caesar would … well, no, actually I'm not sure."

"Oh, Mozart, I have worked so hard to promote a free and open marketplace of ideas. Blind Justice. A free press. The abolition, or at least the reduction, of secret arrests and imprisonments. But I fear the iron fist will soon close and strangle us all again. And your great opera, caught in the crossfire. Haegelin is now officially a murder victim. They dug him up and re-buried him in consecrated ground."

"I know. I stood next to him, perhaps on him, in the grave pit yesterday. But nobody has seen fit to tell the Emperor about his re-habilitation and re-interment. Why not?"

"I really don't know. But with Haegelin's burial I fear they bury the whole progressive wing of our government. A purge is imminent. And it will be the end of all our attempts to be a modern nation, like Britain. Alas, I foresee the immigration of the Mozarts and the score of Figaro to that great country. You know, I saw Haegelin in the theater on the night he died. I wish I could have done or said something . . ."

"You were at the theater too?"

"I was working in the ministry office that night. There was a ruckus backstage. Haegelin came in briefly; he seemed much put out; but it's – it was – hard to tell if his mood was out of the ordinary. He was in a constant state of outrage, wasn't he? Haegelin picked up a packet of papers and left, and shortly afterward Count Gulas came in, ranting and pointing that knout of a cane at me and demanding to know where the Imperial censor was hiding. He was drunk and gibbering that his old ally Haegelin had betrayed him and so had I, a fellow nobleman, although I was a damned Dutchman like that other damned Bohemian von Born. O, Lord, it was he who denounced us, wasn't it?"

"I'm sure of it. Was von Born at the theater too?"

"He was at the play with Count Thun. They were discussing your upcoming premiere when Gulas buttonholed them, swearing and threatening, telling them he would get even, and he knew just how to do it."

"Get even? He said 'get even?'"

"Thun thought nothing of it, but von Born took Gulas at his word. So he told me this morning, as he was packing his effects."

"He is off for the border in Wetzlar's coach."

"Good. Back to my tale…"

"Gulas left, I thought nothing more of it, and I locked the door after him and kept working. They were striking the set and rolling hoppers and yelling and slamming all the doors in the corridor, and heaven knows what sort of mayhem might have gone on under cover of that riot."

"Then you think Gulas killed Haegelin."

"Yes. Although everybody else had a motive also. Even I could have done it, if I had thought that that rusticated oaf was truly capable of bringing down the brotherhood and all its hopes for a modern Empire. In retrospect it seems as if he was."

"What should I do? This is too big for me."

"Think seriously about a London tour. Expect your play to be put off, perhaps withdrawn altogether. I'm so sorry, Amadé. I must be off home now. Be careful!"

⤳ Scene 5 ⤶

Mozart's bedroom, 8:00 P.M.

Mozart and Constanze

"Oh God, Stanzerl, we're ruined, ruined! Not only cancelled by Dear Godfather, but practically exiled from Austria by the Emperor himself! 'Find proof that H.E. is guilty, or no *Figaro*,' he says to me. 'Emigrate to London,' he says to me! What in heaven's name happened today? I'm losing my mind!"

"Lovie, don't worry; we'll be all right. As for your mind, I'm sure it's around here somewhere ... try looking under the bed, darling; it's like the Moon in *Orlando Furioso*; everything ends up there. Now let's get ourselves under the duvet, and cuddle up, put our thoughts in order, and figure out what we know."

"Just let me blow my nose; now kiss me ... again ...

"Ah. You give me the strength of mind to think back on these appalling events and try once again to make sense of them. Here I go...

"Da Ponte is released from jail at dawn on the 26th, and arrives at our house at 7:00 with straw in his hair. To celebrate his love of peace and freedom Da Ponte attacks a man, this Diguri, and knocks out his teeth. Da Ponte is promptly arrested again, and languishes in prison still.

"Thorwart gets the Haegelin suicide verdict reversed and summons me to his office in order to tell me that he is running his own investigation of the suicide-now-murder. He then lies to me, saying that Da Ponte's release was actually the night before on the 25th, and, he says, no sooner had the prison doors slammed behind the Court Poet than he made a bee-line for Fritz Drossel the head usher, and throttled him with a cello G-string, which the police must have given him as a parting gift..."

"Why would Dear Godfather lie to you?"

"He intends to fix both theater murders on Da Ponte, and seems unaware that Rosenberg's intentions are to hush the whole affair up. I do not tell him he is laboring at cross purposes with his boss.

"Instead, I obediently accept the role of *mouche* and pretend to investigate. I – and you – observe very suspicious behavior in a number of members of the *Figaro* cast and interview four of them. Three of them confess at length to all sorts of personal things and manage to cast suspicion on themselves so convincingly that I know they are all innocent of the Haegelin and Drossel murders.

"Signora Bussani admits to me that her husband and Diguri framed Da Ponte, and that it was she who got him out of jail, however briefly, but at great personal cost. She corroborates Da Ponte's story about his being released at dawn on the 26th. I visit him at the *Polizeihaus* today and catch him up on the news of the second murder, the child's incriminating story about Rosenberg's contretemps with Haegelin. I tell him of the heroism of his mistress. He is overcome with gratitude for her sacrifice; he weeps and decides to elope with her. He makes me promise to expose Rosenberg as the murderer so we can all emigrate to a better place. It is a touching scene; I am moved almost to tears, and so I swear to clear his name and free him if it kills me, which it might.

"This mighty oath prompted me, on a whim, which in retrospect I should not have indulged, to set a Mousetrap in the Act III opening duet to shock Rosenberg into confessing. He obligingly bolts from the theater like the guilty King Claudius, but – I should have thought of this beforehand – he cuts the duet and Dear Godfather sticks his boot up my ass and cancels the show. Oh God, God! '*Stelle barbare! Stelle spietate!*'"

"Darling, go on, just talk it all out. We'll see our way clear if you do."

"Act Two, let us sit upon the ground and tell sad tales of the death of *Figaro*. The Emperor dries my tears by giving me a short sharp lesson in European politics and the role of Kings. He officially insists that Haegelin is a suicide and still buried in the potter's field; then he reverses himself and unofficially insists the Masons or the Illuminati murdered him and are plotting his overthrow. When I try to rat a little on the Chancellor, he commands me to come up with hard proof that Rosenberg is involved in any or all of the murders of *Figaro*, or I will never see the inside of the Burgtheater again, not even with a ticket. He suggests that if I don't come up with the murder weapon, some documents or two witnesses, the show will never play, and I am no longer welcome in his Empire.

"I flee the palace, turn the corner and bump into Master von Born, who is leaving that same Empire in haste. He says all hope for our movement is lost. *Then* I meet Swieten, who has been detained and grilled by the police. Swieten! The Imperial Minister of Education and Publications! The cops wanted information about Masonic plots to topple the monarchy. I begin to think that *Figaro* is a mere distraction from some terrible imminent political calamity. A revolution and counter-revolution? Here in Vienna? Oh God, my heart is pounding again! I am, right now, as distracted as it is possible to get. This has to be the worst two days of my life. I am a composer, an impresario, a performer; I'm not cut out for murders and coups and international plots."

"Don't cry, my darling. Now you've got me crying too."

"Oh wait, forgot. Kelly told me that your favorite diva, La Storace, intuiting that she is never going to sing Susanna in Vienna, denounces me to Thorwart and then to Caesar for being a bad moral influence … then she about-faces and suggests to them that I go with her to London … stop laughing; this is awful; all the fates are aligned against us!"

"Even your opera isn't this complicated! Kiss me again."

"So, as it stands now, you and I and Da Ponte, Signora Bussani, Signora Storace *et famille*, and probably O'Kelly are all packing our bags and going on holiday in Britain!"

"There are worse places. Think of Haydn."

"I think of Rosenberg! Rosenberg, who knew I had the cello string! Who sent Casti to shoo me away from the Gottliebs! I think of Rosenberg, who wanted so fervently for Haegelin to remain a suicide, until he didn't…

"Ah! There's my chance! I see it now … when forced to the wall by Thorwart's meddling in the case and fearing that people would find out about the Gottliebs, he reversed himself! He threw down his last desperate diversionary card and told the Emperor that the Freemasons are involved in *Figaro*, and *they* murdered Haegelin! Yes, of course! Now I have him! My opera has gone dark, but he can't hurt me any more and I am free to accuse him! I will have Da

Ponte freed! And I will have vendetta! *L'obliar l'onte, oltraggio, e bassezza...*"

"But you still don't have enough proof to make your case, do you?"

"Well, no, actually. The only hope is extracting a confession out of him. But how?"

"I have an idea, pookybear. Let's pretend to be him. Like actors do. If we can understand what he wants and what he does to get it, maybe we will find a clue, or a way to pressure him into confessing."

"*You* pretend to be him. I'll just curl up next to him – to you."

"Here I go. I'm him. Haegelin, escaping from a drunken Count Gulas, puts his passkey into the nearest keyhole, stumbles into H.E.'s inner office and interrupts me, all busy fucking an actress. Most people would just, you know, 'Oopsie, sorry,' but not our late censor. His morals date from the days of Her August Majesty Maria Theresia, and her linen-sniffing Chastity Police.

"Those morals swell like a boil and burst forth in outrage. He berates and threatens me. I threaten him right back, with all the power of my office and ancient lineage. Haegelin plows right on, such behavior in a member of the nobility and blah blah blah, he is going straight to the Emperor.

"As he turns to go tattle on me, I garotte my censor and censurer with the nearest available cello string..."

"Which you keep in your desk drawer for just such occasions, and besides, you're a flautist."

"I pick it up from the floor where somebody has dropped it..."

"People don't drop new strings. Not on pit musicians' salaries."

"*You* found one, just lying around on the floor."

"The self-same string, the probable murder weapon. There are no more strings lying on the floor; I've been looking.

"Anyway. I drag the corpse out of my office and onto the stage. Drossel sees me and reports me to the Emperor – no, our King and Kaiser is, or are, a skin-flint; so Drossel confronts me and asks me to pay a steep price for his silence.

"I see the perils of being blackmailed by the Imperial snitch, so I kill him, with another cello string. Or hire someone like Diguri to do the deed for me. Diguri uses another cello string, cleverly throwing suspicion on – well, me."

"I so enjoyed that. Now *I'll* be Diguri. Remember how I yelled "It was all their idea, *il loro concetto*," when Da Ponte was swatting at me with his cane and spraying my teeth all over the street? I was not talking about the porn and the poisoning at all, but *the garotting*! Bussani and Casti had come to me in my humble room, where I was moodily playing Bach Suite #2 on my cello, and hired me to quickly and quietly dispose of Haegelin and hang him up in the theater so they could denounce Da Ponte. Herr Drossel witnessed the hanging and also came to my humble room where I was moodily playing Bach Suite #4 on the remaining three strings of my cello, and tried to blackmail me. While he was speaking to me I stopped playing, put the bow down, unwound the G-string and strangled him as well."

"That's pretty good! *My* turn again, sweetie! Now, I am a cabal of Free-masons, Rosicrucians, Illuminati, Hungarian peasants, embittered poets, play-wrights and cellists who sneak backstage and murder their nemesis, Haegelin, who has consistently and insistently censored their inflammatory pamphlets calling for a popular uprising and the overthrow of the Austrian monarchy. First cramming a copy of the Declaration of Independence into the deceased's pocket, they hoist him on high in the Emperor's very own theater house as a flag of defiance and warning, unaware that Drossel, a double agent from the deepest, darkest, most secret society of them all, has broken ranks and is now scampering down the hall to alert the Emperor that the Revolution is at hand. The gang, I mean I, pursue and tackle him as his fist closes on the doorknob; I garotte him and run through the streets carrying his lifeless body until I reach the banks of the Wien, and I tip him in!"

"That's mostly feasible, but the time-line is a little off. But I know it cannot be true because …I confess … it was actually … the famous Mozart."

"You can't be you; that's not fair!"

"I feel a burning need to understand myself, so I get to be me. I am prowl-ing the theater, infuriated as a tigress defending her young cub – in other words, if you don't get my subtle analogy – my precious show. I corner Haegelin and demand that he stop whittling down my play, or else! He laughs in my face and says he was going to cut all of Act IV. I spring at him; I chase him down the hall and onto the stage.

"I reach into my pocket and pull out a cello C-string; never mind that I play viola; the stringmaker sent me the wrong set by accident that afternoon. I planned to lash him with it until he cried uncle, and restored every last cut. But he turns and flees, and I am forced to garotte him from behind. At that very moment I hear the stage crew approaching for the *Figaro* put-in. I know what I have to do; I haul him upright, stick his head in a handy loop of rope … *und der Vorhang rollt herab!*

"Drossel, eavesdropping at the keyhole of the private box where Mandini and Laschi are humping away at each other, looks up and witnesses the whole episode. He demands a large tip. I promise to pay with the proceeds of the gate; I write him an incriminating IOU. Realizing I have put myself in his power, I watch for my chance. I skulk outside the theater cloaked in black; I follow him home, garotte him with the G-string, push him into the river and return to my sweetly sleeping wife, and embrace her like this!"

"Now Gulas. Or the Emperor!"

"My Imperial Majesty, having being discovered cavorting with a housemaid…"

"Gulas, having beaten back a mob of yowling peasants who were demanding the return of their seed potatoes…"

"Oh, how I love you! You're so amusing!"

"I hear bells!"

"No, it's a flute!"

"I kiss you nine squinchillion times, but I admit that tonight my heart belongs to Rosenberg. Our life hangs by a thread, or a cello string. I have to make him confess! 'For murder, though it have no tongue, shall speak!'"

"Wait a moment, wifeykins; that gives me another idea! Not Hamlet-within-Figaro this time but Figaro-within-Figaro! I'll stage the Act IV finale! I'll make Count Almaviva-Rosenberg-Almaviva reveal his misdeeds to the Emperor and everybody else, all at once!"

"Didn't you just do that and land yourself in trouble?"

"Hope is new-crowned again! Listen, my sweet! We're going to the annual Burgtheater fête galante at Galitzins' villa tomorrow evening, after what would have been our final dress. It's a masked costume party, so it will be wild, and now it's also to serve as an ad hoc Figaro closing-night bash. I'm going to arrange matters so that she with no tongue shall speak. You know those little pavilions near the lake, where people always go to make out? I'll spring my trap there. I'll need the little Nanette, and the Baroness – and I need, oh God have mercy, La Storace's help.

"You trust the hussy?"

"No, but I will deceive her. I have no problem telling her some lies concerning our imminent London trip, after what she did to me. And I'll whisper to her that I am already writing an air with clavier obbligato for her and me to perform together there. *Scusatemi se mento!* I'm off to visit our prima donna and then our ingénue, at dawn tomorrow!

❧ Scene 6 ❧

Baroness Waldstätten's house,
April 28, 10:00 A.M.

Mozart and Baroness Waldstätten

"Oh Baroness, I am mortally afraid of doing it, but this ruse I'm concocting is my last and only chance to save my play, my artistic life in Austria, my sanity and my honor; so why should I not take it?"

"This course is much too dangerous, Mozart. You have already set one mousetrap for Count Rosenberg, with no success and with the terrible consequence of having your play withdrawn. Remember what happened to Mesmer. And Mozart, those secret police who took Mesmer away threatened me with the loss of my husband's pension if I harbored any more undesirables under my roof – or did anything they deem unseemly. I am terribly afraid that I will end up a beggar and die in the street if I lose my modest income."

"I understand, and if you like I won't involve you at all. I can find another place for Nanette if you like. It is Nanette's ability to bear witness that threatens the count. I have believed for some time that Rosenberg killed Haegelin. I believe he throttled the man with – well, with a cello string – after the censor threatened to denounce him, Nanette and her mother. This cello string – here it is – is the only remaining solid evidence of a murder. I mean to present him with it tonight, if my first ruse does not breach his defenses. I can't imagine why he chose a cello string to kill Haegelin, or where he even got one. On the other hand, it's an opera house in Vienna, not a chicken farm in Salzburg, so it's not impossible to lay hands on…"

"This is all very difficult to believe, Amadé."

"It is in my best interest at this moment to believe it, Baroness, absurd as it is. So if *Figaro* is to go up this week – or ever – in Vienna, I *must* set this last mousetrap, to catch Rosenberg off guard and force him to utter an indiscretion. In front of witnesses.

"I *would* like to help you, Amadé. I would hate for Vienna to lose you."

"I am terribly grateful, Baronesss. So. My trap involves three couples, in disguise, and the pavilions in Galitzin's garden. The deception is inspired by Beaumarchais himself, and I am haunted by the thought that this may be the only time that the Fourth Act finale of *Figaro* may ever be played in south Germany."

"Who are the couples?"

"Madame Storace and the Emperor, in mask and domino. He always comes to this party in that get-up, and she has agreed to wear it also. He is very fond of her and might just follow her into a dark pavilion if she lowers her eyelashes and begs a private audience, perhaps to denounce another local composer, perhaps to grant the Emperor the amorous attentions he so obviously craves.

"Secondly, Count Rosenberg and Nanette. She will be dressed as Susanna; she will feign muteness and entice the count into the other pavilion by means of a written note. Finally, Baroness Waldstätten and Mozart, masked and costumed as Harlequin and Columbine, who, along with His Majesty, will be the true witnesses to whatever happens next."

"Oh, no, Amadé, this is far too risky! You and I are in dire political trouble and Nanette is so recently recovered and her doctor exiled. Can you really in good conscience dangle her as bait in front of her own ravisher?"

"When he sees her in Susanna's costume he may remember Mousetrap Number One and be severely shocked, or at least I hope so. When he reads the blackmail note I will have her write, he may be shocked enough to say – or do – something rash. And we will be there to stop it if he tries to silence her … with – the D-string…"

"My goodness, you really believe it was him, don't you? Well, Mozart, the least we can do is ask Nanette if she will play a part in this dangerous game. You must offer her a reward, any reward she chooses – except what she wants, of course."

"I know how to make it worth her while."

"I'll go to her room and bring her down here."

❧ Scene 7 ❧

Mozart, Waldstätten, Nanette

"Nannerl, my brave child! How are you getting on? Good! Now, I have a plan to make Count Rosenberg admit that he wronged you, and also to make him agree to let us play *Figaro* tomorrow, so you will get to make your debut in a Mozart play. But if we do not carry out this plan, *Figaro* will never be heard here, and my wife and I will have to leave the lands of the Empire forever. Are you interested to hear my plan?"

"Yes, Maestro."

"Here is the plan. We three will be masked. You will dress as a ladies' maid – like Susanna, in fact – and you must play your part in dumb-show. Some day soon you will sing it too, on a great stage, London or Petersburg or Prague. And not only that; I promise I will write a *prima donna* part in another opera, just for you."

"I want *Figaro* to play," *whispers the ingénue after a long pause, raising her gaze to meet the composer's.* "I want to sing."

"Good, then. This is what you must do … you will write two notes and hand them one at a time to His Excellency. The first note will tell him to meet you at the left-hand pavilion by the lake, during the fireworks. The second note you must hand him when you are inside the pavilion. It will say, pardon me for saying this, that you are willing to be his mistress but you want much more money. This feigned willingness to yield to him is similar to how Susanna fools Count Almaviva at the top of Act III, do you remember?"

"Yes, Maestro."

"Almaviva believes she will consent to be his mistress too, and Susanna assures us all that she is lying, only for Figaro's sake. So you can lie too, for *Figaro's* sake, can't you? Can you play this scene to him if the baroness and I are standing a little way off observing you?"

"Yes, I can do it, for you, Maestro. I want to. I don't like him at all. He is a horrible man, so old, and so wrinkly too, and he pants and drools like a dog in heat. I dream of him handling me every night, and I wake up choking. So what matter if I meet him in the flesh? What should I do first?"

"Write the notes, my dear," *says the baroness*. "I will dictate them to you. You are very courageous to be doing this. Other witnesses will be coming there, watching over you too, so you will never be alone."

"If I call for you will you come?"

"Yes."

"You won't abandon me?"

"No."

"You'll be close by?"

"Yes."

"Now, Nannerl," *continues Mozart*, "you must remember to play the mute. No one but us knows that you can talk and that you have told us everything that happened to you. Do not speak at all unless he threatens you with bodily harm. You may nod and gesture, but don't speak. Can you do it?"

"I am an actress, dear Maestro. I have been working in the theater since I was eight. I can play this part. Or any part you like."

Nanette flashes her eyes at him. The knowledge and the invitation there is unmistakable. *Mozart feels the chill hand of doubt clutch at his innards. He thinks:*

"What is going on in this child's head? What am I missing? I am getting too suspicious; I'll have to give up moucheing or soon I won't be able to trust anybody,"

ᦰ Finale ᦰ

The grounds of Prince Galitzin's palace at Dornbach,
April 28, 8:00 P.M.

All participants

Mozart's old friend and patron Prince Dmitri Galitzin is holding his annual Burgtheater costume ball: a lavish picnic for all the troupes, production crews and administrative staff. A costume ball for theater people is always a wild affair, since their free access to the garderobes and the costume morgues allows the participants to let their creative geniuses off the leash. Dance music for the event is written by the famous Mozart, and – conveniently for that composer's mad designs this evening – contains no viola parts. So Mozart, having written himself out of the dance band, will be wandering at large, merging with the swirling masses of fairy queens, knights in armor, sea-nymphs, Chinamen, gypsies, houris, mages, huntsmen, witches, apes, bears, Bohemian princesses and peasants, sultans and Egyptian pharaohs. He will be preparing to ruin forever the life of Count Franz Xaver Wolfgang von Orsini-Rosenberg – or his own life.

"Look at this fête! It looks like a rowdy version of Watteau!" whispers Mozart to the baroness. *They are both in Commedia dell'Arte costume, and masked.*

"The music, the lights, the food, the acres of silk and satin, the flirting and frivolity! Dear Baroness, this is how Vienna will be remembered in years to come, all whipped cream and no coffee. How we glitter; how we love our good times. And to what purpose, I begin to wonder? My temperament is taking a dark turn, it seems, Baroness. I have no stomach for this mindless gaiety any more."

"Although you still like your dram of punch, I see. Do not take any more,

Amadé; we must be alert, and nobody must identify you. We must go away from this crowd, into the shadows under the trees near the lake."

Mozart walks past the orchestra, which is sawing its way through a set of his "German Dances." The last desk cello is tall and thin and looks vaguely familiar. He thinks: "Ah. The other Gottlieb child. Nanette has managed to bring along her own insurance; it's a good thing he is here tonight." *Mozart notices how poorly the young man is dressed, and that his C-string is so old it has a knot tied in it.*

His eye passes over the orchestra and fixes itself on a dignified personage mingling with the dancers and actors.

"There is His Excellency, Count Rosenberg, dressed as the Barber of Seville. He should have gotten himself up as Almaviva himself, of course. Preening and smirking, as always. You know, Baroness, I hate him, I really do."

"Peace. He is not all bad. He is a loyal chancellor, a good impresario, and a man of culture. He's coming toward the lake! It's getting dark enough for the *feux d'artifice.* Ohhh, how lovely!"

"And there go the Emperor and Storace, toward the pavilions. She is talking to him and taking his arm. In two seconds we'll send Nanette."

As the fireworks begin, the friends disperse into the crowds. Nanette, costumed as Susanna, has been discreetly shadowing Count Rosenberg; at a signal from Baroness Waldstätten, she approaches him, tugs his sleeve, and hands him the note. The count winces and drops his drink; the glass shatters on the terrace. She moves on and looks back at the count over her shoulder, "with frightening expertise," Mozart thinks again. The count reads the note, crumples it into his pocket, and starts almost instantly in the direction of the pavilions. The conspirators begin to stroll there also.

The lakeshore pavilions

Count Rosenberg, Nanette, then Mozart, Waldstätten, Emperor Joseph II

"So, you have decided to pursue me, even after all that has happened?" *the count hisses at her.* "Why are you wearing that outfit? What do you want from me? I am not so sure I can help you even if you desire it. Perhaps when the hue and cry dies down, we can arrange for you ... What's this? Another note? Why don't you speak? Still can't? Well, so much the better; you'll tell no tales, sing no songs. Come here where it's darker. Not quite so shy tonight, I see. All right,

I'll read the damned note."

Approaching the entrance of the pavilion once more to use the light of the next burst of fireworks, the count spreads the note on his knee, hunches over it and reads.

"'*My mother wants more money!*' She wants more money? It strikes me that your mother might be happy to settle for less, much less. Safe passage to Berlin, for instance. Does she really think I am going to pay her for her silence? She ought to be paying me for *my* silence. Look at me, child."

The count grabs Nanette roughly and pulls her into the shadows. The baroness startles and lunges forward, as if she were going to call a halt to the scene; but Mozart, wide-eyed and open-mouthed, keeps his hold on her arm.

"Wait another moment."

Rosenberg speaks from within the pavilion.

"She says that I must pay her twice the agreed-on sum? Or else she will inform the authorities? What madness is this? You are both completely in my power, yet you try to blackmail me! Does she want me to tell the police that she is a procuress and that her child is a whore – and worse? She was there; she saw what you did! By God, I'll haul her in as my second witness to the murder, and you will be convicted of it and die in prison; don't you know that? What's the matter with you?"

Nanette has sunk to the ground moaning, her rigid limbs convulsing, froth oozing from her mouth. She lies there shaking and writhing as the fit has its way with her, eyes rolled back in her head. Rosenberg kneels in the semi-dark. He does not bend his knee in order to aid the child. He bends it because he is staring into the eyes of his King and Kaiser and also into the eyes of the famous English diva Nancy Storace, both of whom have suddenly appeared before him.

"You will attend me in my office tomorrow morning," *says the Emperor, and turns his back on the count. He and Storace walk swiftly away.*

Mozart dashes to the convulsing child, kneels beside her and turns her gently on her side, as her seizure continues. He looks up at Count Rosenberg and meets his eyes, but says nothing.

"No, Mozart, in the matter of the murder at least, my hands are clean. I did not kill him. I didn't hang him up there either. You may continue to surmise who did kill him and you may guess how the body came to rest where it did, but my chief concerns that night were only to protect the Gottliebs and get rid of the body somehow. As you have discerned, Haegelin was strangled in my office. Good evening."

The contortions of the child lessen, and her terrible moaning gives way to light, even breathing. Mozart and the baroness loosen her garment and chafe her gloved hands and arms. At last the composer slides off a white kid-skin glove, turns the limp hand palm upward, and gently kisses the barely healed wire-cut winding around it.

ᥣᄅ Epilogue ᱠᥤ

The Cabinet of His Imperial Majesty, Joseph II
April 29, 9:00 A.M.

They begin to assemble in the Emperor's parlor in the early morning. Mozart is the first to appear. Rosenberg is prompt as always, but he does not stride in arrogantly as becomes a man so close to the sole and central power of the Habsburg Empire. No, he enters cringing, "with his ears laid back like a donkey about to endure the lash," Mozart thinks to himself.

"Too bad for him. He should have thought of it all before he dipped his pen into the company inkwell."

Baroness Waldstätten enters. Da Ponte enters. Casti and Gulas enter together. They speak no greetings, although Da Ponte's eyes dart constantly to the door. "Perhaps he's expecting the police, or the thug Diguri, to show up," thinks Mozart. "I hope Diguri is in Trieste by now."

They all sit staring at the floor and not speaking to each other for the world's longest ten minutes. They rise as one and bow low as the Emperor enters and takes his chair.

"Sit."

The chairs, in their brief moment of emptiness, have taken on the attributes of a carnival Faquir's bed of nails ... their returning asses quiver, feeling too exquisitely reluctant to sit before the Emperor, who sits in judgment over them all ... their spines remain erect and tense.

"Speak!" *snaps the Emperor, glaring at Rosenberg.*

"Your Majesty, I have received an urgent message from Herr Chief Commissioner Pergen. The woman Frau von Gottlieb was denounced as an enemy of the state and taken prisoner at her home last night. She was brought to the *Polizeihaus*, where she has written a document in which she confesses to both murders. Here it is. Shall I read it to you?"

Joseph nods but does not speak. He rises, causing the entire assemblage to pop out of their

chairs. Joseph paces the room. All others turn their eyes to Rosenberg, frozen in various degrees
of shock, dismay – and skepticism. Rosenberg reads in a small, shaky voice:

"This paper is the full, true and uncoerced confession of Anna Maria Gottlieb, widow of Johann Christoph Gottlieb, mother of Christian and Anna Gottlieb, of Vienna. I committed two murderous attacks upon employees of the Burgtheater, and I killed them. The first man I killed on April 20, in the theater. His name was Haegelin, and he worked as the censor for the theater. I murdered him because he threatened to send my daughter and myself to prison.

"My daughter was under the protection of His Excellency Count Rosenberg, who took an interest in her career. Count Rosenberg would not have been able to save her from the threats of exposure that Haegelin was making; I deemed it my duty to prevent the accuser from destroying her chances, and her life.

"The second man was the head usher Fritz Drossel. Herr Drossel came to me and threatened to denounce me and my daughter if I did not pay for his silence. I murdered him in the fashion that I had murdered the first man.

"I have never murdered anyone before. But my family is a theatrical one and my husband had been a fight and fencing coach for the Burgtheater and other theaters. He coached the troupe of the play *Turks and Huntsmen*, in which the Musulman Assassins enter south Germany by stealth. The entire cast, including myself, who was a supernumerary in this show, learned to simulate the unbelievers' foul methods, especially the use of the garotte.

"When Haegelin threatened to send my daughter and me to prison, in my distress I laid my hand in my pocket, to the set of new cello strings I had bought as a present for my son Christian, who plays fourth desk in the *Freihaustheater* orchestra and does free-lance work in dance bands. I drew out the C-string and garotted Herr Haegelin as he turned to leave. The C-string was lost in our ensuing escape, or perhaps, I am surmising, during the mysterious moving of the body that night, in which I played no part and do not know who did.

"Later in the week I murdered Herr Drossel; but in his case I kept my composure. I also kept the G-string. I am sure the music that will issue from it will be just as sweet as from any other.

"The things I did were for my daughter, and in the interests of her artistic

career. She has great talent, which needs proper cultivation. I appeal to Count
Rosenberg to continue to offer her his protection, for she will need powerful
friends to weather this scandal. The Count felt an attraction to her and ex-
pressed willingness to be her patron. It is my hope he will continue to help my
daughter advance in the theater, where many pitfalls lie in the path of one so
young and innocent.

"I am guilty of murder; I confess it freely. Whether I am guilty of shielding
and loving my child the dear God above will judge, and God will mete out my
punishment. Signed, this day, April 29, 1786,

AMG."

Beat.

"*No!*" *It is the Emperor who shrieks.* "No, *not* God! I will see to her punishment,
and I alone! This unnatural monster of a woman! To do murder and then do
it again! She will be punished by the most painful death imaginable! The hot
pincers, the wheel..." *The Emperor sits down abruptly, his fingers twitching, his face
working.*

"There is a further note from Pergen, Your Majesty," *whispers Rosenberg.*

"No mercy, *none*; I don't care what he says! Fix her to the wall and give her
thin gruel!"

"Your Majesty, the woman is dead. She hanged herself with her own
chains an hour ago."

*Mozart opens his mouth and shuts it again. His eyes flick to meet the baroness's eyes,
then dart away. The whole company sits in a frozen silence, watching the Emperor, then the
count, then the Emperor.*

*Mozart stares, fascinated, at the count's face, expressionless on its surface, but burning
with every known distress deep in the eyes. He thinks:*

"Poor mutt. A man of consequence cornered like a rat in an alley,"

"Well," *says Joseph, after a long silence.* "There's an end to it. We have the
confession. That is the official story, and I accept it, officially. The woman will
be buried in the potter's field and denied all the rites. This unpleasant affair is
now at an end, at least in the eyes of the State."

Another long and screaming silence.

"Your Majesty, if I might presume to ask..."

"Yes, Mozart? Will *Figaro* go up in the Burgtheater? Is that what you want to know in this somber hour?"

"Pardon, Your Majesty, but there are many persons in my care hanging upon your answer. They need to be notified."

"Have you done what I asked you, Mozart? Have you extracted a confession of wrongdoing from the count? Are you not satisfied that he is blameless?"

"Your Majesty, I– I am finding that your advice to stick to composing is very wise indeed. But I have reason to believe that the whole story has not been told, by many of us here assembled. I have heard many things, and would like to know many things, but I fear almost any word I say will damage the chances of– of–"

"Your work being seen. I understand. So you are not such a vigorous pursuer of truth as you were three days ago, are you? Not such a seeker after Truth as the Freemasons would have you be, am I correct in this?"

"Playing the lawyer or the policeman is not my metier, but I need to know things. My friend and colleague *Abbé* Da Ponte has been twice imprisoned, on charges brought against him in secret, which I consider to be false and slanderous. His Excellency has confessed before four people, including Your Majesty and myself, that he was a witness to a murder, but he never said so on the day the body was first found, nor any day afterward, to my knowledge. Why did he insist from the beginning that the murder was a suicide? If he was a witness at all to Haegelin's murder, why did he not act to prevent it? Why was a second employee of the theater killed? Was the smut-seller and blackmailer Diguri in His Excellency's pay? What was Diguri doing, and where has he gone since Da Ponte's arrest?"

"Would you like to interrogate Count Rosenberg now, so that the ban on *Figaro* will be lifted?"

"No, Your Majesty. He is a person in authority and has too much power over me, now and in the future. I cannot, and I fear to do so, for – for personal reasons."

"Good. You have learned some wisdom, Monsieur Mozart."

"So, Rosenberg," *the Emperor turns abruptly to his Chancellor.* "You will confess your part in this catastrophe, and explain to us how Herr Haegelin, whom you claim to have seen murdered, came to hang in the rigging of my Imperial theater. You will explain what you did that night, and during the events that followed. Do so now."

Count Rosenberg rises, bows, and puts one hand into his vest and the other behind his back to hide their trembling. The pupils of his pale eyes are dilated and look like black pits in his chalk-white face.

"Your Majesty. There were three of us in my inner office, conducting un-official business. When Haegelin entered he began to accuse us of impropriety, and issue threats of arrest and public humiliation. Miss Nanette Gottlieb was overcome by some storm of the nerves, I believe, and was rendered uncon-scious. What Frau Gottlieb reports in her confession is more or less what I recall."

The composer stirs in his seat, and the baroness lays her hand on his arm.

"After the– the incident, I hid the body under my desk and escorted the Gottliebs to their home. I then returned to my palace thinking of what I would need to dispose of the corpse. Signor Casti found me pacing in the hall and offered his help. I told him there had been a– an accident in my office and Haegelin had died there. Casti said he had a ruffian from Italy in his casual employ, and would rouse him and together they would secrete Haegelin from the theater and install him somewhere else."

"Is this true, Casti?" *snaps the Emperor.*

"Yes, your H-Majesty; those were my orders."

"And did you carry them out, making yourself accessory to this crime?"

"No, Your H-Majesty."

"Casti, we are waiting to hear what went on at the theater that night."

"I would rather not say."

"Casti, confession under torture has been abolished for some time. But I am the State, and if it is necessary to question you intensely I will not hesitate to restore the practice."

"Yes, Your H-Majesty. I roused the ruffian Diguri, and we let ourselves into the th-neater. We found the corpse and wrapped him in a length of masking. We were duly carrying it into the square when we were discovered by someone we thought was a footpad, who was lurking about the alley of the theater. He precipitated himself upon us, shouting and swearing and beating us with a cane. It was, begging your pardon, Count Hn-Gulas."

"So, Gulas," *says the Emperor,* "you also are part of this conspiracy! How charming to know that you are not only without moral rectitude but also brainless and incompetent! Perhaps you would like to augment this already nauseating narrative with some colorful comments of your own."

"I was waiting by the stage door for Haegelin. I wanted to lean on him again about the Beaumarchais play. No, I had not been there the whole night; I went to a place of amusement and refreshed myself, then I thought about Haegelin some more and was even more infuriated the second time, so I went back to see if he were still cowering in the theater waiting until the streets were empty. As it turned out, he was."

"I saw the little rickety one there and his ox-like companion opening the door and smuggling something out of the theater. Something they were stealing, or so I thought. I had no weapon but my cane, but I advanced upon them and took them unawares. After a few good whacks they tried to pull rank by insisting they were on a mission for His Excellency. I didn't believe them, and tore open their bundle. By God, it was Haegelin, garotted and dead as a herring!

"They were headed for the river, but by the time we got ourselves sorted out, it was getting light outside. Then Casti and Diguri came up with a plan to stop the play, ruin Da Ponte and dispose of the body, all in one go. I confess here that I too had my reasons for wanting to stop the play, and teach that little simpering rat Mozart a lesson; pardon me, Your Highness, but his damn play is exactly the sort of propaganda that started the Horia revolt ... even now it causes unrest and insubordination among my musical serfs – my musical staff."

"Stick to the story of that night."

"Yes, Your Majesty. I told Casti I had heard Da Ponte threaten to kill the man earlier in the day, so it seemed the perfect opportunity for all of us to achieve our ends. We carried Haegelin back into the theater and raised him to the sky before Judgment Day, ha-ha-ha!"

"Judgment day is today, Gulas; do not mock the dead or it will go even worse for you than you can imagine. Now, Rosenberg, you now will tell me who denounced Da Ponte."

"Your Majesty, I have no idea."

"I doubt it. And did you know who killed Herr Drossel?"

"Your Majesty, until this morning I did not know."

"He did not come to you with a tale of suspicious doings in your office, and offer to sell his discretion for a small consideration?"

"Your Majesty, Drossel was your confidant. His silence could not be bought. "

"Did you not send him to the actress's mother, knowing that she would take measures in order to protect you and your investment in your daughter?"

"Your Majesty, he never came. I never sent him. My duty was to protect the women. I would not send anyone to a woman to be murdered."

Rosenberg pauses. He is very pale, and tears have started in his eyes and are making tracks down his cheeks. The Chancellor of Spectacles has his hands clasped before him and they are now shaking uncontrollably.

The Emperor stares at him in fury. After enduring several moments of that terrible gaze, the count rallies and speaks again, in a whisper.

"Your Majesty, when my father was very old, in his dotage in fact, he became entangled with a much younger woman, a mercenary woman with a scandalous past. He married her, in the year before he died. During that time my father told me that this woman had made him happier than anything else in his life. I am sure this was true; my mother was a basilisk; perhaps all mothers are basilisks."

The Emperor shifts abruptly in his chair but his face remains impassive.

"My father's intemperate marriage caused a scandal in my family. After his death the family arranged for the marriage to be annulled. The woman was denounced, was deported to England in penury, and soon disappeared. Because of this incident and the bitterness and shame it caused, I vowed never to marry. I have always preferred the more honorable transactions one makes with prostitutes.

"Yet I found myself entangled too, against my own best counsel and my own finely calculated plans for my life, in a shameful liaison. Perhaps this weakness runs in the blood. During this time I was repelled by my actions and the actions of those with whom I was involved. Yet I felt I had a responsibility to these persons which I knew I could not shirk. Perhaps that call to responsibility runs in the blood as well. Evil, great evil, has been done in my hour, some of it by me. I was accountable.

"Mozart, you deceived me and ensnared me in a most dishonorable way.

You are an ungrateful little worm. But you are a diabolically good judge of human nature, and I applaud your discernment while abhorring your deceit. You have learned well from Shakespeare, and from Beaumarchais as well. The 'mousetrap' scene in Act III. The false letter you dictated to the child could easily have been composed by the mother. She was also a false and unscrupulous person."

"Never mind! Is her confession true?" *barks the Emperor.*

A shadow passes over the count's eyes. Mozart, even in his extreme state of alertness and terror, says to himself, "His soul is departing and he feels the pain of it."

"Yes," *says Count Rosenberg.*

"I will take your word to be the truth, Rosenberg. You are a good and loyal chancellor. I believe you have acted in a manner consonant with your high birth and office. You will continue in my service as before. Leave now."

Without a word the count bows and leaves the room.

Another long pause. The King-Emperor looks each participant in the face, until each bows his head in shame. Then he speaks rapidly and decisively.

"Casti, take this purse of money."

"Thank you, but Your H-Majesty, what for?"

"For your journey. You are banished."

"Gulas, you are to go home to your feudal estates and reform them according to the policies of this throne. Failure to comply with the letter of my edicts will result in confiscation of all your property.

"Da Ponte, I believe you are innocent of all wrong-doing. However, trouble dogs your steps. The next ruckus that involves you in the theater will be your last. I understand London is a fine city.

"Mozart, I grant you the only wish that will make you happy. *Figaro* will play the day after tomorrow. You may all go to your various destinations. Everybody get out."

"Your Majesty." *All file out, trying not to look as desperate to leave as they are.*

"Mozart, stay a moment," *says the Emperor.* "Are you content?"

"Yes, Your Majesty; thank you, Your Majesty."

"Lies have been told in this room; you know that."

"Yes, Your Majesty."

"Rosenberg's story was quite touching, was it not? But you think he is lying, don't you? Well, so do I."

"Then why–"

"You see, Mozart, how I have taken your own Contessa Almaviva's strategy of forgiveness to heart. Like her, I am a practical person. The Contessa Almaviva has mercy on her philandering husband, but her forgiveness gives her great power over him, a power she will exercise for the rest of her life. Rosenberg has always been a loyal servant. Now he will be doubly so, because I own him. I can count on him to put my wishes before his until he dies. He is a murderer."

"But Majesty – Frau Gottlieb has confessed to the murder and you have accepted her confession."

"Rosenberg is a proud man. A man jealous of his privilege. Such a man would kill if a lesser man tried to humiliate him."

"Your Majesty, pardon me, but for the first time I believe the count is innocent. He told you of his deep desire to shield the Gottliebs from the consequences of their involvement with him. We need never say who really did the first murder, or who had bought the cello strings as a gift for an adoring brother. The child is very sensitive and high strung. She has convulsive seizures, during which she is not herself; nor does she know what she does."

"That is true, but the count must have done the second murder. It's easy to see, Drossel tried to extort money from him and he wouldn't stand for it. What's the matter, Mozart?"

"It was me! Oh, dear God, *it was me!*"

"What are you saying, Mozart, that you killed Drossel?"

"Your Majesty, I see it all now. *I told her!* It was *me!* Drossel never went to the count. Nor did the count sink so low as to do murder or to arrange for Frau Gottlieb to do his dirty work for him.

"We had heated words, the mother and I! And when I caught her lying about where she was the night of the murder I lost my temper and lied to her! I told her that Drossel had seen and heard her in the theater with Rosenberg and Haegelin, in the office, after the play! Drossel's death is my doing. I have a murder on my conscience as well."

"So. The woman told half the truth, it seems. Drossel went to her, and she behaved like a tigress protecting her cubs. She did the second murder, making it look like the first, planning to take the blame for both and protect the daughter she loved. I admire her sense of purpose, in a way."

"I have blood on my hands…"

"I too have blood on my hands, Mozart. But I expect it. I am more than a man. I am a king. I must bear it, and so must you."

"But Your Majesty, did you guess correctly about the first murder?"

"I was in the pavilion. I have ears, and also some considerable experience with the talents and ambitions of actresses. She is a complicated child. She is truly an epileptic, however, and probably has no recollection of her doings that night in the theater, poor thing. Now, you must do these things for me, Mozart."

"Your Majesty."

"Tell Da Ponte to leave the Bussanis alone. Without Casti to urge him on, Bussani will accept his horns with more grace, and keep his well-known pornography collection to himself. Yes, I have seen those prints before, and I don't blame his wife for seeking a slightly less depraved companion. Have you quit the Masons? I notice you don't wear the gold key on your fob."

"Almost, Your Majesty. My emblem is in the cemetery nestled in the bosom of Herr Drossel."

"I don't have time to hear that story. And now the decision is yours, Mozart. Do you want your murderess in prison or in the cast of *Figaro*?

Beat. A short one.

"In the cast."

"And the false accuser, do you want him in the cast too?"

"Which false accuser? They all denounced each other. Except Benucci. He was busy cultivating his art. Of course I want them, Your Majesty. I want them all."

"I thought so. Go rehearse."

"Yes, Your Majesty."

✺ Stretto ✺

Backstage, after the premiere of Le Nozze di Figaro,
May 1, 1786, 10:30 P.M.

Mozart is cordially shaking hands with Madame Storace, congratulating her on a stellar performance and promising her that her aria with clavier obliggato is in the works, and that they will perform it together at her farewell concert. She gives him one long last, sad, forgiving, valedictory look, and sweeps off to join the Emperor.

"Mozart, it's fabulous, simply fabulous! The mercurial speed, the invention! The plumbing of the human soul! What a glorious evening!"

"Signor Salieri, praise from you is praise indeed. I myself thought the audience reception was a little muted. Empty boxes, and so on."

"Oh, but no! Never mind the provincial country boobies who hold those boxes. The intelligentsia down front, and the shopkeepers up in Paradise, all those who are really in the know, see the dazzling cleverness and real, deep human feeling in the thing!"

"My God, Mozart, the finale of Act II – I could barely breathe! Not to diminish the Act III or IV finales, but Act II is a miracle! By all the gods, man, you really are a genius."

"Well, enough people liked it. They all laughed at the funny parts and didn't talk during the serious parts. I like the silent rapture better than the easy laugh. That's all one can hope for, I guess, at a premiere. Let's go for a late dinner; what do you say? I haven't eaten anything for weeks."

"Wait till you've soaked up all the adulation, then we'll go."

Out of the tail of his eye, Mozart observes his cast, falling ecstatically into each other's arms, chiming "You were simply divine, my dear – never before have I heard such exquisite vocalità…"; he sees Signora Laschi and Signora Mandini exchanging air kisses, the pressures of the show and of petty rivalries all being released in great gurgles and gushes of goodwill and collegiality. Happy now, friends forever, until tomorrow's rehearsal, when the cycle of snipery and bitchery will begin anew.

"Ah, tutti contenti saremo cosi…"

As he glances around the other way, Mozart sees Signora Bussani primly offering the back of her hand to Da Ponte, who takes and firmly shakes it, English style. His eyes – and hers – glisten with tears. He looks away and is startled to spy his little prodigy and co-conspirator Mademoiselle Nanette Gottlieb, tall and elegantly swathed in a new blue silk gown, sweeping out of the hall on the arm of Count Orsini-Rosenberg. She glances over her shoulder at her Maestro, and smiles, a secretive little smirk of a smile, as if they share a little joke between them.

Mozart winces, as he realizes that she is now orphaned and utterly dependent on the man who has so unceremoniously taken her young maidenhood; and that he, Mozart, is partly responsible for her present plight. But that ironical smile of hers! The composer extricates Da Ponte from a crowd of female admirers and takes him to a quiet corner.

"Da Ponte, what do you surmise about our little Barbarina and her Contino? I wonder sometimes, did she seduce him or he her? Does she even know? Does she know she strangled a man with a cello string after being raped, or was her memory erased by the epileptic fit? Did she go willingly to the count that night, and kill the censor to protect herself and her mother from public shaming and prison? Was she really struck dumb? Did she tell Mesmer and me the truth, and in doing so did she rat out the count and, incidentally, her own mother? Did she even think her actions through? Or did she just play whatever scene she happened to be in, to see how it would turn out? I can't fathom it. Such a sweet young girl, but perhaps not as much the *ingénue* as I thought. And yet…"

"We can take up that thorny philosophical conundrum in our next opera, which would be *Don Juan* of course … but first let us rejoice in the certain triumph of this one."

"It is sublimely good, isn't it?"

"My dear man, it is an oeuvre for the ages. I do my best work with you. Let's do dozens more; what do you say?"

"Let's start soon. Think of it! A moonless night. The servant waits under

the balcony. A rape – or is it a seduction? A woman screams, the father inter-
venes, death is swift ... the libertine escapes ... oh dear, we've got first-hand
experience for this one, don't we?"

"It's the human condition, dear fellow. You can't avoid it."

"Then let's not."

Finis

www.ingramcontent.com/pod-product-compliance
Lightning Source LLC
Chambersburg PA
CBHW070747180626
46818CB00007B/3024